THE
RANGE HAWK

Arthur Henry
GOODEN

D1428849

CENTER POINT LARGE PRINT
THORNDIKE, MAINE

This Center Point Large Print edition is published
in the year 2012 by arrangement with
Golden West Literary Agency.

The text of this Large Print edition is unabridged.
In other aspects, this book may
vary from the original edition.

Set in 16-point Times New Roman type.

ISBN: 978-1-62899-462-9

Library of Congress Cataloging-in-Publication Data

Gooden, Arthur Henry, 1879–1971.
The range hawk / Arthur Henry Gooden. — 1st US ed.
p. cm.
ISBN 978-1-62899-462-9 (library binding : alk. paper)
1. Large type books. I. Title.
PS3513.O4767R36
813′.52—dc23
2012021355

Printed and bo
by TJ Internati

To My Mother and Marion,
Enthusiasts

CHAPTER ONE

Almost overnight the wildflowers were up, spreading gaiety and beauty across the harsh face of the land. The breath-taking panorama lulled old Mark Severn's usual vigilance and his stern face wore an oddly softened look as his gray horse rocked him homeward from the town of Coldwater. It was always that way with him when the desert wildflowers bloomed. Mary had loved the coming of spring . . . the wildflowers.

The old cattleman's long gaunt frame sagged as he thought of his daughter. She'd had no mother . . . he'd been too harsh . . . his own fault she ran away with the man she loved. And now Mary was dead these long years . . . but the wildflowers always returned . . . brought memories that hurt.

Mary had never returned to the old Bar 7 ranch, and only once had she written to him, not a letter, just a small picture of herself and the baby, with Mary's girlish scrawl, *Dear Daddy—with love from me—and your little granddaughter—Mary Cameron.* Never another word . . . only news of a train wreck . . . a little baby girl left tragically orphaned and seemingly lost forever to a longing grandfather.

Mark had never been able to learn what had become of Mary's baby. She would be all of eighteen now, a grown woman. He longed for her desperately, wanted her to have the ranch when he'd gone. Little Mary Cameron was his grandchild . . . the old Bar 7 must be hers.

If he had been less engrossed with the baffling mystery of his lost granddaughter, the old cattleman would have noticed the coyote and shrewdly suspected the reason for the little gray prowler's sudden burst of speed as it passed close to a thick clump of greasewood above the trail. He was a wary old-timer and, like the fleeing coyote, he instantly would have known that death lay in wait behind that scrubby upthrust of brush. But Mark Severn's vigilance was at low ebb for the moment. He rode on his way, the warning unseen. Suddenly thin bluish smoke curled from the bush.

As the rifle's crashing report blasted the stillness of the desert hills, old Mark Severn toppled sideways from his startled horse. The gray came to a snorting standstill and looked back inquiringly at the limp form prone across the flower-bordered trail.

The echoes of the gunshot faded and presently the ambusher emerged cautiously from his hiding place behind the greasewood. He stood on the slope above the trail, beady eyes intent on his victim.

He was a smallish man of middle age, scrawny

and swarthy with a high-boned face deeply scored with lines of evil. He wore a red calfskin vest and leather brush-scarred chaps. A black forelock strayed over slant brows from under his wide-brimmed hat.

He stood there making and lighting a cigarette, his dark visage devoid of emotion, only his vicious eyes restless, glittering, the rifle in lowered hand, a low-slung holster brushing thigh. One of the killer breed, this man who had lain in wait for old Mark Severn.

Apparently satisfied, he tossed away the thumb-nailed match and turned unhurriedly into the chaparral, smoke curling from nostrils. Soon, the brooding stillness was again stirred by the sound of drumming hoofs as the assassin fled from the scene. The gray horse swung up his head, listened with cocked ears to the fading hoofbeats, nickered softly, then fell to nibbling the sparse short grass striving hopefully with the carpeting desert verbena for a place in the sun.

The echoes of the rifle shot that blasted Mark Severn out of his saddle were not to pass unheard. Jack Fielding, down in the sands of the Chuckwalla wash, reined in his tall red horse. There were reasons why the crackle of gunfire in the wild region of the Chuckwalla always caught his immediate interest. With the border conveniently close, men living beyond the law were numerous in the maze of desert hills south of the river and there were times when a sheriff's posse rode the land.

He listened tensely for a few moments. The silence was not again disturbed and presently he relaxed and thoughtfully made a cigarette. He was curious about the man who had fired that lone shot. He was not far distant, not more than a quarter of a mile.

He lit the cigarette and stared frowningly at the high bluffs of the mesa beyond the wash. There was a butte there where a man could get a good view and himself remain unseen. He wanted to get a look at that rifleman and find out his business in the Chuckwalla.

Jack pinched out the cigarette and soon the red horse was forging up the steep slope to the boulder-strewn mesa. Leaving the animal concealed in a thicket of mesquite, young Fielding went scrambling up the final precipitous rise of the butte. Almost instantly his quick eyes saw the lone rider, heading fast for the narrow mouth of upper Topaz Canyon. He whipped out binoculars, stared intently. The man was a stranger, but Jack was sure he would recognize him if they ever met, also that bald-faced pinto he rode. In another moment horse and rider were lost to view.

Jack returned the glasses to the leather case and reflectively made another cigarette. The unknown rider was obviously in a hurry to put distance between himself and the scene of the shooting.

The implication was sinister. Jack now knew the answer to that rifle shot. Murder had been done.

Another thought came crowding as he crouched there on the butte, an unpleasant thought that chilled him. He knew the trail down below the mesa bluffs. It was the cutoff old Mark Severn sometimes used and it was four or five miles shorter than the wagon road from the Bar 7 to Coldwater. More than once Jack had warned Mark he was taking chances by using the Topaz Canyon cutoff. There were men in the Chuckwalla who would jump at a chance to potshot the fearless and forthright old owner of the Bar 7 ranch. Mark was poison to the rustlers and border desperados infesting the Chuckwalla.

Spurred by a dreadful certainty, Jack hurriedly clambered down from his high perch and ran to his concealed horse. If his hunch was right, there was a chance, just a chance.

He was forced to follow along the rimrock almost two miles before he could break through to the lower slopes and turn into the trail winding up the dark gorge of the lower Topaz.

It was a seldom-used trail, little more than a cattle track, choked in places with slides of rock and shale, but Jack sent the big red horse along at reckless speed. Overhead two buzzards circled against the blue sky, sable-winged undertakers of the desert. Jack's heart sank. He dreaded

11

what the next bend in the trail might disclose.

The gloomy gorge of the lower Topaz suddenly widened into a vast clearing, perhaps some two miles across to the mouth of the upper canyon where Jack had glimpsed the lone horseman. Giant boulders lay in tumbled confusion and the trail now twisted between great hummocks covered with bristling cacti, tipped with pink and white blossoms.

Jack reined his horse and gazed around. It would be somewhere here, in Topaz Basin, that he would find what he sought. The place was ablaze with sunlight and gay with wildflowers and the low, encircling cliffs flung back gorgeous reds and greens and pinks. Jack had never seen the basin more savagely beautiful.

His horse flung up head, cocked his ears and Jack's roving gaze suddenly fastened on a thicket of white-plumed yucca. Something moved there. Behind the bristling green barrier appeared Mark Severn's gray horse. Jack spurred up the trail and in another minute was bending over the man lying face down among the wildflowers.

The old rancher was still breathing. Jack turned him over, propped him against his knee and after a moment the wounded cattleman's eyes flickered open.

"That . . . that you, Jack?" he muttered faintly, "how come . . . you here?" He gazed up at the anxious face bending over him, an odd mingling of suspicion and bewilderment in the pain-drawn eyes.

"Heard the shooting," the young man said briefly. "Hurt bad, Mark, old-timer?" He knew the question was idiotic, knew that old man Severn was dying.

"Reckon that bullet had my name on it," muttered the rancher, "won't be long . . . *now* . . ." He continued to stare up at the other man with suspicious, questioning eyes. "Was it you pulled that trigger?" His voice was suddenly strong and harsh. "Was it *you* who shot me?"

Young Fielding's tanned face paled. "No, Mark," he spoke huskily, "I'm not *that* kind of skunk."

Old Severn gazed up intently as if reading the other's soul, then something like a grin flickered across his stern features. "I'm believin' you, son, but you turned up so quick, so johnny-on-the-spot like, you got me to wonderin'. You see, I know things about you that other folks don't. . . ."

"You mustn't talk any more," Jack said firmly. "Take it easy, old-timer. I'll have a look at this bullet scratch, then it's the home ranch for you, and Doc Brown coming to fix you up as good as new."

The old man's grin was skeptical. "You're not fooling me, young fellow. That bullet was wearin' my name in big letters." His eyes closed. "The home ranch," he murmured drowsily, "the old

Bar 7 . . ." His voice trailed off to scarcely more than a whisper. "Reckon it will be dark . . . when I get back to the home ranch . . . dark . . . and then the sun, lifting over the old Bullions . . . always the sunrise, yonder . . . over the Bullion hills . . ." His head lifted and he gave Jack a grim smile. "No, son, you don't fool me . . . Doc Brown won't be fixin' me up . . . I'm going fast . . . no sense pretending I'm not . . . time is short and I've things to tell you . . ."

"I'm listening," Jack said. The old man was speaking the truth. No sense pretending. "What's on your mind, Mark?"

Mark Severn's smile was faint but grim. "I know about that hombre they call the Hawk . . ."

"The Range Hawk," murmured Jack, after a brief silence. He gestured. "You know more than most people, I'm thinking." His dark eyes hardened. "What do you know about the Hawk?"

"You're him, Jack," the old rancher whispered. "*You* are the Hawk, young fellow." Again a long silence, the two men staring at each other. "I'm not blamin' you," Mark Severn said. "You had a tough deal . . . your dad murdered . . . your cows rustled . . . your range stole . . ."

"Forget it." The young man's tone was harsh. "No need to worry about my troubles."

"Don't cut in on my talk." Severn's voice crackled. "I said I wasn't blaming you for fighting back. Your dad was my friend before you were

14

born . . . no finer man lived than John Fielding." Distress looked from his pain-dimmed eyes. "You haven't known I've been sidin' your play against Bert Cross and his Arrow crowd o' thieves."

"Bert Cross and his bunch have five thousand posted for the Range Hawk," Jack said thinly. "Plenty of folks would turn the Hawk in, if they knew what you think you know." He smiled affectionately. "You've been a mighty good friend to me," he added huskily.

"I've kept your secret, boy," muttered Severn. A chuckle rasped from his laboring throat. "Queer thing about the Range Hawk, he never bothers honest cattlemen, only rustles the Arrow outfit and the highbinders Bert Cross runs with."

"You said you'd important things to tell me," reminded the young man. He smiled faintly. "Don't you waste time worrying about this Hawk hombre. I reckon he can take care of himself."

"It's about my daughter's baby, Jack. You never knew I've a granddaughter . . . don't know where she is, but I want you to find her . . . the Bar 7 must be hers . . ."

"No," exclaimed Jack Fielding, astonished, "I sure didn't know about her, Mark. Never heard you had a granddaughter."

"Most eighteen by now," went on the old man. "Her name is Mary, same as her mother's, Mary Cameron, it is now. I lost track of her when she was a yearlin'. Never could find her." He

15

straightened up against the supporting knee, and his voice was suddenly strong. "I'm trusting the Range Hawk to find her. He's the one man I can trust to see that she gets the ranch, and if you don't find her, Jack, I've fixed up papers for you to own the Bar 7."

"You're trusting the Hawk plenty," murmured the young man, staring wide-eyed.

"He's a man I can trust," old Severn said simply. "Give me your hand, son . . ." His long gaunt frame was suddenly limp. "Mel Destrin . . . knows about the papers . . ." His voice faded.

Jack thought he had gone, but after a moment Mark Severn stirred, said in that feeble whisper, "You'll do your best, son . . . hold the old Bar 7 in trust . . . for, for Mary . . ."

Jack nodded, unable to speak. The rancher's hand tightened its clasp. "You can talk to the governor about it . . . Jim's my friend . . . made him executor . . ." Again that fleeting and grimly impish smile. "Jim don't know what I know about the Range Hawk. You needn't worry . . ."

He was suddenly silent, and Jack knew that Mark Severn had uttered his last words. He knew too they were words he would never forget.

He stood up presently, stared sorrowfully at the form lying so still among the wildflowers, and gradually from the confusion of his bewildered, grieving thoughts, he began to comprehend certain astonishing facts.

Mark Severn had long known the truth regarding the mysterious rustler called the Range Hawk, dreaded by some, beloved by others; yet despite his knowledge, the owner of the Bar 7 ranch had given all he possessed into the keeping of Jack Fielding as a sacred trust for an unknown granddaughter.

There was a dazed look in the young man's eyes. The prospect staggered him. If he failed to find the lost granddaughter, this Mary Cameron, he would himself become the owner of the Bar 7 ranch. And where would he look for the girl? There was no certainty that she still lived.

The possibility of there being no Mary Cameron appalled him. He could never rest until he found and installed her as the rightful owner of the Bar 7 ranch. It was in his thoughts too, that the Range Hawk must fly no more, so long as the solemn trust imposed by Mark Severn remained unfulfilled.

Jack's keen sun-browned face hardened as he pondered. There was strength in his long hard-muscled body, a seasoned, capable look about him. The hair under dusty black Stetson was dark, touched with reddish lights. The resolute dark eyes under shadowing brim were alert, and at this moment fiercely implacable as his gaze roved up the chaparral slope. The cowardly killer had lurked somewhere nearby, in those clustered brambles of greasewood.

His look went back to the limp form, prone among the wildflowers. There was nothing he could do for Mark Severn now, save bring to justice the assassin who had slain him from ambush, and fulfill the mission he had given.

Jack's eyes narrowed. He had reason to know the difficult trail to justice in the lawless reaches of the Chuckwalla. It came to him, as he pondered there by the side of his murdered friend, that perhaps after all the Range Hawk would again spread wing in relentless warfare.

He went soberly up the slope and presently found where the killer had lain in wait behind the clump of greasewood. Nothing of value as a possible clue, a few cigarette butts, carefully pinched out; the imprint of bootheels; an empty rifle shell, which he examined and pocketed. Scores of riders in the Chuckwalla used rifles of similar caliber, but the empty shell at least proved the assassin had used an old model .44.

He followed the boot tracks to where the horse had been concealed. Here his careful scrutiny met with some reward, for he found a broken piece of hair rope snagged in the brush.

Jack patiently worked the entangled strands free from the thorns. It was a valuable find. His eyes glinted as he studied the frayed end of rope, a skillful weaving of red, black and silvery hairs, the last from the tail of a Palomino, he decided. With a satisfied grunt, he pushed the foot-long strand of rope into a pocket. Some day he would meet that lone rider he had glimpsed disappearing into the portal of the upper Topaz, the owner of a hair rope woven in red, black and silver and he would be the murderer of old Mark Severn.

He went back down the chaparral slope to the flower-bordered trail and gently carried the slain cattleman to his gray horse where he tied him across the saddle for his last ride.

Mark Severn had spoken the truth. It would be dark when he reached the old home ranch.

CHAPTER TWO

Mrs. Kelly was glad to escape from the glaring sunshine into the cool dimness of the store. It was still uncomfortably warm, despite the waning afternoon, and a group of riders bent for Ace Coran's saloon had lifted choking clouds of dust as they tore past her.

Those Arrow men had no manners. In fact, Mrs. Kelly shrewdly suspected they had raised the dust on purpose to annoy her. She had recognized Curt Quintal, had caught his derisive grin as he spurred past.

She put down her basket and fanned her flushed face with a handkerchief. It was always pleasantly cool in the store. Jake Kurtz had a way of using the sprinkling can on the heavy planked floor and the walls were adobe, three feet thick. Jake took an enormous pride in his prosperous General Merchandise Emporium, a business he had started from a peddler's wagon.

He beamed at her from behind the counter, a rotund little man with a florid round face and a pink dome fringed with sparse grayish hair.

"*Ach*, Mrs. Kelly . . ." The storekeeper broke off and quick concern wiped the smile from his face as he saw the worry in the comely widow's eyes. Jake thought he knew the cause of her distress. He wagged his head dolefully. "*Ja*, it is bad news about Mr. Severn, a terrible t'ing . . ."

"It's devilish!" Mrs. Kelly's voice was weepy. "Me heart's fair broken, such a fine upstanding old man Mr. Severn was."

Jake Kurtz nodded vigorously. "A goot man . . ."

"An' that worthless Sheriff Slade coolin' his lazy feet across the street in Ace Coran's place, guzzlin' beer with that killer runnin' loose." Mrs. Kelly spoke fiercely.

Jake glanced around uneasily, shook his head reprovingly. "You must not egzited be," he warned, "it is no goot to say t'ings about Mr. Slade."

"I'll say what I want and say it to his face!" retorted the widow heatedly. "We need some *real* law in Coldwater, I'm tellin' you."

"It was dot Range Hawk kill Mr. Severn," the

storekeeper opined solemnly. "Such a rascal."

Mrs. Kelly's handsome eyes flashed. "Jake Kurtz, you're a bigger fool than I thought! I've a notion to put you out of me house this very day, sayin' such lies about the Range Hawk!"

The rotund storekeeper's face paled and he gave her a horrified look. He was her star border and partial to her famous corn beef and cabbage. Also it was no secret that Mr. Kurtz had romantic designs on the comely Widow Kelly. He lifted a plump protesting hand.

"It is the talk," panic made him stutter, "it is the talk people bring me . . ."

"Well," Mrs. Kelly spoke crisply, "don't you be repeatin' such idle chatter, or I'll never be speakin' to you again, Jake Kurtz." She gave him a shrewd look. "I'll wager a week's board 'tis talk that comes from Bert Cross of the Arrow outfit," she charged bitterly.

Jake Kurtz, breathing hard, kept a discreet silence. Mrs. Kelly looked at him, her expression softening. After all, Jake Kurtz was one of the few honest men in the cowtown of Coldwater and a decent soul if his dumb adoration *did* irk her at times.

"I'm needin' a few things I forgot this morning," she said, smiling at him, "and Jake, don't you be late for supper, there's corn beef and cabbage tonight."

Amicable relations restored, she went briskly

out with her purchases in the basket on her arm. Two young cowboys riding up the street drew rein and greeted her with cheerful grins.

"Hi, Ma! What's on the bill of fare tonight?"

"You can drop in and find out for your own self, Johnny Archer," chuckled the widow. She was mother to half the reckless young punchers in the county. They were always certain of a hearty welcome from Ma Kelly as she was fondly known, and there was always room for one more lonesome or sick young rider in her boarding house where she served absurdly big meals for absurdly small prices, and sometimes for no price at all.

Johnny Archer, stocky, sandy-haired and laughing-eyed, tipped back his dusty Stetson and turned a mock lugubrious look on his companion. "Give Ma the bad news, Smoky," he said brokenly, "I, I ain't got the nerve . . ."

"Johnny means we're broke, Ma," explained Smoky in a solemn voice. "We're sure a pair of busted cowpokes, Ma."

"Go on with you," placidly commented Ma Kelly. "I ain't got time to be listenin' to yer nonsense." Her pleasant eyes twinkled. "I'm warnin' you to come early or you'll be missin' the corn beef and cabbage."

"Honest, Ma," Johnny Archer's tone was embarrassed, "we're kind of shy on the *dinero* . . ."

"Who said anything about money?" retorted Ma

Kelly tartly. "You'll have a pay day comin' . . ."

"You're lookin' at two top-hand cowpunchers out of a job," Johnny informed her. "We ain't workin' for the Arrow no more, ma'am. Bert Cross give us the sack."

Mrs. Kelly was silent for a moment, her gaze intent on something down the street.

"You might try Jack Fielding," she said finally. "Jack's bossin' the Bar 7 now, since poor Mark Severn got killed. I just saw Jack go into Mel Destrin's law office," she added. "He's sure to be over to my place tonight an' you can have a talk with him. Jack always stops with me at the 'Dobe House when he's in town." She was fumbling in a pocket of her print dress as she spoke. "In the meantime, you two young scamps'll be needin' a bit of change and I'll stake you to a little something."

Johnny and Smoky lifted protesting hands. "You're sure one white man, Ma," proclaimed the abashed pair in unison.

"We ain't brung up that way, ma'am," added Johnny Archer virtuously.

"Go on with you," chuckled Ma Kelly, "as if I haven't staked the pair of you these many times." She flipped the gold coin up to Johnny's ready hand. "Only don't be spending it on Ace Coran's rotten whiskey," she warned.

Grinning their thanks, the two young cowboys rode on their way to Pop Shane's

Livery & Feed Stables at the end of the street.

"We'll be gettin' a haircut with all the fixings," the long, dark-browned Smoky Tucker called back to her.

Mrs. Kelly watched them for a moment, a fond look in her pleasant eyes. Nice youngsters, a bit reckless, but clean and honest. She'd put in a word for them with Jack Fielding. Her gaze swung to the Coldwater Palace Hotel down at the corner across the street. Hardpan Jones had just halted his San Carlos stage in front of the place and was lowering his long gaunt frame from the driver's seat to the accompaniment of rumbling abjurations to his sweat-lathered six horse hitch.

Ma Kelly's eyes suddenly widened. A young girl was climbing down from the high seat, assisted by Hardpan's reaching hand. She stood in the dusty street, gazing timidly around.

"Looks like she's scared to death," reflected Ma Kelly compassionately. "Not one of them brazen hussies that Ace Coran gets for his dance hall I'm betting." Her eyes hardened. "And speaking of the devil, there's Ace himself, and that black-hearted Bert Cross, standing there and looking as if they'd like to eat the poor little thing for supper. I declare . . ." Mrs. Kelly was already hurrying across the dusty street, red flags in her cheeks.

The saloon man, with the tall, sardonic-faced foreman of the big Arrow ranch listening at his shoulder, was already talking to the girl when Ma Kelly bustled up to them.

"But, I, I can't afford to stay at the hotel," the girl was protesting in a low, frightened voice, "I haven't much money . . ."

"No need to worry about the bill, Miss," the saloon man interrupted in his suave voice. "I'm part owner of the Palace, and if you're hard up I reckon we can fix up a job for you . . ."

"You'll fix up nothing, Ace Coran," broke in Ma Kelly's voice sharply. "A job in your nasty dance hall, you're meaning. Well, you can just run along. I'm taking care of this young lady."

"You keep your nose out of this," snarled the saloon man. Bert Cross kept silent, but the avid look in his eyes added fuel to Ma Kelly's wrath. Ignoring the two men, she smiled at the girl who was looking at her with something like relief in her dark blue eyes. She was a slim little thing with hair like delicate spun gold. It was evident that she was both frightened and perplexed.

"You come along with me, dear," Ma Kelly said. "I've plenty of room at my place, and you must be worn out after the long ride in from San Carlos." She tucked the young stranger's arm under hers.

The girl hesitated, glanced at Hardpan Jones coming round from the boot with a small, shabby bag. The gaunt old driver nodded reassuringly. "You go along with Ma Kelly, young lady," he said, and flung a scowl at the glowering Ace Coran. "Reckon you'd best leave it that way, Ace," he added gruffly and climbed up to his seat.

Ma Kelly picked up the bag and without further protest the girl accompanied her down the street toward the adobe building nestled among the tall feathery tamarisks.

"You'll be in time for supper," Mrs. Kelly chatted, "and after you've rested maybe you'll be tellin' me what brings you to Coldwater so lone and friendless like this."

"You're very kind," the girl said. Her voice was low and sweet, and the yellowing light of the setting sun glowed softly on her hair. "I, I was frightened when that man spoke to me. I didn't know just what to do."

Ma Kelly patted the cold hand tucked under her arm. "Don't be givin' him another thought, lass."

The girl gave her a shy little smile, and her dark blue eyes were suspiciously bright, as though she easily could have given way to tears. She was startlingly lovely, Ma Kelly realized.

"I think it's lucky I met you. . . ." There was a falter in the low voice. "Only, you see, I really have no money . . . a dollar or two left, and that man did say something about a job . . ."

"Ace Coran has no job for the likes of you," said Ma Kelly firmly. "You needn't be worryin' about the money, lass. You're welcome to stay with me as long as you please. As for a job, you can have one. I run a boarding house," she added, "the 'Dobe House, I call the place, and if you don't mind waiting on table you've a job this very minute."

"I'd love it," said the girl simply. Tears sparkled on long curling lashes.

Ma Kelly chuckled, paused in front of a gate set in a neat white picket fence. "Well, here's the 'Dobe House, and welcome you are, lass." There was pride in her voice and involuntarily she touched the little cross of carved wood resting on her bosom. It had been fashioned by the fingers of a weary and thirsting Franciscan padre who a century earlier had rested in the shade of the tamarisks and paloverde quenching his thirst at the eternally bubbling springs hereabouts. He had bestowed grateful blessing, and the name of *Agua Frio* on the desert oasis that had refreshed him. The passing of the years and the coming of the gringos had changed it to Coldwater.

The little cross of paloverde wood profoundly affected the young widow Kelly when she chanced to find it still embedded in the same tree from which it had been carved. It was a sign and the abandoned old adobe house nestled among the green trees, beckoned her. Truly it was an oasis in the desolation of her widowhood, and like the trees by the flowing springs, Mrs. Kelly took deep root in the same soil that nourished them. She was proud of the home she had made on the spot where once a weary holy man had rested and upon which he had bestowed his grateful blessing.

She drew the girl inside the gate. Through the trees showed glimpses of a red-tiled roof and gray walls festooned with scarlet flowers.

"It's like Heaven," said the girl softly.

"It's taken a heap o' work to make it so," chuckled Ma Kelly, "but it's the truth, child, that we've each of us got to make our own heaven."

The thud of horses' hoofs swung them round to the street. The riders reined up at the gate.

"Hello, Ma!"

"Hello yourself, Tim, hello boys!" Mrs. Kelly beamed at the bearded man and his grinning companions. "Are you tellin' me you'll be in for supper after a bit?"

"You've guessed the dark secret, Ma," chuckled the grizzled giant with the beard. He rode on, followed by the cowboys who flickered admiring glances at the girl as they passed.

She stood there watching them, tense and wide-eyed, hand pressed to her breast. "Who, who is he—that old man?" There was an odd breathless note in her low voice.

"Tim Hook," informed Mrs. Kelly. "Tim owns the Diamond D, and a rare man he is." She looked at the girl curiously. "What's wrong with you, child? You're as white as a sheet, an' your heart's goin' like mad."

"Oh, I, I don't know. I'm just, just tired and nervous I suppose." The girl drew a long breath, suddenly smiled. "You must let me help wait on the tables tonight, Mrs. Kelly. It'll be fun to wait on those nice cowboys."

"I'm thinkin' I'll be needin' your help," admitted Ma Kelly. "I wasn't lookin' for the Diamond D crowd in tonight."

As they went on down the flower-bordered walk, there was a mystified look in Mrs. Kelly's pleasant eyes.

"Stared at Tim Hook like he was a ghost," she mused. "Wonder what queer business brings the child to Coldwater?"

For some reason, vague forebodings troubled Ma Kelly and her thoughts went again to the sinister talk as to the slayer of old Mark Severn. She had come to learn the amazing truth about the Range Hawk's identity, and was frightened for him.

CHAPTER THREE

"You've been a long time coming," grumbled Mel Destrin, "over a week since the funeral . . ."

"Spring roundup," explained Jack Fielding, "and old Buck Wells is laid up with a busted leg.

Haven't had a chance to get in for a talk with you about things."

"It's a queer business," fretted the lawyer. He was a thin, grayish man with sharp features and shiny restless black eyes. Two protruding upper teeth lifted his lip in a perpetual fox-like grimace. "Mark Severn is trusting you plenty, young fellow." He tapped the papers on the desk with tobacco-stained fingers. "If you can prove there is no granddaughter you get the Bar 7 ranch, lock, stock and barrel."

"We'll take the line that sooner or later we'll find her," Jack said curtly. "In the meantime I'll hold things down at the Bar 7 like I promised Mark."

"I'm trying to tell you that if you don't find this Mary Cameron you become owner of the Bar 7," snapped Destrin. "You're in a tough spot. Folks will talk if you don't find her."

Jack stared at him, his eyes coldly contemptuous. He had never liked Mel Destrin.

"Meaning I don't want to find the girl?"

The lawyer's fangs showed in a crafty smile. "There are some who wouldn't try too hard," he said.

"I don't like your kind of talk," growled the young man. He looked tired and worried. Things were not going well at the Bar 7. The outfit was shorthanded and with the foreman laid up with a broken leg, the thousand and one details incidental to preparing for the spring roundup all devolved on him. "Tell me what you know, Destrin, and keep to facts."

He listened gloomily while the lawyer went over the papers.

"Mark never heard from his daughter but once after she eloped with young Cameron . . . this picture . . . nothing else . . . no letter . . ." Destrin passed a small photograph over to Jack who studied it in silence.

Mark Severn's daughter was very pretty, fair-haired and laughing-eyed. Jack judged the baby in her arms must have been only a few months old. There was an inscription in a girlish hand, the ink faded. *Dear Daddy—with love from me, and your little granddaughter—Mary Cameron.*

"Poor old Mark!" Jack's voice was husky. "He sure kept it secret." He handed the picture back to the lawyer.

"That's the only word he ever had about a granddaughter," said the lawyer. "Mary and her husband were killed in a train wreck and from that day until this very afternoon there has been no trace of the baby."

Jack's long frame jerked upright in the creaky chair.

"This afternoon?" He spoke sharply. "What do you mean, Destrin?"

The lawyer's grimace was more fox-like than ever. "I've been working on this thing myself,

Jack," he said complacently. "Ever since old Mark Severn got me to draw up these papers, I've been busy, and this afternoon I got this letter at the post office. It came in on the noon stage."

"Let's see it!" Jack almost snatched the paper from Destrin's hand. It was addressed to the lawyer and written on cheap hotel stationery with an El Paso date line.

Dear Sir:

I happened to see your advertisement in a paper here and think maybe I'm the Mary Cameron you want to find. I don't remember my mother—she died in a train wreck, but I've got an old letter her father wrote when she sent him my baby picture. His name was Mark Severn and he had a big cattle ranch from what the letter says, only I don't know where, because the letter doesn't say and I was too young when my mother died for her to tell me about him. I've made a copy of his letter and if you think I'm the Mary Cameron you want to find, I'll come and see you as quickly as you let me know.

"Sounds like she's the girl, right enough," muttered Jack, frowning at the signature. He looked exultantly at the lawyer. "My God, Destrin, if only old Mark could have lived to read this!"

"Here's the letter she enclosed," grunted the lawyer. "A copy, of course."

The copy of Mark Severn's letter to his daughter was written on the same cheap hotel stationery.

My dear Daughter:

I was very happy, Mary, to have the picture of you and my little grandchild. I want to see her, and I must see you, too. I am lonesome and longing for my dear daughter. The old ranch is your home and will be yours and little Mary's some day. Come as quickly as you can and tell your husband he is welcome. I want him to be a son to me and help me run the ranch. I'll make a good cattleman out of him.

Lovingly your Dad,

Mark Severn

"Poor old Mark," muttered Jack. He was deeply moved by the pathos and longing of the words written so long ago by the proud and unhappy owner of the Bar 7. His hopes had been shattered so cruelly. "If only he could have lived for this," repeated the young man regretfully. Mel Destrin's high nasal voice broke in on his reflections.

"How does it sound to you, Jack?"

"Best news I've heard for a long time!" Young Fielding's tone was jubilant. "Get word to her at once, Mel. There's no doubt in my mind. She's our Mary Cameron!"

Mel Destrin nodded. "I'll send a man over to San Carlos with a telegram," he decided. "I'll tell her to bring any other proof of identity she can dig up, but of course the original of old Mark's letter is good enough for me—good enough for any court."

Jack grinned happily. "Sure is one big load off my mind," he declared. "How quick do you reckon she'll get here, Mel?"

"Inside of the week," guessed the lawyer. "I'll wire her the fare," he added.

Jack nodded agreement to this. "I'm leaving it to you," he said. "I've got plenty on my mind these days, the way things are at the Bar 7." His tone was grim. "Mark has been losing too many cows to rustlers. Reckon he was slipping, the way I size things up."

"The Range Hawk," murmured Mel Destrin. "You clip that bird's wings, Jack, and there won't be any more Bar 7 cows rustled—or any other fellow's beef, either."

The young man was silent, meditative gaze bent on the cigarette he was making.

Destrin watched him with sharp black eyes. "There's talk in the town about the Range Hawk being the killer of old Mark Severn," he said softly.

"I've been hearing that talk," muttered Jack. He lifted cold eyes. "I reckon Bert Cross is one of the loudest talkers, huh, Mel?" The young

34

cattleman gave the lawyer a hard smile. "Bert Cross needn't worry. I'm getting the man who killed Mark Severn."

"You'll have plenty of help," nodded Destrin.

Jack shrugged his indifference to this, and after a moment he said curiously, "I've been wondering about something you were saying awhile back, about my being in a tough spot if I didn't find Mary Cameron. What made you talk that way to me, Mel? You already knew about this letter, knew the girl was found."

The lawyer gestured placatingly. "I was afraid you might be sore," he confessed. "Wasn't sure how you'd take my trying to locate the girl without talking to you before going ahead and advertising."

"Glad you did," reassured Jack. He heaved a relieved sigh and got to his feet. "Let me know when she gets in, Mel. I'm only hoping she'll prove to be our Mary Cameron." His voice took on a regretful note. "I'd give a lot if poor old Mark could be here to welcome her to the ranch." He broke off, swung round to the door and stared coldly at the newcomer framed in the entrance.

"Hello, Bert," the lawyer said, waving to a chair. "Come in and listen to some good news. We've located Mark's lost granddaughter, or think we have."

The tall Arrow foreman gave Jack a frosty nod

and dropped into a chair. There was a scowl on his darkly handsome face.

"I'm fed up with that nosy old Kelly woman," he grumbled.

"What's she done this time, Bert?" The lawyer's lip lifted in his foxy grin.

Cross told them about the girl Hardpan Jones had brought in on his stage.

"Ace Coran was only trying to be decent—told her she needn't worry about any hotel bill—told her he'd fix her up with a job, and then that snooty Kelly female horns in and fairly drags the girl off to her own dump."

Mel Destrin chuckled. "Must be a good-looker," he commented. "Ace always was one to spot a good-looker for that place of his." He winked knowingly at the tall young boss of the Bar 7. The latter was staring with cold scorn at the Arrow man.

"I'm swinging my rope for her," Bert Cross said, as he turned his head to look at Jack. It was plain that no love was lost between these two big men. "I'm swinging a loop for the girl," he repeated, and there was arrogant insolence in his tone, a note of warning. "You can tell your friend, Ma Kelly, I said so, if you want, Fielding."

Mel Destrin broke in hurriedly, as if fearing a clash between the two. "I was telling you we think we've found Mark's granddaughter," he said. "Listen to this, Bert—" He read the letter aloud.

"Sounds good," admitted the Arrow foreman, nodding. He looked at Jack. "What do *you* think, Jack?"

"Mel knows what I think." Jack's tone was curt and throwing the lawyer a brief nod he pushed out to the street.

The last remnants of twilight were fading as he made his way to Pop Shane's livery barn. A paunchy man wearing a white apron was lighting the big swinging kerosene lamp in front of the Royal Flush saloon. Jack slackened his stride as he passed the line of cow ponies drooping at the long hitch rail. The bartender climbed from his stool and grinned at him.

"Hear you're bossin' the Bar 7, now old Mark's gone," he greeted. "How's the old spread makin' out these days?"

Jack halted, a smile softening the hard light in his eyes. "Hello, Monte!"

Monte Boone picked up his stool and cocked a critical gaze at the lamp. Jack had known him for years. Monte was an old-time cowhand, a former member of the Fielding JF outfit in his younger days. He was gray and fat now and there were heavy pouches under his washed-out blue eyes. Jack had a fondness for the old rascal in spite of the fact that he was now tending bar for Ace Coran whom he heartily disliked.

"Goin' out tonight, Jack?" The barman spoke in a husky whisper. "Got somethin' to tell you."

37

"Tell me now."

Monte flicked an uneasy glance at the swing doors. "Ain't safe," he muttered. "Quintal's back inside."

"I'll be at Shane's at eight," Jack told him.

Monte nodded, his gaze on three riders drifting up the street and trailing little riffles of dust that made a thin golden haze in the fading sunset.

"Looks like that Mex feller, Don Vicente," he said aloud, and then, in a low whisper, "watch yorese'f, Jack, keep yore eyes wide open while yo're in town." He pushed through the swing doors with his stool.

Jack stood for a minute, making a cigarette, his gaze traveling down the line of horses at the hitch rail. There was purpose in his apparently idle scrutiny. He was looking for a red and black hair rope with a silver thread, a rope that would match the broken end in his pocket.

The three horsemen drew up in front of Jake's store. Two of them wore the tall steeple hats common below the border. The third rider was tall and young with a trim black mustache. His more resplendent attire and elaborate saddle gear proclaimed him as a man of some consequence. Silver braid adorned his flat-brimmed hat and short jacket, and dark tightfitting trousers belled over fine leather boots inset with large-roweled silver spurs.

As he tied his sleek Palomino to the gnawed

hitching post the young caballero looked across at Jack. The latter lifted his cigarette in an almost imperceptible gesture and passed it from right hand to left. The young Mexican withdrew his blank gaze and muttered something to his companions who came jingling across the dusty street. Without glancing at Jack, they pushed through the swing doors into the saloon. The caballero went leisurely across the boardwalk and paused under the glow of the big kerosene lamp swinging above the entrance to the store. He stood there for a minute making a cigarette. He lit it, then passed it to his left hand, his look slowly coming over his shoulder to Jack as he sauntered into the long store.

Jack moved on, his expression thoughtful. Once he halted and stared intently at a pinto horse. The killer of Mark Severn had ridden a pinto. Jack's gaze went to the rope coiled on the saddle, a well-worn rawhide, not a hair rope. He continued on his way to Pop Shane's livery barn.

Pop was seated in his old much-mended rawhide chair. He was an elderly, leathery-faced man with sleepy-lidded eyes that usually saw more than people suspected. But Pop was a cautious individual and not given to prying into things he observed. All sorts of men were numbered among the patrons of his livery stable, and if there were times when he suspected the worst of some of them, he wisely kept his mouth shut. It was only with certain friends that he chose to be confidential. Jack was a friend, the son of a man who had been one of his best friends. He waved a greeting and spat a dark brown stream into the litter of straw at his feet.

"Well, son, what's on yore mind? You look doggone solemn."

Jack squatted on his heels by the side of the rickety chair and frowned at the glowing tip of his cigarette.

"You maybe can tell me something, Pop." He fished the broken end of hair rope from a pocket. "Ever see a hair rope like this one around your barn?"

The old liveryman took it between bony fingers. "Looks like Tomi's work," he speculated. "There's a number of fellers that stable their broncs here has Tomi's hair ropes." He shook his head. "Ain't been seein' one with that twist of silver which is in this here piece."

Jack stuffed the frayed end of rope into his pocket. He knew Tomi, an old Shoshone who sometimes drifted in from his desert abode with a supply of his cunningly braided hair ropes. Two or three times a year he would be found squatting on his haunches in front of Jake Kurtz's store in solemn barter with the cowboys eager for his wares.

"When do you reckon he'll be in town again?"

"No tellin'," answered Pop. "Ain't seen Tomi

for months. He's awful old, that Injun. Mebbe he's dead, for all I know."

"Any idea where he lives?"

The liveryman shook his head, ejected another brown stream into the straw at his feet. "You'll have a hard time findin' that hombre," he prophesied. "Tomi holes up some place in the hills, but he ain't tellin' nobody his address."

"Pop," Jack said, after a moment's thought, "you keep your eyes open for that old Indian. Next time he comes to town you hang on to him and send me word."

"I'll keep him for you if I have to hog-tie him," promised the liveryman. There was a question in his eyes that he did not voice. Jack gave him a grim smile.

"I'm thinking this piece of rope will hang the man who killed Mark Severn," he said.

"I get you, son." Pop Shane spat again and his sleepy-lidded eyes were suddenly sharp and hard. "There's more than one man behind that killin'," he declared.

"You're not one of those saying it's the Range Hawk, huh, Pop?"

"No, son." Pop's sleepy eyes took on a faraway look. "I ain't sayin' it's the Range Hawk that killed Mark Severn." His gaze came round to Jack. "The Range Hawk ain't popular in this cowtown, no more than you are, son." His voice lowered, took on a hard, grim note. "You watch

41

yoreself, Jack. I sit here an' see a lot o' things an' my ears listen plenty good, so you mind what I'm tellin' you."

"Thanks, old-timer." Jack stood up. "I'll be heading back to the ranch at sunup, Pop. You tell Miguel to give Red his grain early." With an affectionate parting smile he turned on heel and went clattering up the boardwalk.

The liveryman watched the tall form disappear into the gathering darkness, then with a grunt, got out of his chair and vanished into his office. When he reappeared, he bore an ancient Sharps rifle in his hand. He resumed his seat and set to work cleaning and oiling the gun. There was a hard light in the old man's eyes as he worked away with his oiled rag and words came from his lips in scarcely audible grunts.

"Wasn't thinkin' I'd ever use you again, doggone you. No tellin' though, plenty varmints needin' a dose of yore lead poisonin'. Aim to have you ready, doggone you."

He sat back presently and gnawed off a corner of plug tobacco and the gloom deepened over his leathery countenance. He was fond of the young man who had just left him. Pop's somber thoughts went down the long lane of the years to the day when he had ridden stirrup to stirrup with Jack's father. Young and lusty riders of the range they were then. With Mark Severn, he and Fielding had followed the great herds of longhorns up from

Texas more than once, had shared the perils of Indian raids and had weathered many a storm together.

The old man shook his head sadly. Those had been days to test the mettle of a man—floods and Indians and rustlers—death always lurking near. John Fielding had finally realized his ambition and lived to see great herds wearing his JF brand, while Mark Severn's Bar 7 reached across the hills to the border. Men had said they were lucky, but Pop knew it was not luck, but the good, honest metal in his two friends of those epic days when cattle and the cowboy were making frontier history and wresting an empire from the wilderness under the western horizon.

Pop's bony fingers tightened around the hard steel of the long rifle between his knees and bitter rage looked from his eyes. They were dead now, those two gallant comrades of his youth, slain from ambush by cowardly assassins, and John Fielding's once prosperous cattle ranch a remnant of its former greatness. John's son himself was now marked for the same death that had overtaken his father and the owner of the Bar 7.

The old man's thoughts went to the mysterious man known as the Range Hawk, the Robin Hood of the Chuckwalla. It was significant that the Range Hawk had made his first appearance shortly after the murder of old John Fielding. It was also a curious fact that only certain ranches suffered from the depredations of the daring raider and his riders. The big eastern-owned Arrow ranch was the heaviest loser. Who the Range Hawk could be and where he came from was a baffling mystery. It was known only that his band numbered some half score men and that the smaller outfits of the honest cattlemen were immune from their despoiling attentions. Indeed there were certain cattlemen whose hearts were gladdened by the mysterious return of long-lost stock. Horses would be found in their corrals and cattle again feeding on their own lawful range. Gradually the myth of the Range Hawk had grown and it was whispered that more than one grateful rancher was always ready to give aid, and a temporary hiding place to the unknown Nemesis of their powerful and ruthless neighbors. The latter, among them the big Arrow outfit, made it a point to charge all the rustling and the killings to the Range Hawk. Sheriff Slade, elected to office by unscrupulous interests headed by Bert Cross and Ace Coran, was notoriously lax in his duties save only in following the phantom trail of the elusive Hawk.

Old Pop Shane's eyes narrowed to grim slits as he sat there, the long rifle between his knees, gaze boring up the street where lights made yellow gleams through the darkness. The enigma of the Range Hawk was still a baffling mystery to the sheriff, but there was no telling when the Arrow's hireling lawman might stumble upon the amazing truth. The rewards now totaled more than five thousand dollars and there were those who might be weak enough to succumb to the temptation to take the Judas silver for betrayal of the man Sheriff Slade had sworn to hang.

The old liveryman's fears for Jack Fielding would have risen to fever heat could he have overheard the talk behind the lighted windows of Mel Destrin's office. Jack *was* in mortal danger that night, though not for the reasons that were troubling Pop Shane.

"Took the letter the way a hungry trout takes the hook," gloated the fox-faced lawyer. "It's in the bag, Bert."

The Arrow foreman's eyes narrowed thoughtfully. "Don't be too sure," he warned. "Jack Fielding's smart."

"He's dumb," sneered Destrin.

"He's smart," reiterated Bert Cross, "and he's a fighting fool, same as his dad was, same as old Mark Severn."

"And where are those two old-timers now?" The lawyer's lip lifted in his fox-like grin. "Don't you worry, Bert. I'll have that young man where his dad is, before long." He paused, fixed his restless black eyes on the other man. "Let's go have a drink," he said abruptly. "I've a word to whisper in Curt Quintal's ear."

45

The Arrow man nodded, his smile ugly. "I gave Curt your message," he murmured. "Told him to get hold of Fargo. Reckon he's over at Ace's place now."

The lawyer stuffed his papers into a drawer and sprang like a jack-in-the-box from his swivel chair.

"Let's go. Wasn't thinking Quintal would have Fargo in town so quick."

As the two men hurried into the street, Destrin came to an abrupt standstill and stared intently at a tall shadowy form moving past Jake's store.

"That's him, now," he muttered. "That's young Fielding, heading for Ma Kelly's." His gaze came round to his tall companion, and there was wicked mirth in his sharp button eyes. "It'll be a setup for Fargo, huh, Bert?"

"No telling," grunted the Arrow man. "Jack is fast with his guns, fast as lightning."

"Fargo is faster," declared Destrin confidently. "Fargo always gets his man."

The swing doors of the Royal Flush closed behind them.

CHAPTER FOUR

Mel Destrin was wrong in his guess that Jack was heading for Ma Kelly's at that moment. Ma Kelly was in his thoughts, and also the good food he knew would be waiting to satisfy a healthy appetite, but he had a certain matter to attend to before he could relax and enjoy the widow's hospitality.

He passed the store at a leisurely walk and mindful of the two warnings he had already received that evening he kept his eyes alert. He knew that a lot of Arrow riders were in town, including the bull-shouldered Curt Quintal. The latter was Bert Cross's right bower, unscrupulous and dangerous, and in active command of the ruthless operations that were browbeating the smaller ranchers. It was thus that the Arrow outfit was gradually gaining an iron-handed domination of the range.

Almost automatically Jack's roving gaze covered the horses drooping at the lines of hitch rails on both sides of the street. The town was full tonight and most of the animals wore the Arrow iron, with a sprinkling of the DX brand. Tied in front of Moraga's *cantina* were four Flying A horses. These three outfits had always bitterly

47

contested for the range with his father and old Mark Severn.

Grim lines marked the young man's lean face as he made his way up the street. He smelled trouble, trouble that might demand the Range Hawk's attention, and the thought depressed him. The gathering of the clans in Coldwater that night was ominously significant. Besides, there was Don Vicente Torres. His presence could mean but one thing.

He came to the long stretch of darkness between Moraga's *cantina* and Ma Kelly's 'Dobe House. Behind, the lights gleamed softly yellow in the windows, and in front, he could see the twinkle of Ma Kelly's lights through the tamarisks bending gently to the night wind.

His tall form made a vague shape in the black night, still moonless, with only the stars twinkling overhead. He halted, quickly removed his scraping spurs and drifted on soundless feet down a deep and narrow gully.

He moved cautiously, eyes wary, seeking out every shadow of boulder and bush, until finally he came to the large stump of a lightning-blasted sycamore. He stood beside it and stared intently up through the darkness toward the street. Presently a shape took form, came toward him on feet as soundless as thistledown.

"*Bueno*, it is you my frien'."

The shadow materialized into the elegant young

Mexican, teeth gleaming white in a pleased smile. "It is good you are in town, Juan," the newcomer continued in soft Spanish. "I have news that means work for the Hawk this night."

"I guessed as much when I saw you riding up the street," responded Jack gloomily. "I can't say that I'm glad to see you, Vicente, or to hear your news."

"It is another blow at these enemies who would destroy you, my friend," pointed out the young caballero. His tone showed surprise. "Have you not sworn to avenge your father's death and to despoil those who have despoiled him—and you?"

"I'll not rest until the men who killed my father are destroyed as well as those who plotted his death and ruin," admitted the owner of the ravaged JF ranch. He spoke in Don Vicente's mother tongue. "But the debt we must collect has grown since I saw you last, and new cares have come to me, Vicente." Rage made his low voice tight, almost inaudible. "Mark Severn has been murdered, shot down from ambush."

"I had not heard," muttered the young Mexican in a shocked voice. "*Por Dios*, this is sad news, my friend. A gallant hombre was Señor Severn, an honest man, and brave in his fight against infamous scoundrels."

"He left a trust to me," Jack said grimly. In brief words he gave his friend an account of the charge Mark Severn had put upon him.

49

"Mark as much as said he knew that I am the Range Hawk," he finished. "I'm wondering how many other people are beginning to suspect the truth."

Don Vicente flashed his white teeth in an amused smile. "A beeg joke, thees bol' bandit of the border, no?" he chuckled in English, and then his tone grave, he said in Spanish, "Do not forget, my friend and brother, that I am fighting always by your side. You have saved the life and honor of Don Vicente Torres, and Don Vicente Torres does not forget a debt."

"You've repaid the debt many times, Vicente," smiled the young cattleman. "If I have saved your life, do not forget that you have saved mine more than once. It would have gone hard with the Hawk had you not flown so bravely by his side." Jack paused, gestured for silence as the Mexican started to speak. "Listen, somebody's up there in the road."

Faintly they caught the sound of stealthy footsteps, then again only the stir of the night wind in the brush, the sounds of revelry from the saloon, the tunking of a banjo in Moraga's *cantina* and a voice suddenly lifted in a plaintive love song. Don Vicente said softly, "Estevan and Diego watch for me. No one will escape their eyes."

Jack nodded. "I grow nervous," he muttered. "Two warnings have been given me tonight to be on my guard." He shrugged his powerful shoulders. "What is this news, Vicente, that you bring?"

"Word has come to me of another raid to be charged against the Range Hawk," said the young Mexican. "Our enemies plan an attack on Señor Cole's ranch. It will be a very complete destruction, buildings burned and horses and cattle run across the border." Don Vicente gestured expressively. "The sign of the Hawk will be left for men to see."

"I was smelling trouble," muttered Jack. "So it's old Bill Cole this time. Means his finish. He'll pull up stakes, clear out for keeps, and that means another slice of the Chuckwalla grazing Arrow steers." He scowled. "The sign of the Hawk, huh, Vicente? Smart trick those devils thought up, always leaving a hawk's feather stuck in a man's door."

"You and I know that the Hawk does not boast of his deeds. He leaves no feather at the door," said Vicente Torres harshly. "It is as you say a devil's trick to fool the Señor Slade and make him believe it is the Hawk who kills and steals."

"I'm not so sure Sheriff Slade is fooled," declared Jack. "He knows more than he lets on. He knows the men back of all this. Slade's one of the gang."

"*Si*," agreed the Mexican, and added in English, "I t'ink some day thees sheriff hombre weel 'ear the Hawk scream death ver' close to heem."

"We can't let them do this to old Cole," broke

51

in Jack. "I reckon you're right, Vicente, the Hawk flies again this night." They talked for a few minutes, discussing plans.

"It is agreed then," Don Vicente murmured. "We will meet in Topaz Basin at the rising of the moon and fall upon the thieves in the bottle-neck of the lower Topaz as they drive the stolen cows to the border." He nodded contentedly. "It is a good plan, Juan, and this time we must not let one man escape our guns."

They went back up the dark gulch, pausing in the shadow of a great boulder. The Mexican made the soft hoot of an owl. There came an answering hoot and two men suddenly stood in the road above them.

"All is well," muttered Don Vicente. "It is Diego and Estevan who wait for me."

One of the steeple-hatted men spoke softly to his chief.

"A man went past us, a gringo unknown to us." The Mexican gestured toward Ma Kelly's place. "He waits concealed in the paloverde near the gate."

"It's a good bet he waits for me," muttered Jack. He slid gun from holster.

"*Bueno*," grunted Don Vicente. "We will give thees hombre the beeg surprise, no?" A gesture sent his two men drifting into the darkness. "We will circle round and come up from behind him," he told Jack.

They moved stealthily through the night, vague shapes that gave out no sound, and presently drew close to the clump of paloverde. Voices reached them from the 'Dobe House, the clatter of dishes. Jack recognized the booming tones of old Tim Hook of the Diamond D. Tim would be the next on the list, most likely, he reflected. The waters of the Ox Bow would be a valuable addition to the Arrow ranch. He wondered grimly if the big eastern cattle syndicate was aware of its manager's activities. He was beginning to suspect that Bert Cross was furthering his own personal ambitions, that he schemed to make himself lord of the entire Chuckwalla country and eventually even to absorb the Arrow itself. An obstacle in his path was Jack Fielding, an obstacle to be ruthlessly removed.

The young man's fierce gaze, probing the black shadows of the paloverde, suddenly discerned a huddled shape crouching there.

He looked about him, picked out the motionless shapes of his fellow-stalkers. It was not possible to get closer to the paloverde undetected. Jack flattened behind a low boulder and suddenly his voice cut through the night like cold steel.

"Drop your gun. We've got you covered."

A muttered oath came from the clump of trees. Jack repeated his warning.

"Stand up," he said, "walk this way, and keep your hands up or you're a dead man."

There was a moment's silence, a stirring in the brush and the huddled form became an upright shape. It moved reluctantly into the fifty foot clearing. Jack stood up, gun leveled.

"All right, boys, get him—"

In a minute, the two Mexicans had the prowler securely lashed with a rawhide lariat one of them carried over his shoulder. Jack proceeded to question him.

"Waiting to pot shot somebody?"

"Was just layin' there waiting for a friend." The man's voice was a mixture of sullenness and fright.

"You lie," Jack told him. "You were waiting for a chance to empty your gun into me."

"I never seen you before," answered the man. "What for would I be taking a shot at you?"

"Who are you working for?" demanded Jack. "Talk up, mister."

"I told you I was waiting for a friend."

"What's his name?"

The man hesitated, looked about him desperately, cringed under the implacable eyes of the men staring at him. Don Vicente spoke in a soft aside to Jack.

"We will take him with us and keep him safe until he tells what we want to know," he said.

Jack nodded assent, his gaze intent on the vicious, sullen face of the prisoner. The man was a stranger to him—not the man he had seen riding away from the scene of Mark Severn's murder.

"Where are you from?" he asked.

"Come down from Montana. Only just got into Coldwater."

"What's your name?"

"Fargo Laben, and I'm telling you I was just laying here waiting to meet a friend."

"Take the skunk along with you," Jack said disgustedly. "No time to waste with him now."

"*Si*." Vicente's tone was silky, his eyes agate hard. "Diego has ways to make thees kind talk."

Jack stood for a minute watching his friends until the darkness hid them, then he made his way into Ma Kelly's garden by way of the back gate. He would have a full hour before the long ride to Topaz Basin, time enough to eat and have a chat with the widow. Mrs. Kelly was one of the few friends he had in Coldwater. Time was when the names of Fielding and Severn stood for something in the little cowtown. There was no need in those days for a sheriff. John Fielding and Mark Severn had always stood for justice to all men and the border bad men had shied away from the place.

Ma Kelly greeted him with a beaming smile.

"I was beginnin' to think you were not comin', lad," she said, "an' sorry I was for you to miss the fine supper we have tonight."

"It's always a fine supper when I come to the 'Dobe, Ma," chuckled the young man. "Let me have it fast. I'm riding soon."

Ma Kelly bustled away and soon the waitress was placing hot food before him. She was new to him, slim and appealing with her blonde young loveliness. She gave him a timid smile and he saw that her eyes were a dark blue and shyly wistful.

"Who's the new girl, Ma?" he queried, when Mrs. Kelly returned from the kitchen and sank into the chair opposite him.

"She's new to the town, Maisie is," the widow told him. "A nice little lass if she is sort of timid-like, and kind of mysterious-actin'."

Jack recalled Bert Cross's account of the girl who had come in on the stage.

"She's the same," Ma Kelly said. "I was just in the nick of time to save her from the clutches of that Ace Coran devil. She's broke, she tells me, and glad she was to take the job with me, and glad I am to have the lass." Mrs. Kelly shook her head. "She's a bit of a puzzle to me, kind of lost-actin'. Also 'tis very strange the way she keeps watchin' old Tim Hook—the way she's doing now, if you'll take a look at her."

Tim Hook and his two riders were sauntering from the dining room, on their faces the contented expressions of men who had enjoyed a good meal, and Jack saw that the young girl was gazing with a curious, almost breathless eagerness at the big, bearded owner of the Diamond D.

"You see what I mean, Jack?" Ma Kelly gave him a bewildered look. "She has me guessin'."

"I'd say that Tim reminds her of somebody," was the young man's comment. He smiled at the widow. "It's mighty lucky you got her away from Ace Coran." His face darkened. "Bert Cross gave me a message for you, Ma. Said to tell you he's swinging a loop for this Maisie girl of yours."

"The black-hearted devil!" exclaimed the widow. She flushed angrily. "I'll give him a bit of me tongue, bad cess to him."

"He'll have plenty of rivals," chuckled the young man. "Tim's boys could scarcely see the door for looking sideways at her."

"Not to mention young Johnny Archer and Smoky Tucker," laughed Ma Kelly, obviously not displeased with the hit her new waitress was making. "Them two young cow wallopers have been groggy ever since Maisie give 'em a smile." Ma lowered her voice. "It's lucky you're in town this night, Jack. I'm wantin' to put in a word with you for them two boys. They've been fired from the Arrow and I'm thinkin' you could give 'em a job out at the Bar 7."

"I sure could use a couple of good hands," Jack said, staring across the room at the two young cowboys now attempting a bashful conversation with the new girl, "but you know how I feel about the Arrow outfit. That brand is no recommendation."

"Johnny tells me Bert Cross give 'em the sack," answered Ma Kelly. "I'd say that was recommendation enough. Bert Cross wouldn't want a decent body on his pay roll." She tossed her head.

Jack nodded. There was truth in the widow's canny viewpoint. "I'll talk with them," he decided. "Tell them to come over as soon as they have finished supper."

"Good lads they are," declared Ma Kelly. She got briskly up from the chair. "They've been finished this long time," she chuckled. "All they're doin' right now is callin' for more cups o' coffee so they can get in some words with Maisie, the young rascals."

Her message brought the two punchers clattering across the room to Jack's table, eager, expectant grins on their brown faces.

"Ma said you was wanting to talk to us," Johnny Archer began. "Sure would like to get on the Bar 7 pay roll, Mr. Fielding."

Jack put down his coffee cup. "I think I know you two boys," he said. "Used to work for Bill Cole's Circle C outfit, didn't you?"

Johnny and the taciturn Smoky Tucker nodded. "Bill had to let us out," Johnny said laconically. "The Circle C is about busted, no *dinero*."

"Bill's been rustled to the bone," put in Smoky Tucker tersely.

"How come you got on the Arrow pay roll?" Jack was studying the pair with growing interest. He liked them, liked their straightforwardness and their clear-eyed appraisal of himself.

"A job's a job, and the Arrow was shorthanded, Curt Quintal told us. We only stuck for the roundup." Johnny gave his companion a bleak smile. "Smoky and we wasn't liking things at the Arrow, if you want to know the truth, and Curt Quintal wasn't liking it because we told him there was a bunch of Circle C steers in his herd." Johnny's tone was hard. "We was quittin' when Curt fired us, and some day I'll sure fill that coyote full of lead."

"You're hired," Jack said.

The pair exchanged ecstatic grins, and Johnny the spokesman asked, "Want for us to push out to the ranch tonight, boss?"

"Be a good idea," assented Jack. "You know Buck Wells?"

"Sure do," chorused the young punchers. "Denny Wells was a pal of ours before he was killed by the Bantry gang."

Jack nodded a bit grimly. Old Buck Wells had never been the same since his son was slain during a fight with the Bantry gang of rustlers a year earlier.

"Tell Buck I sent you," he told his new hands, "and . . ." he hesitated, "tell Buck I maybe won't be back at the ranch till tomorrow afternoon."

Johnny and Smoky promised and went cheerfully on their way, sending broad smiles in Maisie's direction.

"Hope you'll be here when we come in next

payday," called Johnny. "We got us a job ridin' for the Bar 7. Looks like you brought us luck."

"Sure did," grinned Smoky.

The girl smiled and lowered her eyes under their frank admiration. "I'm glad you got good jobs," she said as she went smiling and flushed to Jack's table. "Another cup of coffee, Mr. Fielding?"

He shook his head, aware of an odd thrill as he met her clear-eyed gaze. Her voice was low and sweet. She was, he realized, no ordinary person, and also she was extraordinarily lovely.

"A little lady," he reflected, as he made and lit a cigarette, "a thoroughbred, whoever she is, and she's got all the courage of a thoroughbred looking out of those blue eyes."

She was suddenly speaking to him again, her voice a bit breathless. "Mr. Fielding, I, I, well I'm wondering about that nice Mr. Hook, of the Diamond D. I suppose he has a family . . ."

"Tim Hook?" Jack chuckled. "Well, I reckon not, Maisie. You see, Tim's an old bachelor."

"Oh!" Her tone was disappointed. "Oh, well, thank you, Mr. Fielding." She went out with her armful of dishes and he saw that her slender shoulders drooped dejectedly.

"Wonder what's on her mind about old Tim?" puzzled the young man as he sauntered out of the dining room. "Went pale when I told her Tim had no family."

He found Ma Kelly in her little office, going over accounts at her littered desk. There was concern in the faint smile she gave him.

"I'm that worried about you, Jack," she said bluntly. "I'm hearin' talk that fair makes me heart turn over with fears for you."

"You should know better than let talk worry you, Ma," grinned Jack, "an old-timer like you."

"Old-timer!" Mrs. Kelly tossed her head and flashed her handsome eyes at him, "an' me only a year past forty!" She chuckled. "It's all I can do to keep Tim Hook an' Jake Kurtz from smokin' guns at each other, for all I'm the old-timer you say."

His eyes twinkled. "You've got the grand looks, Ma. You're the prettiest woman in the state, and the smartest."

"Young impudence," chuckled the widow, "get away with your blarney." She was suddenly grave again. "But you'll no be turnin' me away from what's on me mind. I'm not likin' the talk I hear about the Range Hawk bein' the murderer of Mark Severn." Mrs. Kelly gave him a shrewd glance from blue-gray eyes. "I'm in mortal fear that there's others in this town maybe knowin' your secret, Jack."

"I wouldn't worry, Ma." He shrugged his shoulders. "You know, and Pop Shane. I'd say my secret is safe with you two."

"How about some of 'em that fly with the Range

Hawk?" she fretted. "All that money posted for him, dead or alive and a crooked sheriff hatin' the son of the man who hung his brother for cow stealin'. You'll be rememberin' Dirk Slade, if you was only a boy when your father caught him red-handed and dangled him from a cottonwood tree down in Coyote Gulch. Slade's Tree it's been called ever since."

"Maybe there'll be others dangling from that same tree some day soon," Jack said grimly.

"You'll be careful, lad," begged Mrs. Kelly.

"I've reason to be careful, these days," he told her, thinking of his promise to Mark Severn.

"You're a brave lad," said Mrs. Kelly as she gave him a fond smile. "I'm thinkin' you'll win out, Jack, and bring peace and real law back to Coldwater County."

He changed the subject abruptly. "I've been talking to Mel Destrin," he told her. "Mel thinks, and I think too, that we've found Mark's granddaughter."

"Jack!" Mrs. Kelly's eyes widened with delight. "Of all the grand news!"

He told her about the letter from the girl in El Paso.

"Mel is sending her a telegram for her to come as soon as possible," he finished. "Only wish Mark could have been here to welcome her home to the old ranch."

"He'll be restin' the easier in his grave, poor

man," said Mrs. Kelly fervently. "I'm prayin' it's true, an' I'm prayin', too, that the girl is a good girl, worthy of him and the Bar 7 ranch."

"We'll soon know," Jack said. He bent down and kissed her smooth, flushed cheek. "*Hasta la vista*, Ma," he said.

He left her staring after him, the beginnings of a slight frown on her brow. Mrs. Kelly had small use for Lawyer Destrin.

"Sure an' it's hard to believe a good word can come from that imp of Satan," she reflected dubiously.

A heavy footstep aroused her from her troubled thoughts. She looked round at the door and met the smiling gaze of Jake Kurtz.

"I'll be working late at the store tonight, Ma," he said. "I must mein accounts make to send to the bank in San Carlos."

"You keep too much money in that old safe of yours," censured the widow. "Some mornin' you'll find you've been robbed."

"You t'ink so, Ma?" The storekeeper's voice was startled. "Mein Gott, I got a thousand dollars in that safe right now."

"And the town full of border scum," reminded Mrs. Kelly. "You're a fool, Jake Kurtz. I declare you try me patience!" But the storekeeper was gone.

Mrs. Kelly sighed, shook her head, attempted to put her mind on the papers in front of her, but presently she got out of her chair and went through a side door into the garden. A vague shape in the darkness moved down the walk to the gate. Mrs. Kelly hesitated, then quietly followed. The girl leaning over the gate turned and looked at her as the widow gently drew her arm through her own.

"A sweet night, lass," she said.

"I love it here," Maisie spoke softly, "and yet I, I feel that something is, is going to happen."

"We'll pray that whatever happens is for the good of all of us," Mrs. Kelly said. Her fingers touched the little wooden cross on her bosom.

They stood there, arm in arm, leaning over the gate, silent under the spell of the starry night, and presently a horseman drifted past, spurs jingling, dust lifting in tiny whirls. His hand raised in a salute and they caught a glimpse of a grave smile on his lean, hawk-like features.

"Jack Fielding, God bless the lad," murmured Ma Kelly.

"He's nice," Maisie said softly. "He, he seems so strong and fine."

"He's the salt of the earth," declared the older woman. "God go with him this night, for he rides always in the shadow of death these times."

The girl shivered and Ma Kelly felt the press of her slim body against hers.

"We'll not worry," she added confidently, "we'll not be worryin' about Jack Fielding. He's a man that can take care of himself against any of 'em."

"He looks like that sort of man," Maisie said quietly. Her smile reached up to Mrs. Kelly as they turned from the gate.

CHAPTER FIVE

The late moon pushing over the jagged peaks of the Chuckwalla Range, faintly silvered the landscape and made weird shapes of the bristling cacti. Jack reined the red horse in the dense shadows of a thicket of tall, slender ocotillos. He had made a fast ride and the horse was breathing hard. Swinging from the saddle and giving the animal a friendly slap, he moved stealthily up the slope. He knew that Red would not stir from the spot unless called.

He reached the crest of the low ridge and hugging close to the shadow of a boulder, he stood listening intently, gaze raking the dark depths of the narrow canyon below.

The sounds that drifted up from the lower reaches of the chasm were unmistakable. He heard the muted bawls of harried cattle, slowly growing in volume as the herd pressed up toward Topaz Basin.

Satisfied, the young man hurried down the slope

to his horse. Red greeted him with a soft nicker.

"Got your wind back, old man?" Jack rubbed the velvety nose affectionately, then climbed into the saddle.

For some ten minutes he kept the horse moving at a fast running-walk, following a trail that twisted down to the wide floor of the basin. Again he reined the horse in the shadows, and after a moment the silence of the night was broken by the soft call of an owl. Jack returned the call and suddenly, from behind great boulders and clumps of cactus emerged moving shapes. The soft clink of horses' shoes striking stones mingled with the jingle of spurs.

"*Amigo!*" greeted one of the riders as he rode up. "*Bueno*, they come, but we shall give them the beeg surprise, no?" Don Vicente's tone was jubilant. "This night the Hawk strikes to the death, no, my friend?"

Jack gave him a hard smile. "What have you done with the man, Fargo Laben?" he asked.

"By now Diego has him safely across the border. He is secure, that hombre, until you have the time to ask him the questions." Don Vicente cocked his head, listened intently. The bellowing of the cattle came distinctly on the night wind. The Mexican smiled, gave Jack a dancing-eyed look. "*Si*," he went on, "the dog's meat will be safe at Rancho del Torres, my friend, and when we have finished with him there is a great tree in

66

the yard where he will make a pretty picture, swinging in the breeze."

"You're a blood-thirsty devil," Jack said grimly.

"I thirst for the blood of your enemies," the young don said simply. He looked proudly at the circle of horsemen at his back. "These men I bring serve me as their forefathers have always served mine. They fight for you as they fight for me." He swept the score of swarthy-faced men with a questioning look. "Is it not so, men of El Rancho del Torres?"

"*Si!*" Their voices came fiercely staccato, eyes gleaming. "*Si!* Our Señor's friend is the friend of all of us! We fight by the side of the Hawk."

"*Gracias!*" Jack's tone and smile thanked them. "It is my hope that soon the Hawk will fold his wings in peace, but your loyalty and courage will never be forgotten, men of the Rancho del Torres."

"They come," repeated Don Vicente. He straightened in his big saddle, a proud and gallant figure. "Not one must escape. It is my command."

"*Si!*" chorused the fierce-eyed riders.

Jack was silent, a bit sick at the thought of the coming slaughter. There seemed no other way. The law was a farce in the Chuckwalla country. There was no law, save the law of the gun. Ruthless as it seemed, justice demanded the extreme penalty from those who behind the cloak of Sheriff Slade's protection were ravaging the land.

"If Curt Quintal is with them, I want him taken alive," he finally said to Don Vicente. "Even though we destroy these men, the thing is not finished until we have the fiend whose orders they obey."

"It shall be as you wish, if possible," assented the Mexican. He rode away with his followers to take their agreed posts where the narrow defile of the lower Topaz broke into the basin. Jack watched until they melted into the shadows, his expression hard and grimly resolved. After all, those men coming up the lower Topaz were killers of the worst sort, among them perhaps the men who had slain his father and Mark Severn. To destroy them was no worse than destroying rattlesnakes, and the ruthless execution done by Don Vicente's riders would be a grim warning to those who plotted in secret against the peace of Coldwater County.

The clamor of the oncoming herd increased and he could hear the yipping cries of the rustlers urging the cattle up the steep ascent. Suddenly they were pouring through the gap into the basin now faintly silvered with moonlight. A lone horseman rode at the spearhead of clashing horns. Jack flung out of his saddle and ran down the slope, following around a thicket of densely growing greasewood. Even in that elusive light he recognized Curt Quintal. He made no attempt at quietness. The bawling of the cattle and the thunder of their hoofs made stealth unnecessary.

The Arrow man glimpsed Jack's vague shape as he leaped into the trail, and with a startled oath reined his horse. The animal reared, then frightened by the press of horns behind sprang forward with a snort. Quintal, nearly unseated, was jerking frantically at his gun and as his terrified horse fled past, he sent a bullet at the shadowed form crouching in the thicket. The next moment the cattle broke into a dead run on the heels of the runaway horse.

Jack leaped for the shelter of a big boulder. His attempt to take Quintal had failed miserably, but there was yet a chance to turn the stampeding cattle away from the outlet of the upper Topaz. Almost with the thought, he was emptying his gun into the horned bodies charging past. Four steers went down, piling across the trail. He fired again at a big steer and with an agonized bellow the animal swerved to the left, went crashing through the chaparral. The cattle behind followed blindly and in an instant the stampede was broken as the herd surged along a circling rampart of boulders.

Horsemen came streaming through the gap and went scattering into the chaparral as guns spouted red flame and death through the darkness. Startled cries and screams rose above the clamor of the herd, as Don Vicente's riders poured their deadly fire into the scurrying rustlers. Those of them who were left alive hastily sought the protection of boulder and bush, their own guns now sending out winking flashes of crimson.

Jack went stumbling up the slope to his horse. He desperately wanted Curt Quintal, now on the dead run for the upper canyon of the Topaz. Again in the saddle he tore into the trail, almost collided with a horseman spurring around a great cactus-covered hummock. Flame lanced from the man's gun and Jack felt the searing breath of hot lead against his cheek. There was no time for an answering shot and as the two horses crashed together, Jack's hand fastened on the rustler's gun arm. With a frightened oath, the man dropped reins and clutched wildly at his attacker. Both went tumbling from their saddles locked in desperate embrace. Dazed for a moment as they crashed into the boulders, Jack lay across the prone body of his opponent, then slowly he staggered upright. A glance told him the rustler was unconscious, a red smear widening across one cheek.

Gasping for breath, his head ringing, the young cowman looked over his shoulder at the scene of the fight at the gap. The gunfire had subsided, only intermittent flares stabbed the darkness as Don Vicente's men relentlessly sought out the rustlers. A horseman drifted out of the shadows.

"You are hurt, *amigo*?" Don Vicente's tone was anxious. "You sway like a tree in a storm."

"Took a knock on the head," Jack told him. "Be

all right in a minute." He stared down at the prone rustler. "Reckon this hombre feels worse than I do."

The Mexican lifted his gun. "We will finish him, no?"

"You'll leave him alone," rasped Jack. "We're not murderers, Vicente."

"You are too soft," grumbled the young don. Then with a low laugh, "I think it is all over, Juan. But two of the dogs still remain." He broke off, listened, head turned. A voice lifted, cut through the night hard and triumphant. "It is done, Señor, not one has escaped."

Don Vicente's smile came down to Jack, leaning against the boulder. "Estevan," he said softly, "he says it is finished with them."

"Quintal got away," interrupted Jack. "He's in the upper Topaz by now and no chance to head him off."

"*Por Dios!*" ejaculated the Mexican, "is not this hombre on the ground here the Señor Quintal?"

Jack's eyes widened as he stared at their lone prisoner. "Looks like Quintal for a fact," he muttered. He rubbed his aching head. "I'd gamble he was Quintal, if I hadn't seen the man who got away from me when the herd stampeded." He scowled. "That sure was Quintal, though, and I'd have nabbed him too, if this man hadn't bumped into me."

The prisoner sat up with a low groan and stared

71

at them. "What kind o' hell's broke loose?" he wanted to know. "Who are you fellows?" He gazed around stupidly. "What's happened?"

"Plenty," Jack told him. "You're in a tough spot, whoever you are."

Estevan rode up with several of his companions and the rustler looked up at them with something like horror in his eyes.

"Where's the boys?" he demanded wildly, "where's Curt—where's all the fellers?"

"Dead," Jack said curtly. He stared at the man with growing surprise. "You could pass for Curt Quintal," he added.

"I'm Curt's brother," sullenly muttered the prisoner. He was looking uneasily at Estevan who with exaggerated deliberateness was uncoiling a rope.

"How long have you been with the Arrow?" Jack asked him curiously.

"A week or two," answered the rustler sullenly. "Curt sent for me. He said he was sending a trail-herd up to Montana and could use me."

"Whereabouts is this place in Montana where you were going to drive the cattle?"

"Curt didn't say," muttered the man.

"I think you're lying." Jack's tone was grim. "And it wasn't Montana." He looked at Don Vicente. The latter nodded, gestured over his shoulder. "It was planned to hold the cows in the Arroyo Los Coyotes," he said. "It is there the brands would be changed before drifting them across to the Arrow range." The Mexican shrugged. "You well know their custom, Juan." He spoke in Spanish.

"I know," replied Jack in the same tongue, "but I want the truth from this man, if he will talk."

"I'm swearing I wasn't knowing what Curt was up to," broke in the prisoner. He licked dry lips, glanced fearfully at Estevan's rope.

"You understand Spanish," Jack said grimly. "You've lived down below the line, huh?"

"Been down there some," admitted the man. He pressed a hand to blood-smeared face. "Curt never told me this was a rustlin' job," he went on, and then, his tone suddenly defiant, he added, "I ain't believin' it even now. It's you fellers that's the rustlers. You're the Hawk's gang."

"There's a tree in the Arroyo Los Coyotes," Jack told him softly, "it's called Slade's Tree. Maybe you've heard of Slade's Tree."

The growing terror in the prisoner's eyes was answer enough.

"I'm swearin' I wasn't in on Curt's plans," he gasped, and getting unsteadily to his feet he looked through the moonlit night at the cattle massed in dark groups against the granite cliffs. His gaze came back to the implacable faces of the men surrounding him. "Dead," he muttered, "all of 'em layin' there in the chaparral *dead*—an' Curt dead . . ."

"Like you will be very soon," said Don Vicente with a grim smile.

Jack shook his head. "Turn him loose," he commanded. "I'm thinking he won't like the Chuckwalla after what's happened."

The man looked at him with renewed hope. "You've said it, mister." He spoke vehemently. "I'll be ridin' a long ways from this damn place—ridin' so far it'll cost a thousand bucks to send me a post card. What for should I stick round, now Curt's dead?"

Jack did not choose to put him straight about Quintal's escape. He was sick of the business and he sensed too that this young brother of Curt Quintal was perhaps not entirely guilty, that the older man had dragged him into the thing.

"Catch up your horse," he said with a gesture. "I'm letting you go, but keep traveling, and don't ever come back."

"I ain't forgettin'," muttered young Quintal. He went unsteadily toward his horse, a dazed look on his battered face. He was finding it hard to believe this thing that had happened, this miracle of mercy that had given him back his life. "I ain't forgettin'," he repeated huskily from his saddle and staring fixedly at Jack as though he would impress the latter's features firmly in his mind. "If we do ever cut each other's trail again, Starke Quintal's guns will be smokin' on your side." He rode away into the night without a glance at the men of the Rancho del Torres.

Don Vicente's smile was bitter as he met Jack's gaze. "You are soft," he muttered, "the man would have made a pretty picture, swinging from some tree in the moonlight." His smile warmed and his voice took on an affectionate tone as he added, "*Por Dios*, it is like you, Juan, which is why you and I are friends and brothers. Did you not do as much for me that night in Ensenada?"

Jack gave him a cheerful grin. "A lucky night for me, Vicente. I made friends with men that are men." His smile swept the circle of swarthy faces. "Well, let's bunch those cattle and start them back to their range," he added briskly. The vaqueros rode away, spurs jingling. Jack whistled a soft note and the big red horse trotted up with a low nicker.

"All creatures obey your voice," admired Don Vicente. He lit a cigarette, looked at his friend with dancing eyes as the latter climbed stiffly into his saddle. "You are very much of a man, my friend."

"*Gracias*." Jack's tone was grateful, "I owe you much for this night's work, Vicente."

The young Mexican was silent for a moment, the end of his cigarette making a red dot in the darkness. He was recalling a certain night in Ensenada when this quiet-voiced gringo had fought and disarmed him in the *cantina* of Ramon García.

"You remember, Juan," he said softly, "that night you came so boldly and accused me of buying your stolen JF cows from your enemies? It was true I had bought many of your stolen cows. I did not know you then from any other gringo, but your talk enraged me and I did my best to kill you. Instead, you took my guns, gave me my life and your friendship, when you might have killed me, as you might have killed the young hombre you just sent on his way unharmed." A solemn note crept into the young don's low voice. "You changed the way of my life, Juan, made me see things in a new light. You taught me the way of honor and justice."

"The honor of a Torres has always been above reproach," Jack said. "You're a good scout, Vicente." He smiled cheerfully. "We'll be getting old Bill Cole's cows back to his range."

"*Si*," chuckled the Mexican, "the Señor Cole would have the big surprise could he see his cows now."

They rode slowly toward the gap, where Bill Cole's cattle were streaming into the lower Topaz, urged by the shrill yells of the vaqueros. Jack was aware of a keen disappointment as he thought of Curt Quintal. The man's escape might prove disastrous to his plans. He was not sure that Quintal had not recognized him. He hoped not, hoped that the night's work would not link the name of Jack Fielding to the much-wanted Range Hawk.

"Do not worry," reassured his companion lightly. "I doubt that he could have recognized you in the darkness and in his hurry and fright."

"I reckon you're right, Vicente," agreed Jack.

"Before the sun rises you will be back at the Bar 7, sleeping soundly, and happy that you have driven one more nail in the coffins of your enemies," exulted the Mexican.

"I reckon that's right," the young cattleman said again. And oddly enough he found himself thinking of the new girl at Ma Kelly's, wondering if she would still be there when he again went to Coldwater. He hoped he would see her soon again.

CHAPTER SIX

Bill Cole called out a whoa to his laboring team and stared apprehensively at the lone horseman approaching across the wash. His wagon was piled with a jumble of household goods that showed signs of hasty stowing. A small tow-headed boy sat on the seat by his side and trailing the wagon was a buckboard driven by his wife. An older girl rode with her, the youngest Cole baby in her lap. A twelve-year-old boy riding a pinto brought up the tail end of the procession with two horses on a lead rope.

"What are you stopping for, Bill?" There was

fright in the woman's voice as she peered tensely through the gray dawn.

"Feller comin'," Cole called back in a low voice. He was reaching for a rifle under his feet. "Grab hold of the lines, Tommy," he said to the boy by his side. The youngster seized the reins and his father leveled the gun at the rider showing vaguely against the paling horizon.

"Who be you, feller? Pull up quick and talk, or I'll start shootin'."

"Hello, Bill." The horseman reined to a halt. "What's going on here?"

Cole lowered the rifle. "My God, that you, Fielding?" Relief made his voice husky. "I was ready to pull the trigger, Jack." The rancher glanced over his shoulder at the woman in the buckboard, her peering face showing pale and strained in the gray of the false dawn. "It's all right, Ma, it's Jack Fielding."

"What's up, Bill?" Jack rode down the grade to the wagon. His tone was worried, as though he already knew the answer.

"I'm pullin' up stakes, Jack." Cole spoke dully. "I've had another warnin' to clear out. Found the paper tucked under the door when Minnie an' me come home from town."

"Don't you be too hasty, Bill." Jack's tone was cool, reassuring. "I'm thinking that warning you found won't come to anything."

"It was from the Hawk," the rancher said in the

same lifeless tone. "I ain't buckin' the Hawk, not with Minnie and the kids to look out for." He shook his head. "I'm quittin', Jack, before it's too late."

"It wasn't the Hawk who left that warning," Jack said quietly. "Don't you believe it, Bill."

"Threatened to burn the place an' all of us in it," went on Cole. "Same as they burned your place, Jack, when your dad was killed." He sat humped forward despondently on the wagon seat, nursing the rifle across knees. "Run my cattle off, killed Pete an' Shorty."

"Your cows are back on your range, Bill, and if I were you I'd turn round and head back for the ranch. There'll be no burning your place down."

Cole stared at him, disbelieving, bewildered. "What d' you mean, my cattle back on the range?" His wife's excited voice interrupted him.

"What's that he's saying about the cows, Bill?"

"Says they're back on the range," called out her husband. His bewildered gaze clung to the young man on the high red horse. "How come you say it wasn't the Hawk?" he asked wonderingly.

"You've been listening to lies, Bill. You know the Hawk doesn't bother men like you."

"Reckon that's right, come to think of it," muttered the rancher after a moment's thought. He nodded. "Come to think of it, there's the times Bert Hoskins an' Sol Bench was rustled or thought they was, until they found their cows back on the range like nothin' had happened."

"Bert Hoskins never would tell us how he got his cows back," called out Mrs. Cole. "Was always awful mysterious about it, Bert was."

"Listen, Bill, I want to tell you something." Jack swung his horse up the grade a few yards away from the wagon. "You, too, Mrs. Cole," he added.

"You hold the team, Julie," said the woman. She climbed hastily from the buckboard and joined her lanky husband as he clambered from his high seat.

"I don't want the youngster to hear this," Jack told them as the two came up. His face was stern as he looked at the pair. "What I'm telling you must not pass your lips."

"Sure," muttered the rancher. "Minnie an' me won't say nothin' to nobody."

His wife, more shrewd, looked at Jack with startled eyes. She was beginning to understand why Bert Hoskins and Sol Bench had been so mysterious about the amazing recovery of their cattle.

"I'm the Hawk," Jack told them quietly. "I've some good friends who work with me, Bill. They helped me get your cows back tonight."

"My God!" The startled rancher's voice trailed away to a whisper. "You, *the Hawk!*" His eyes bulged and he gaped around at his wife.

"I was beginning to figure it that way," she said simply. "That explains why Bert Hoskins acted so queer about his cows. He wouldn't say a word, and we won't say a word, either," she added, looking hard at her husband.

"You bet we won't," muttered the dazed man.

"I've sworn to get the men who murdered my father and stole our JF range," Jack continued in a low voice. "We've a war on, and some day soon I'll be calling on you people for help; you, Bill, and Bert Hoskins, and Sol Bench and half a score more of you who have learned the secret of the Range Hawk."

Bill Cole looked at the rifle in his hands. "I'll be riding with you, Jack," he said simply. "You can't be calling on me too soon."

"Go back to your home," Jack told the pair. "You won't be raided again, after what happened tonight in Topaz Basin. Only one man got away from us . . . and he won't dare talk about it for fear of giving his game away."

"We're trusting you, Mr. Fielding," declared Cole's wife. There was new hope in her eyes, a kindling of fresh courage that wiped the haggard look from her still pretty face. "We're going back to our home and we're fighting the same as you . . ." She broke off, stared at the tall young man with widened eyes. "Land sakes!" she gasped, "it wasn't the Hawk that went and killed and robbed poor Jake Kurtz in his store?"

Jack gave her a horrified look. "Jake murdered!" He spoke harshly. "When?"

"Tonight," faltered the woman, "I, I mean last night. It's most daylight now."

"Jake was found with a knife stuck in him," said her husband. "Ma Kelly got worried because he didn't show up at the 'Dobe House where he lives an' sent out for him. Jake was layin' there by his safe, dead."

Jack stared at them, wordless, his face pale. He was recalling Monte Boone's curious behavior, the old barman's furtive hints of trouble. He had promised to meet Monte at Shane's livery barn after supper. Don Vicente's news about the planned raid on the Cole ranch had driven all thoughts of Monte Boone from his mind. It was possible the old man had learned of the murderous plot against the honest and too-trusting store-keeper. Mrs. Cole was speaking.

"They're saying in town that it was the Hawk who killed Jake Kurtz. The sheriff was getting up a posse when we left. Folks in town is awful wild about that killing," she finished.

"What do *you* think, Mrs. Cole?" Jack's tone was hard.

"Why," exclaimed the woman, looking at him, breathless. "It *couldn't* have been the Hawk. You, you wasn't in Coldwater when Jake was killed."

"Thanks, Mrs. Cole." Jack's smile was bitter. "But you see how it is, there's no way now of proving it wasn't the Hawk."

They stood there, watching in appalled silence

as he spurred down the grade, tore past the wagon and buckboard, past the wide-eyed boy on the pinto pony.

"It's sure hell, Minnie," muttered the gaunt rancher. "He's just done told us he's the Hawk, an' there he goes heading for Coldwater."

"He'll be lynched if folks find out who he is," quavered his wife. "Oh, Bill, just supposin' somebody goes an' tells on him!" She looked at her husband with terrified eyes. "There's a lot of reward money up for him."

"I'd sure kill the man who tells on him," said Bill Cole fiercely. He turned back to the wagon. "Come on, Minnie, let's get started back for home."

Hot rage seared Jack Fielding as he sent the big red horse into the short-cut trail for Coldwater. The news of this latest outrage was ominous warning that the unknown leader of the sinister force slowly gaining a stranglehold on the community was growing impatient. He had struck two blows in one night; the attempted raid on Bill Cole and the murder of Jake Kurtz.

There was more to the affair than a murder committed during a robbery, Jack told himself. The looting of Jake's safe was only incidental, a blind to cover up the real motive, which was the removal of honest, sturdy Jake Kurtz. Men of his caliber were not wanted in Coldwater these days.

Uneasy premonitions chilled the young man as he rode furiously along the winding trail. Ma

Kelly would be another marked for removal from the scene. The arch fiends would contrive some way forever to still the fearless widow's biting tongue. All thoughts of returning to the Bar 7 had left him. There was no knowing how swiftly the enemy might strike again, and this time at the woman who had been the good-natured store-keeper's best friend. It was risky, showing himself in Coldwater, not knowing when he might be betrayed, not knowing whether or not Curt Quintal had recognized him in that brief moment in Topaz Basin; but the impulse to be with Ma Kelly drove him on. For some reason which he made no attempt to analyze, thoughts of the girl, Maisie, were bewilderingly mixed up with his fears for Ma Kelly. Ace Coran had attempted to lure the girl into his employ, and Bert Cross had openly boasted of his purpose to make her his property.

Dawn's red fires lay on the dark Bullions as he turned into the arroyo behind the 'Dobe House. Jack suspected there was wind, and perhaps rain in those clouds massing over the rugged peaks. It looked like one of those lashing desert storms with dust devils dancing on the lower levels while torrential cloudbursts roared down the canyons. He should be out at the Bar 7, he reflected. Old Buck Wells would be suffering torments, what with his helplessness and the roundup at a standstill.

Leaving the tired horse in a thicket of mesquite he made his way cautiously into the back garden. A young Mexican, watering a potato patch with a hose, looked at him with surprise and some alarm. Jack's sudden appearance through the tamarisk hedge, his fierce, questioning eyes, startled the swarthy youth. He dropped the hose and turned to flee. Jack's hand fastened on his shirt collar.

"Jose! It is I, Ma Kelly's friend!"

Jose recovered from his fright. "The Señor came so quickly," he stammered. "I, I . . ."

Jack interrupted him. "Jose, go you and tell Señora Kelly that I wait here in the garden, and Jose, do not tell anybody that you saw me."

"I obey," muttered the youth. He darted away, bare feet pattering the hard path.

Jack turned to the concealment of the thickly massed willows through which he could glimpse the dark waters of the pond. It was fast growing lighter, although the sunlight was not yet in the garden.

Ducks were quacking on the pond. Jack came to a surprised standstill, startled gaze on the girl standing by the trunk of a fallen tree. She held a tin can in one hand from which she had been feeding barley to the noisy flock, but the birds were now neglected as she stared breathlessly at the man who had come upon the scene.

"Oh, I was sure it was you talking to Jose," she said. Confusion sent the color waving into smooth

85

cheeks. "I was feeding the ducks," she added.

Jack recovered his composure with an effort. "I'm afraid I startled you, but perhaps not as much as you startled me."

She smiled at that and tossed a handful of barley into the limpid pool.

"You look dreadfully upset," she said frankly. "Something must have happened to bring you here so early in the morning asking for Ma Kelly. You see," she smiled at him again, "I know it wasn't just seeing me that upset you."

He looked at her silently, not so sure that she was right. The unexpected sight of her affected him profoundly. She was utterly lovely, standing there in the glamorous dawn, the rising wind fluttering her short print skirt and soft fair hair. The color in her cheeks and the bright look of her told him that she was pleased to see him.

She was looking at him curiously, and suddenly she said in a startled voice, "Why, Mr. Fielding, you're hurt! Your face, it's bleeding!" Instantly she was by his side and dabbing gently at his cheek with a handkerchief.

"A scratch," Jack said. "Reckon I ran into some catclaw. Lots of it in the canyons."

Maisie ran to the pond's edge, rinsed the handkerchief and was back in a moment. "It's more than a scratch," she declared. "It's a nasty cut, and your cheek is bruised."

He smiled down into her concerned face. The

light touch of her fingers was pleasant, and he was disturbingly aware of her fragrant hair.

"Just a scratch," he repeated. "Thanks just the same, Maisie."

Her dark blue eyes went up to his briefly and something like a smile quirked the corners of her mouth. "Catclaw must be awfully hard," she said, "hard like granite, to make you black and blue like this."

They laughed softly and the girl stood back and looked at the wound critically. "I'll ask Ma Kelly for something to put on it," she told him.

"Might have been a lot worse," Jack replied, thinking of Starke Quintal's hastily-flung bullet. "We get used to these things out on the range."

She regarded him with grave eyes. "The range," she repeated in a low voice. "It gives me a queer feeling when you talk of the range, as though I've always known it. As though I've always belonged to this country of yours."

Footsteps approached down the hard path and they heard Ma Kelly's voice, guardedly low and anxious. "Jack! Where's the lad gone to?"

"In the willows, Ma." It was the girl who answered, and as the widow, pale and haggard-eyed, pushed into view, Maisie said with a gesture at her companion, "Mr. Fielding hurt his face, Ma. Where can I find something to put on the cut?"

"Sakes alive!" exclaimed Mrs. Kelly, "an' what in the world did you run into, lad?"

"Maisie's been doctoring me," grinned the young cowman. "Nothing to worry about, Ma."

"You'll find me medicine box in the cupboard in me office," Mrs. Kelly told the girl. "Run and bring it to us here, child."

Maisie disappeared on swift, light feet, and Mrs. Kelly looked solemnly at Jack. He saw that her eyes were bright with tears.

"They got poor Jake," she said. "Dead the poor man is, an' me warnin' him these many times not to keep all that money in his old safe."

"I got the news up the trail," he informed her. "I came as fast as I could, Ma."

She shook her head. "I'm sorry you came, lad. It's the talk that the Hawk killed Jake for his money."

"You know different."

"Of course," Mrs. Kelly stared at him with troubled eyes, "but it's risky for you to be in this town, what with the feelin' high an' Sheriff Slade swearin' to hang the Hawk, and all that money posted for him dead or alive. I'm fearin' one of these men you've been helpin' will turn you in."

"I had to come," Jack interrupted. "Ma, you know as well as I do that Jake was not killed for his money. They wanted him out of the way, and they'll not stop with him."

"Meanin' the devils will be after me own scalp?" The widow's eyes flashed. "They wouldn't dare touch me, Jack."

"That gang will dare anything," he muttered.

"Every honest cowpuncher in the country would ride to me help," declared Mrs. Kelly, "like your own fool self, bless your heart."

"I don't like you being in this town," persisted the young man. "I've got to be out at the Bar 7 looking after things."

"I'm not afraid," Mrs. Kelly said. "I'll not be driven from the home I've made for meself." Indignation flushed her cheeks.

"I want you to go away for a bit," Jack urged. "You listen to me, Ma, and take a nice trip, you and Maisie." His tone was grim. "I'm thinking it won't be long now, until we have a showdown."

Mrs. Kelly gave him a shrewd look. "Maisie," she repeated, "oh, so it's *Maisie.*"

He reddened, and after a moment Mrs. Kelly said musingly, "Well, maybe I can be sendin' the lass off some place while this trouble is on us." A low exclamation interrupted her and turning they saw the girl looking at them with dismayed eyes. She approached hesitantly, a small box in one hand.

"I, I heard you," she faltered.

"Jack is wantin' me to close the 'Dobe House and go away for a spell," explained Mrs. Kelly. "I'm tellin' him he talks nonsense, but he's fearin' there'll be trouble in this town."

"I'm not afraid," declared the girl with a quick proud lift of her head.

"I'm thinkin' that's the truth," mused the older woman, looking at her intently, "yet maybe 'twould be the wise thing to send you off some place, child. I've friends in San Carlos who'd be that glad to have you for a bit."

Maisie's look went to Jack's inscrutable face. "I'm not afraid!" she repeated almost fiercely. "You've no right making Ma frightened for me."

"He's meanin' the best for you, child," gently reproved Mrs. Kelly.

"I don't want to go away and leave you!" protested the girl. "I, I belong here. This is my country. I won't be afraid. I can fight, too!"

They looked at her curiously, with some wonder, and they were not a little stirred. Mrs. Kelly nodded approvingly.

" 'Tis the high spirit you've got, child," she said softly. "I'm likin' your courage and the true heart of you."

"You won't send me away?"

"I'll not send you away," promised Ma Kelly. "I'm thinkin' you're the sort that belongs in this fightin' land. You're no weak clingin' vine for all you're so pretty and soft."

Maisie gave Jack a look in which was a mixture of defiance and triumph. His answering smile was grave, but there was a light in his dark eyes that brought the sudden color into her cheeks. Her long curling lashes lowered.

"Oh, here's the medicine box, Ma," she said a bit breathlessly.

"You fix him up, lass," directed Mrs. Kelly, twinkling a mischievous look at Jack. "You've the light touch that'll soothe the poor hurt man."

Maisie set to work, her color high, but her fingers were cool and steady as she applied the antiseptic and dabbed the cheek clean of dried blood. Mrs. Kelly watched, her eyes dancing. Jack scowled at her over the blonde head.

"You're a born nurse," admired Ma when the girl stepped back. "You can run along, now. I've a bit of a word to say to Jack."

Jack's gaze clung to the girl until the trim figure vanished through the willows. He drew a long breath, touched the ministered cheek tentatively and fixed embarrassed eyes on the widow. She gave him a wise smile.

"A rare sweet lass," she said softly. "I wouldn't be blamin' a man for feeling the heart of him warm to her." She shook her head. "A bit of a puzzle, I'll admit, but I'm gettin' as fond of her as if she were me own daughter."

"She's a thoroughbred," muttered the young man. He changed the subject abruptly. "I'm telling Pop Shane to keep an eye on you," he went on, frowning thoughtfully at her. "We'll get a couple of good men to stay with you, Ma."

"Every man in the house will look after me," reassured the widow tartly. "Don't you worry about me, Jack Fielding. It's yourself that's in the shadow of death these days and nights."

He shrugged dusty shoulders as he thought of those hectic moments in Topaz Basin. Twice death had reached hungrily for him, and had failed.

"I've made a new friend, or I should say friends," he told Mrs. Kelly.

She listened with breathless attention to his account of the Cole raid and his encounter with the rancher and his family.

"You can trust them," he assured her. "If you need help at any time, you can trust Bill Cole and his wife. Don't forget."

Mrs. Kelly promised. She knew Minnie Cole, she said, a nice little woman, and it was God's work Jack had done that night.

"There were men killed," he reminded gloomily.

"When I see a rattlesnake, I smash its wicked head," returned the widow dryly, "and Jack, them two nice boys, Johnny an' Smoky, they're a pair of fightin' fools, fast on the draw with their guns. I'm wantin' that you keep 'em close to you wherever you go."

"I'll think it over," he smiled.

"We can't risk losin' you at this time," scolded Mrs. Kelly. "Them two harum-scarums'll likely save you from a shot in the back."

He gave her a hug. "Sorry about poor Jake," he said. "Wish I could stay to help with things."

"I'm knowin' you would, lad, but 'tis not

possible for you to stay with all you've got on your mind." She dabbed at her eyes. "I've sent word to Tim Hook. Tim will be in."

Jack nodded, relieved. "I'll be loping," he said. "*Adios*, Ma." He disappeared through the willows.

"God ride with him," murmured the widow and touched the little wooden cross on her bosom.

CHAPTER SEVEN

Monte Boone jerked around from the array of glasses he was polishing, displeasure in his sunken eyes, as the swing doors flew open with a bang.

"What's yore hurry," he began, "aim to bust them hinges?" He broke off, suddenly recognizing his early-morning patron. "Hell, Curt, you scairt me," he finished in a milder tone.

Quintal lurched into the long barroom and leaned heavily against the bar, reaching a shaky hand for the bottle the barman promptly placed in front of him. He drank deeply, disdaining the glass Monte slid expertly along the polished top.

"Where's Ace?" The Arrow man put the bottle down and drew a hand across his lips.

"Dunno whar-all Ace is," returned Monte, staring wonderingly at the other. Quintal was in a bad way, eyes bloodshot, with a wild look in them, and dust covering him from head to foot. His face was crisscrossed with deep scratches encrusted with dried blood. "Been in the catclaw," conjectured Monte. "Ain't seen Ace sence supper last night," he said aloud. "I ain't workin' nights this week."

Curt Quintal scowled and tipped the bottle again to his lips. "Who cares about when you work," he snarled. "Bert Cross been in this morning?"

Monte made a vicious snapping sound with his wet rag. "Talkin' to me?" he asked thinly. He leaned over the bar, big-knuckled hands spread wide apart on the shining surface, chin thrust out belligerently, "Or mebbe you was yelpin' at some coyote."

Quintal glared at him, then growling an imprecation he hurled the bottle splintering to the floor and stalked to the door.

"You're owin' the house two bucks for that!" yelled the old barman furiously. "Come back here an' I'll l'arn you manners." He grabbed up broom and dustpan and went muttering to sweep up the broken glass. "Sure is ugly this mornin', that poison sidewinder. Looks like he's been through plenty hell at that." The thought brought a grin to Monte's leathery face. He had long nursed an ardent dislike for the sneering-eyed Curt Quintal.

The latter was clattering hurriedly up the boardwalk to the Palace Hotel. Ignoring the elderly clerk at the desk, the big cowman went up the stairs three at a time. A disgruntled voice responded to his hammering on the door of Room 17.

"Who's that?"

"Let me in, Ace, got to see you *pronto*!"

There was the sound of bare feet padding across the floor. The door drew open and displayed Ace Coran's startled face.

Quintal pushed into the room and Ace Coran closed the door, staring with narrowed eyes over his shoulder at his obviously highly-excited visitor.

"What's up?" The saloon man went back to the tumbled bed and sat down on its edge, hand reaching for his clothes.

"Plenty!" rasped Quintal. "All hell busted loose on us last night over in the Topaz. That's what's up!"

Coran stared at him, rubbing the red stubble of unshaven beard.

"The Hawk jumped us again," Curt Quintal told him. "Makes five times that hombre and his gang has cut our trail." The Arrow man choked out an oath. "Sure would like to know who puts the Hawk wise to our plans."

Coran drew on his trousers and reached for his shiny brown boots inset with silver spurs. The saloon man was a fastidious dresser. "Looks like some hombre in your outfit wears too loose a tongue," he grumbled.

"Jumped us in the bottle-neck of the lower Topaz," Quintal went on. "Ace, they was layin' for us and blasted us out of our saddles. We didn't have a chance." Sweat beaded the Arrow man's scratched face. "My, my kid brother," he muttered. "My God, Ace, it's my fault for gettin' him in with us."

The saloon man looked down at his feet. "Sure tough, Quin. Maybe he got away, like you did."

Quintal shook his head. He was the only one to escape, he declared.

"Recognize any of the gang?" queried Coran.

"Wasn't stoppin' for introductions," snorted Curt Quintal. "All I saw was plenty of gun flashes, an' a feller comin' on the run down the slope. I couldn't make him out in that dark. He was jest a quick-moving shadder." The Arrow man swore. "Would have plugged him if that fool bronc o' mine hadn't gone crazy when the damn cows come proddin' on his heels."

Ace Coran finished knotting his loose red silk tie and after a moment's scrutiny of his face in the mirror, he thoughtfully made a cigarette, gaze fixed on the other man.

"Sure is bad news, Curt," he mused. "The big boss'll go crazy when he hears you've pulled off another flop."

"I'm leavin' it to Bert Cross to break it to him,"

muttered Quintal. He licked dry, cracked lips. "Bert can handle him." He considered a moment. "I'll head for the ranch as soon as I've had some breakfast."

"Bert stayed in town last night," the saloon man informed him. "You won't need to head for the ranch, Quin. Bert's in the hotel—Room 17."

"I'll go wake him up," decided Quintal. His tone was nervous. "You come with me, Ace."

The latter shook his head, rubbed his unshaven face. "I'm getting me a shave," he said. "See you later, Quin, down in the dining room."

It was half an hour before Coran saw Quintal again. The Arrow man was sitting at a table with his handsome and debonair superintendent. The latter's darkly-tanned face wore a disgruntled look.

"Hello, Ace." He gave the saloon man a somber nod. "What do you think of this business?"

Coran drew out a chair and sat down, eyes signaling the hard-featured waitress. "I'm thinkin' if we don't clip this Hawk hombre's wings we're in for a hell of a lot of grief," he grumbled. "Looks like he's awful well posted about things."

"One thing sure," Bert Cross said slowly, "is that it wasn't Bill Cole who got up a gang to lay for you in the Topaz. He was in town late last night, waiting to see Mel Destrin about a new loan. His wife was with him."

Ace Coran was staring at him with frowning

97

intentness. "Queer about Fargo," he broke in. "He never come back after he left us at sundown. Ain't seen hide nor hair of Fargo from the time he left."

There was a silence, the three men exchanging uneasy looks.

"Fargo wouldn't be leavin' without the money he was to get for the job," went on the saloon man. "What do you make of it, fellers?"

There was another silence while the waitress placed dishes and coffee in front of Coran. When she hurried back to the kitchen, Bert Cross said slowly, "I reckon it'll be a smart idea for you to send old Pedro over to the Bar 7, Curt. Have him get in touch with Carlos and find out if Fielding got back last night."

Quintal nodded. "Them Bar 7 fellers don't suspect Pedro, him bein' Carlos' foster uncle an' hangin' round there lots o' times."

"Queer thing about Jack Fielding," mused Coran, "every time we send a man to get him, we don't see that man no more. Fargo Laben is the fourth."

"Here's Mel," muttered Quintal. He rolled apprehensive, bloodshot eyes at his companions, and got heavily to his feet. "Reckon I'll be headin' for the ranch," he added. "So long, fellers, I'll have Pedro mosey over to the Bar 7. It will be a good idea to find out about Fielding." He clattered out through a side door, careful not to look at the lawyer as the latter paused to speak to a thin-faced, tired-appearing elderly man at a table near the main door.

"When is the inquest, Doc?" the lawyer was asking.

"Ten o'clock," Doc Manners told him. He shook his head. "Poor Kurtz. A good man, Destrin."

"A cowardly murder," declared Mel Destrin. "I'm hoping Slade tracks the killer down. We'll get the man, Doc, we'll get the Hawk for this last crime."

"Sometimes I wonder," murmured the doctor. "Sometimes I wonder if Slade is on the right track. Why pin all these killings on this mysterious Hawk person?" The doctor's keen eyes lifted in a shrewd glance at the dapper little man standing by his side. "Plenty of desperados in this country, Destrin."

The lawyer grimaced. "It's the Hawk all right," he declared. "Didn't Slade find his card, that feather the killer bird always leaves, stuck in his victim's fingers?"

"Might be a trick," murmured Doc Manners. He drummed the table with long capable surgeon's fingers. "I tell you, Destrin, I sometimes wonder if the man Slade wants is not so far from Coldwater, or *in* Coldwater."

"I wouldn't do too much wondering, Doc." The lawyer's tone was thin. "Stick to your doctoring and leave such things as catching murderers to our friend Slade." He passed on with a curt nod.

Doc Manners watched him covertly and there was a slight tremble to the hand that reached for a coffee cup. His had once been a name famous and honored in his profession.

"Give a lot to be able to leave this hell-hole," he reflected. "My own fault, my own damn fault . . ." With a sudden gesture he abruptly pushed back his chair and went into the street. Mel Destrin watched him go with speculative eyes as he joined Bert Cross and Ace Coran.

"The doc's getting ready for another drunk," he said with his fox-like grin. "Always can tell when he gets to craving his whiskey."

"You'll be needing a long drink yourself, Mel, when you hear what happened in the Topaz last night." Bert Cross smiled sourly. "You tell him what Curt told you, Ace," he said to the saloon man.

In his dingy little office across the street, Doc Manners dropped into his desk chair and jerked open a drawer.

"I'm shaky this morning," he muttered, as he reached for the bottle in the drawer. "Need a good drink." Suddenly the reaching hand jerked back. "My God, I don't need it, only think I do!" The doctor slumped back in his chair, face haggard and drawn. "I'm an intelligent human being, or used to be, and can be intelligent again if I want to be."

For long minutes he sat there, staring at the bottle in the open drawer, then slowly he reached out and pushed the drawer shut. "I'm going to be able to look at you without wanting you," he said aloud. Smiling grimly, the doctor got to his feet and again went into the street.

Tim Hook and Mrs. Kelly were standing in front of the General Merchandise Emporium, and after a moment's hesitation, the doctor joined them.

"Mornin' to you, Doc," greeted the widow none too cordially.

Big, bearded Tim Hook gave him a brief nod. "When's the inquest?" he asked curtly.

"Ten o'clock." Doc Manners was looking at Mrs. Kelly speculatively. "By the way, Mrs. Kelly, I'm thinking of leaving the Palace. What's the chance for a room at the 'Dobe House?"

Ma Kelly gave him an astonished look. "I've a room, sure enough, now poor Jake Kurtz is gone," she admitted.

"I'd like to take it." The doctor's tone was eager, almost pleading. "That is," he added wistfully, "that is, if I may enjoy the privilege of your hospitality, Mrs. Kelly."

"I'm tellin' you now that there's no bar in the 'Dobe House," Ma Kelly told him frankly, growing wonder in her eyes. "I'm thinkin' a place without a bar would not be suitin' you, Doc Manners."

"Madam," the doctor drew himself up, "madam,

I am not interested in bars, or the stuff they sell over bars."

"If that's the way of it, you can come an' welcome," exclaimed Mrs. Kelly heartily. Smiling kindly at him she added in a low voice, " 'Tis glad I am for you to be usin' your brains an' givin' up what's been pullin' you down."

"Thank you, Mrs. Kelly." Doc Manners bowed. "You're an outspoken woman, Mrs. Kelly, but I quite agree with you that it's time I used my intelligence." He went smilingly back to his office.

"Thank the good Lord the man's had a look at himself," murmured the widow. "I'm thinkin' he means it, Tim, and it's a rare turnabout. He's a fine man and a good doctor."

The big Diamond D man nodded. "He'll make the grade, Ellen," he prophesied. He gave the comely widow a fond grin. "Another chick for you to mother, huh?"

"We'll be gettin' things ready for the funeral," Mrs. Kelly said. "Come along with you, Tim." She looked up at him, a soft light in her eyes. "It was good of you to come with your help, and you so busy with the roundup."

"I hope I'll always be on hand when you're needin' me, Ellen." Tim Hook spoke gruffly, striving to cover his emotions. "I'm your, your friend."

Mrs. Kelly gave him a soft-eyed look, and then,

her expression suddenly alert, she exclaimed, "There's Bert Cross an' his friends comin' pell-mell from the Palace, an' by the looks of 'em they're in an awful kilter about somethin'. Bad luck to their black hearts."

CHAPTER EIGHT

Buck Wells hiked himself awkwardly across the yard to the long figure draped over the corral fence.

"Gettin' myself real agile, Jack." The Bar 7 foreman grinned wryly. "Old bones get some brittle," he grumbled, leaning his weight against the split rails. "Now you take young uns like them two yonder an' they can bust their legs an' be friskin' round forkin' broncs in no time a-tall."

Jack grinned sympathetically from his perch. "You're doing all right, Buck, and the way you've kept the roundup moving is a wonder. I was worried, not being able to help you."

"Carlos is right smart with cows," Buck said contentedly. "He took hold o' things fine for me and he gets along fine with the boys, even if he is half Injun." Buck paused to put a match to his cigarette. "You ain't met Carlos Montalvo, have you, Jack?"

"No." Jack was watching the efforts of Johnny Archer to slip a rope on a distrustful-eyed gelding. Smoky Tucker stood near, holding a saddle and making low-voiced jeering comments. The brown gelding suddenly squealed and charged at the young cowboy with bared teeth. Johnny saved himself with a sideway leap.

"You sure broke the world's record with that jump," chuckled Smoky.

Johnny glared at him. "If you'd keep yore big mouth shut maybe I'd get somewheres with this bronc," he complained. "Laughin' jackass, that's what *you* are." He stalked after the snorting horse, stiff-legged and gently swinging his loop.

"Johnny's bound to fork that wall-eyed outlaw," Buck Wells observed. He shook his grizzled head. "Wastin' his time, I told him. That brown horse is bad clear through. He's jest plain outlaw an' won't be rode."

"I've an idea Johnny will ride him at that," commented Jack.

"The boy is good," agreed the old foreman, "an' that Smoky Tucker, both of 'em top-hands. Glad you picked 'em up."

"I'm putting them under my direct orders," Jack told him.

"All right with me. You're the boss of this outfit."

"I'm looking after the ranch, Buck, but you're still boss of the outfit, giving orders to the boys. It's only Johnny and Smoky I'm holding out on you."

Buck Wells was silent for a moment, and if he was surprised about Jack's wishes concerning the two new hands, no hint of his thoughts showed on his inscrutable weather-beaten face. He returned to Carlos Montalvo.

"Carlos used to ride for the Arrow. He quit them when Bert Cross took hold there. Went over to Mexico for a spell and when he come back to the Chuckwalla, Mark give him a job with us. Smart hand with cows, he is," Buck repeated. "Keep him down at the Chuckwalla Crossin' camp most of the time. Carlos is half Mex, you know, 'long with his Injun blood, an' the camp being close to the border an' him speakin' Mex like a native, he's useful down there. He keeps things friendly with them hombres below the border."

Jack absorbed this bit of news about Carlos with an interest he carefully concealed. He would have a look at old Buck's halfbreed, he decided. He had wondered more than once where Don Vicente obtained his valuable information, such information for instance as the planned raid on Bill Cole. Perhaps Carlos Montalvo was the answer. If true, there was a lot more to Carlos than even Buck Wells suspected.

He slid down from his perch on the fence. "Tell Johnny and Smoky to come over to the house when they get finished foolin' with the colt," he said.

"If they can walk that far when they get done tryin' to ride that piece o' dynamite," grinned the old foreman.

Jack made his way leisurely to the house and after a brief chat with the wrinkle-faced old Chinese cook he went to the room Mark Severn had used for his office. There he began to rummage through the desk drawers. A long envelope came to his fingers. Jack stared at the inscription, penned in Mark's hand, the ink faded. *Mary and my granddaughter's picture.* He slowly drew the picture out. It was an enlargement of the one he had seen in Destrin's office. Under the likeness of the young mother and babe, the rancher had written in bold heavy hand, *My dear daughter, Mary, and my little grandchild, Marita.*

Jack gazed long at the smiling face of the girl-mother, vaguely aware of an odd feeling of familiarity with the features of Mark Severn's daughter.

"Must have some look of old Mark in her," he reflected. "Reckon that's what makes me think her face is familiar." He held the picture at arm's length and studied it critically, endeavoring to see the grizzled weather-beaten features of Mark Severn in the laughing-eyed girl. "Doesn't look like Mark for a fact," he muttered, "but then, those things are queer. It's something indefinable, something you kind of feel, more than you can see. Reckon it's Mark she reminds me of, and that's the answer."

He transferred his attention to the baby girl. The name, Marita, he guessed was Mark's own invention, a pretty diminutive at that, Jack thought.

He returned the picture to its envelope and locked it away in the drawer. Then he put his mind on the tally sheets of the roundup given him by Buck Wells. The figures brought a frown to his brow. The calf crop was absurdly small.

"Looks like Bar 7 cows have quit having calves," he grumbled aloud. "I make it less than two hundred three- and four-year-old steers in the cutout. Should be a thousand ready for the drive to market."

Jack leaned back in the swivel chair and glowered at the long rows of figures. A bad leak somewhere, and he shrewdly suspected just where that leak was. The Arrow's gradual encroachments had given the Bar 7 an unscrupulous neighbor. It was easy to visualize Arrow riders at work. No doubt the calf crop in the Arrow range was extraordinarily good. A lot of Bar 7 cattle were wearing the mark of the Arrow iron these days.

Footsteps and the rasp of dragging spurs pulled him from his gloomy musings. He looked around to see the grinning faces of Smoky and Johnny at the door.

"Come in, boys."

"Howdy, boss!" Johnny Archer pushed in,

followed by his taciturn friend. "Buck said for us to come over."

"I said for you to come when you got finished with the colt," smiled Jack. The young cowboy's dusty clothes told him there had been strenuous activities in the corral.

"The colt got finished with him," chuckled Smoky.

"I ain't got finished with that piece of wild meat yet," Johnny said good-naturedly. "You can laugh yore fool head off, Smoky, but I'm forkin' that wall-eyed piece of sin, or I'm handin' you my first month's pay check."

"I'm no sure-thing gambler," retorted the dark-browed Smoky. "I wouldn't be robbin' you, feller."

Jack interrupted the good-natured banter. "You were telling me Quintal fired you because he didn't like your being too particular about whose cows he had in the Arrow roundup," he began. "Circle C cows, you said—Bill Cole's brand."

The pair looked at him soberly, exchanged glances, and Johnny Archer said slowly, "We could have told you more, boss. We know for a fact that there's plenty of cows on the Arrow range that should be wearin' the Bar 7 iron on their hides." He shook his head. "Awful lot o' calves in the Arrow herd that Smoky an' me figgered wasn't born on that range." He looked significantly at the tally sheets spread out on the desk.

"That's right," muttered Smoky.

"I get you." Jack's tone was grim. He pondered for a moment, staring at the two thoughtfully. The playfulness had left them. Their young faces were hard now, their eyes bleak and with a hint of cold fire in them.

"I'd sure like to bust that Quintal jasper wide open," Johnny declared with sudden vehemence. His tone was hopeful. "It's about time that Arrow bunch gets what's comin' to 'em."

"Maybe you'll soon have a chance to bust Quintal," Jack said quietly. "I'm telling you boys that trouble is coming fast, and it will be a showdown. I want to be fair to you. A showdown will mean a fight . . ."

The two exchanged grins. "You ain't scarin' us, boss." Johnny's voice was brittle and he was suddenly sober and hard-eyed again. "Smoky an' me aim to be right with you if a fight comes. We cut our teeth on the lead that comes out of these guns." He tapped the six-shooter in low-slung holster.

Smoky Tucker made no comment, but the way his hands went lightly to his gun butts, and the cold gleam in his unwinking eyes, sent an odd prickle through Jack. The dark-browed young puncher was chilled steel all through, and the fact that he wore two guns was significant. Smoky was a natural gunfighter. Ma Kelly had been right about this pair.

His thoughts went to the widow and her peril. She had scoffed at him for warning her she was in danger, nevertheless, the danger was very real. And then there was Maisie.

Jack came to a decision. "I'm sending you to Coldwater," he told his new hands.

Their faces fell, and after a moment, Johnny said disappointedly, "We figgered you'd be needin' us out on the ranch. Nothin' for us to do in Coldwater."

Jack silenced him with a gesture. "I'm sending you to Coldwater because I trust you, because Ma Kelly's life is in great danger."

The two looked at him with renewed attention, a quick flame in their eyes.

"Jake Kurtz was murdered in his store last night," Jack continued. "It's the talk he was killed for his money, but I know why he was killed, and the same scoundrels will be having a try at Ma Kelly."

"My Gawd!" muttered Johnny. His face paled. "Is this straight talk, Boss?"

"Ma Kelly will likely try to run you off the place," smiled Jack. "No matter what she says I want you to stay on the job. My orders, savvy?"

"Boss," Johnny spoke earnestly, "we'll stick to her like the way a tick sticks to a maverick."

Smoky Tucker nodded, hands tightening over gun butts. "When do we start?" His tone was bleak, the look in his eyes a promise of sudden death to the man who would harm Ma Kelly.

"You start now." Jack reached into a pocket. "You'll be needing money."

They pocketed the gold pieces and turned hastily to the door.

"Keep your eyes and ears open," called Jack. "Keep me posted, and don't forget you'll be there to watch out for Ma Kelly and," he hesitated, "and that new girl, Maisie."

"You're tellin' us!" exclaimed Johnny as he clattered out. There was an odd brightness in the look he flung back over his shoulder.

Jack turned back to the tally sheets and slowly stuffed them into a drawer. The thought of Johnny and Smoky on the watch at the 'Dobe House brought him vast relief. He sensed their devotion to the widow, and sensed too, a new-born unswerving loyalty to himself. They were of the breed that knew no fear.

Buck Wells came in, hobbling painfully and leaning on his home-made crutch. "The boys say you're sendin' 'em to Coldwater," he commented from the doorway. "Wouldn't say what for."

"Got a job of work there for them," replied Jack. He was secretly pleased at the boys' cautiousness. Their reticence even with the Bar 7 foreman was comforting proof they could think fast, as well as shoot fast. He thought best to mollify Buck who was obviously hurt at this secrecy. "Want them to keep an eye on things in Coldwater for me, Buck. That town's getting to be nothing but a stamping ground for cow thieves."

The old foreman nodded gloomily. "We've been losin' a lot of beef, Jack," he confessed. "I'm guessin' old Mark was gettin' wise to the gang, which is why he was dry-gulched."

"What do you know about this rustling?" Jack's tone was blunt.

"Well, Jack," the foreman hesitated, "I'm admittin' I ain't been much use to Mark the past year or two. Gettin' too old for the job, an' that's the truth."

"You've been with Mark ever since there was a Bar 7," reminded the young man gently. "He thought a lot of you, Buck."

The veteran range man smiled sadly. "Too long, son. Told Mark more'n once to put a younger feller in my place. He was awful stubborn, Mark was." He shrugged wide, stooped shoulders. "I reckon it's my fault, and his, too, that we've been lettin' the old ranch slip. Both of us too old for the game, what with all this rustlin' goin' on."

Jack felt sorry for him. Buck was suffering torments, inwardly raging at his own inability to cope with the situation that was ruining the ranch.

"Mark thought a lot of you," he repeated. "You've done your best, Buck, and your best is always good. You can give most of us younger fellows points on the cattle business."

"Should know about cows by now," admitted the foreman, brightening. "Well, I'll mosey along to the shack. Jennie takes a look at the leg about this time o' day." He limped away toward the low adobe building set back in a grove of cottonwood trees. Jack had asked Buck and his wife to move into the rambling old ranch house, but the couple preferred to remain in the cottage that had been their home since Jennie was a bride.

The foreman's limping steps came to a halt.

"*Buenas dias*, Pedro! What's on yore mind?"

Jack pricked up his ears, listened with quick interest. The man talking to Buck was asking for Carlos Montalvo.

"Carlos ain't round right now," he heard Buck answer. "Carlos is over at Chuckwalla Crossing."

Jack went to the door. He wanted a look at the man who was inquiring for Carlos Montalvo. Buck's roving gaze fastened on him.

"It's only Pedro," he called, "wanting to see Carlos."

Jack stared curiously at the middle-aged, paunchy Mexican. "What's your business with Carlos?" he asked in Spanish.

"I come just to make him the visit," answered the man.

"Where do you work?"

"I have a small place where I keep a few sheep," Pedro informed him readily enough.

Buck nodded his grizzled head. "Sure," he said,

"some no-count mesa land Mark give him to run a few sheep on. Pedro's been livin' there for years on the Chuckwalla rimrock." He looked at the Mexican sharply. "Them Arrow fellers troublin' you, Pedro? Some of that mesa spreads over into Arrow range," he added in an aside to Jack.

"No, Señor." Pedro shook his head. "Sometimes they stop and water their horses at the spring, but they cause me no trouble." He gestured. "The land, it is worthless, and always I am most careful to be polite. So I keep friends, like I do with you, Señor."

"You know what we think of the Arrow," gruffed Buck.

"*Si*, Señor." Pedro darted a nervous look at Jack. "But what can I do, but keep friends with them?" He gestured helplessly.

Jack smiled reassuringly. "I think you are wise to keep friends, Pedro. No sense making trouble for yourself."

"*Gracias*!" The Mexican looked at him with a curious intentness. "You are the new Señor?"

"I'm helping Buck for awhile," smiled Jack.

"The old *jefe* was very good to me," Pedro said. "He was my friend."

"Any idea who killed him, Pedro?"

The Mexican gestured. "*Quien sabe*," he muttered. His eyes lowered. "One hears it is the Hawk, or at least such is the talk of the vaqueros of the Señor Cross when they come to my place."

His glance went to his horse. "I go now, Señores. It is a long ride to the Chuckwalla Crossing Camp."

"Buck," there was a hint of excitement in Jack's low voice, "I want to see this Carlos Montalvo."

"I'll have old Pedro tell him," Buck said. His voice lifted. "Hi, Pedro!"

"I don't want Carlos to know I'm wanting to see him," Jack added quickly. "Savvy?"

"Sure," grunted Buck, whose puzzled tone indicated he did not savvy.

The Mexican had halted his horse and was staring back inquiringly. "If you're ridin' over to the Crossin', you can tell Carlos I'm wantin' him soon as he can get here," called the foreman.

"*Si*, Señor, I tell him," promised Pedro. He rode on his way.

"Thanks, Buck." Jack smiled and went back into the office.

CHAPTER NINE

Mel Destrin pulled the buckboard team to a standstill and pointed his whip at the cluster of ranch buildings in the distance.

"There's the place where your mother was born," he said to the girl sitting by his side.

"Looks awful lonesome." Her tone lacked

enthusiasm. "Wish she'd been born some place that wasn't a thousand miles from nowhere." She stared discontentedly at the ranch house showing like a gray dot in the blur of green in the wide bosom of the valley below. "Of all the gawdforsaken dumps!"

"You don't know your luck." The lawyer gave her an impatient glance. "You watch your step, Belle, and play this game right."

"Don't you worry," returned the girl airily. "I ain't kickin' at a few hayseeds in my hair." She was small, trim, blonde, and decidedly pretty in her hard way.

"You'll never make ten thousand more easily," Mel Destrin said with his fox-like grimace.

"Guess I can stand it for a few months," agreed Belle Gerben agreeably. "Won't hurt me to rusticate on the old home ranch." Her laugh had a hard note.

"Don't forget all the things I've told you," warned the lawyer, "and watch your talk, Belle. Cut out your dance-hall chatter. You've got to remember your mother was a refined lady."

"Say!" interrupted the girl, "I'm remembering my mother was killed in a train wreck when I was a baby. It ain't her fault if I was brought up kind of rough. Gives me a good alibi if I act natural, don't it?" She tossed her head. "At that I guess I can be a lady with the best of 'em. You leave it to me."

Destrin touched the team with his whip and they started down the long descent into the valley. The girl's hard blue eyes took on a softer light as they neared their destination. The rambling old ranch house in the trees looked less lonesome, loomed homey and comfortable through the towering trees, and there was a prosperous look about the wide spread of outbuildings and the great barns back of the corrals where horses drowsed in the afternoon sunshine. A man was shaping horseshoes in the old blacksmith shop under a big cottonwood tree, the sound of his hammer on the anvil beating mellow music, above which rose the sudden barking of a dog, as the buckboard wheels ground through the coarse sand of the creek that flowed below the gate.

Destrin handed the reins to the girl and climbed from the vehicle.

"Looks kind of nice and homey," Belle Gerben murmured half to herself, while the lawyer unfastened the chain and swung the wide gate open. He motioned her to drive through. Belle slapped the team's dusty backs with the reins, her gaze intent on the man who suddenly appeared on the ranch house veranda. As the horses jerked forward, a gust of wind snapped the gate from the lawyer's limp grasp and banged into the hind wheel. There was a crash and startled snorts. In a moment the buckboard went careening up the avenue, the horses on a dead run, the reins, pulled from the girl's unaccustomed hands, trailing under flying heels.

Jack, watching from the veranda, heard the girl's frightened scream and went leaping across the stretch of Bermuda grass. A ten-foot water ditch lay between him and the drive. He took the jump in his stride. No time for the footbridge if he was to keep the runaway buckboard from piling up in the barbed wire fence. The girl, white-faced and limp with terror, glimpsed him crashing through the shrubbery, then hid her eyes as the tall young man dived headlong at the oncoming runaways. The next moment the buckboard was careening to a standstill.

Belle opened her eyes, saw her rescuer firmly holding the horses by their bridles and smiling reassuringly at her. This was the man the lawyer had told her about, Jack Fielding, *the* Jack Fielding. She smiled back, a faint, pathetic little smile and scrambled from the buckboard.

"Oh! I, I'm afraid I, I'm going to faint . . ."

Jack dropped bridle reins and was at her side in a moment. He caught her in his arms as she collapsed.

Mel Destrin hurried up from the gate, dusty and excited. Belle lay limply against Jack's shoulder, her eyes closed.

"Your friend has fainted," said Jack with some anxiety.

There was a grunt from the lawyer, and then,

"Haven't you guessed who she is, Jack?"

Belle Gerben felt the strong arms tense, and then heard Jack's voice, thrillingly deep, *"Mary Cameron?* Well I'll be . . ." His voice trailed off and the girl felt the impact of his startled eyes.

"Mark Severn's granddaughter," chuckled the lawyer. "And mighty lucky you were on the job, Jack, or she'd have been in that barbed wire. That would have been a damn poor welcome home."

"I'll carry her to the house," Jack said. Belle stirred in his arms and opened wide blue eyes.

"I, I'm all right now," she said faintly. "You, you see, coming home like this and thinking of poor mama and how she was killed in a wreck, and then this happening so, so suddenly . . ." Belle smiled wanly up at the rather stern face so close to hers. "I sort of went to pieces," she finished. From the corner of a fluttering eye she glimpsed Mel Destrin's face, knew that she was not fooling him. He was on to her act. The lawyer's expression was cynical, but pleased. "I'm sure I can walk to the house," Belle said in a stronger voice.

For answer, Jack lifted her bodily and started by way of the footbridge for the house where Wong was watching from the kitchen door, a pitcher of water in hand. The girl's reference to her mother profoundly affected the young superintendent of the Bar 7. Naturally she would have been greatly moved by this homecoming, thinking of the mother she had never known and the grandfather

119

she would never know. It was enough to cause any girl to faint.

He placed her gently on the big horsehair sofa and handed her the glass of water Wong handed him. The aged Chinese was staring at the girl intently. Something like disappointment lurked in his slant eyes as he turned, wordless and without a glance at Jack, and padded softly from the room. The blonde girl's gaze followed him uneasily for a moment, as if vaguely sensing an unspoken enmity. Lawyer Destrin also flicked a sharp look at the stoop-shouldered old cook shuffling to the door.

"Too bad Mark Severn isn't here to greet his granddaughter," the lawyer was saying smoothly. He smiled at the girl. "Feeling yourself again, Miss Cameron?"

Belle sipped daintily at the water and gave the glass back to Jack. "It's wonderful to be here in the old home where mother was born," she said softly. Her smile lingered on Jack's grave young face. "It, it's all so romantic coming home like this, *you* saving my life and carrying me across the threshold in your strong arms."

He flushed, a bit disconcerted at her pointed reference to him carrying her across the threshold. Decidedly a naive sort, this Mary Cameron, he reflected. Aloud he said heartily, "It's a happy day for the ranch to have Mark Severn's grand-daughter home, Miss Cameron." He took his first real look at the girl and was conscious of an odd dismay. He had expected something quite different from this rather bold-eyed young woman. Pretty, in a hard way. He had seen her kind before, in the dance halls. He hadn't expected Mark Severn's granddaughter to be like this girl; and yet, why not? Lost as she had been for these long years, she had lived the life circumstances had made for her. From the dance halls undoubtedly, but what of it? She was nevertheless entitled to her birthright, entitled to the loyalty he had sworn to give Mark Severn's grandchild.

Angry that he should feel as he did, Jack grimly rose above his disappointment. "I'll send for Mrs. Wells," he said cheerfully enough. "She'll help you get settled, and then, of course, you will be making your own household arrangements for servants, a housekeeper, perhaps . . ."

Belle nodded carelessly, displaying perfect white teeth in a slow smile. "I think I'm going to like you a lot," she declared. "I hope you will like me, too, even if you are losing a great big cattle ranch just because Mr. Destrin has found Mark Severn's long-lost granddaughter."

Jack flushed again, this time from annoyance. "I'm sure we'll get along and be good friends." His eyes hardened at mention of Mel Destrin. "I think Mel must have misquoted me on your grandfather's written wishes about the ranch.

Mel knows I regarded the matter as a sacred trust."

"Jack is mighty touchy about it," broke in the lawyer hurriedly. "Forget it, Miss Cameron. He's tickled pink that we've found you." Destrin's voice took on an oily tone. "Jack doesn't care just how quick you give him his walking papers."

"Not so fast, Mel." The younger man's mild tone belied the chill light in his eyes as he stared at the lawyer. "Not so fast," he repeated, and vaguely aware of a startled exchange of glances between the other two, he went on, "it was Mark Severn's declared wish that I continue in charge of the Bar 7. You must understand and agree, Miss Cameron."

"Hotsy totsy with me," declared the girl. Then under Destrin's flick of eyes, she laughed, "I mean you can stick with the ranch till the cows come home. Oh, you know what I mean!"

"Miss Cameron used to be on the stage," Mel Destrin said with a lift of his brows. "Used to play tough girl parts, she tells me."

"Find myself talking the same lingo when I'm excited," Belle added. She smiled demurely as she smoothed her scanty skirts over her knees.

"I just wanted Miss Cameron to understand the situation." Jack's tone was stiff. "I'll have Wong tell Mrs. Wells to come over," he went on. "Speaking of Wong, he's been here for years and you'll find him a great help."

"Say!" The blonde girl sat up, her hand brushing

at a yellow curl. "I'll tie a can to that chink. I hate chinks." She broke off with a confused giggle. "There I go again with my tough girl talk."

Her embarrassment was so genuine that Jack grinned in spite of his annoyance. "Wong is a square shooter, Miss Cameron. Your grandfather thought the world of old Wong."

"Oh, call me Mary," laughed the girl. "I'm here to stay, and so are you. Might as well get used to each other."

It was on the tip of Jack's tongue to tell her of the name Mark Severn had written on the picture hidden away in the drawer. For some reason the impulse passed. This rather hard-faced girl was not the Marita old Mark had in mind when his big-knuckled hand had penned that pretty diminutive. He smiled and shrugged the shoulders that Belle Gerben was secretly admiring. "Back in a few minutes," he said, and went from the room.

Lawyer Destrin's fox-like grimace went to the blonde girl on the sofa.

"Doing fine," he muttered. "He's swallowed you all in one piece."

Belle nodded indifferently, admired her outstretched shapely legs. "I kind of like him." Her tone was musing. "Kind of stern and icy, but I'll bet he could be awful nice to a girl if he liked her a lot."

"Let me tell you something." Destrin sat down on the sofa, his voice low against her ear. "Your job is to make Fielding so damn sick of you and the Bar 7 that he'll walk out on you, promise or no promise."

The blonde girl looked at him, and something she read in his shiny black eyes made her head draw back as if from a threatening rattlesnake.

"I'm getting rid of him one way or another," Destrin said in his venomous whisper.

"My Gawd, Mel." The girl was pale. "You're a devil . . ."

"You're working for me, and I don't let anybody working for me, double cross me."

Footsteps sounded from the hall. Destrin slid over to the end of the sofa and lit a cigarette he drew from a silver case. "Yes, Miss Cameron, you'll find Jack knows cattle from A to Z. You couldn't find a better man in the state." He spoke loudly, smile fastened on the girl, still tense and distrait. "Snap out of it," he added in a low whisper.

Belle straightened up, her lips parting in a smile, as Jack came in with a plump, pleasant-faced elderly woman. Behind them limped Buck Wells, leaning on his crutch. The latter darted an excited look at the blonde girl on the sofa.

"Jack's just been tellin' us the big news!" he rumbled. "Sure am pleased to be meetin' old Mark's granddaughter. Big day for us, huh, Jennie?" He leaned on his crutch, his delighted gaze fastened on the girl. Mrs. Wells was at her

124

side, arms opening wide. "Indeed it is a happy day for us!" she cried. "My dear little lamb, bless your sweet face, it's many the time I used to dress dolls for your darlin' mother when she was a bit of a girl."

Belle embraced her with a little inarticulate cry. "She used to tell me about you, and how you used to make her dolls to play with." She broke off, conscious of a warning scowl from the lawyer, conscious too of a little gasp from the older woman.

"That would be strange!" Jennie Wells exclaimed, drawing back. "You was but a babe in arms when your mother was lost to us in that terrible wreck."

"It is strange," affirmed the girl. "You see, I don't mean that she *actually* talked about you— of course I was too young." She gestured tragically. "I used to have dreams, as if she was leaning over me in bed and telling me things, about dolls, about you . . ."

Mrs. Wells nodded solemnly. "Of course, my sweet lamb. Those queer things do happen to us. I dream too, like that about the loved ones who have gone." She embraced Belle again. The latter kissed her, then ran to old Buck and flung her arms about him.

"Buck is your foreman," Jack said in a somewhat puzzled tone. "I didn't know you knew of him."

"I've been telling Miss Cameron all about the

ranch," Mel Destrin broke in smoothly. "It's her hope that the outfit will continue to work for her, including Buck and Jennie."

"Yes, indeed," exclaimed Belle, smiling up at Buck's pleased face. "Mr. Destrin said you've been with the ranch for years and years, Buck."

"Used to tote yore mother on my shoulders when she was nothin' but a kid," chuckled the veteran. His voice was suddenly gruff. "But as for roddin' the spread for you, Mary, I reckon I'm gettin' too old."

"Oh!" Belle seemed taken aback and she darted a glance at Destrin.

"That's bad news," murmured the latter. "You were Mark Severn's best friend."

"Mary'll have Jack on the job," went on the old foreman. He smiled at the girl. "Yore grandpop thought an awful lot of Jack. He knows cattle with any of 'em."

"So I was just telling Miss Cameron," chimed in the lawyer.

"I heard you, Mel." Jack's smile was a trifle thin. He was beginning to resent the lawyer's praise. He disliked Mel Destrin and was quite aware that Destrin disliked him. "I think Miss Cameron understands that I am in charge of the Bar 7 and intend to remain in charge."

Belle gave him a slow smile. "I'm not caring, or worrying about anything just now." She drew a long breath. "It's just too wonderful to be here on the old home ranch where my mother was born."

"You dear, sweet lamb!" cried Jennie Wells, quite overcome and dabbing at her eyes with a corner of her apron.

"Jennie will show you over the house," Jack said.

"Indeed I'll be glad to make her comfortable," declared Mrs. Wells.

"I'm not staying now," the blonde girl informed them quickly. "I, I'll be in Coldwater for a few days at the Palace Hotel."

"It's my suggestion," explained Destrin. "Some papers I'll be wanting Miss Cameron to sign. Be handy to have her in town for a time."

"I'd rather you put up at Mrs. Kelly's 'Dobe House," Jack said firmly. "I don't like the idea of the Palace, Miss Cameron. No place for Mark Severn's granddaughter."

Belle Gerben looked helplessly at the lawyer. He nodded. "Fine, Jack, same thought was in my own mind. Ma Kelly's is just the place for Miss Cameron. You'll like Ma Kelly," he added, looking at Belle.

"And in the meantime I'll have the house cleaned from top to bottom," promised Mrs. Wells, "and don't you be too long in Coldwater, Mary. We'll be wantin' you at the old ranch, and a grand party we'll have with all the boys on hand to meet the new mistress of the Bar 7."

They trooped out to the buckboard, and Belle

Gerben climbed in between the high wheels, a hand modestly smoothing down her fluttering brief skirt.

"A pity poor Mark isn't here this day," said Mrs. Wells tearfully, as the buckboard whirled down the long avenue. "A sweet child she is."

There was no comment from Jack Fielding. He went thoughtfully into the ranch house kitchen. Wong had a large canvas bag on the floor. Jack gave the old Chinese a questioning look.

"Me go." Wong's tone was curt. "Me go allee same damn quick."

"What's the trouble, Wong?"

"No likee missie," Wong said blandly. "No likee missie, missie no likee me."

"Don't be a damn fool," Jack told him crossly. "Put that bag away." He stared frowningly at the wrinkled, inscrutable face. "Why don't you like her, Wong?" His voice was troubled.

Wong looked at him intently. "I think so you no likee missie," he said finally.

"I don't, for a fact, Wong." The young man spoke gloomily.

"Mark here, he no likee missie," muttered the old cook in a curious voice. "Mark mebbe tell her go away damn quick."

"What do you mean? Why would Mark tell her to go away if he were here?"

"You soon find out." Wong gave him an inscrutable look from slant eyes, went on stuffing his strewed effects into the yawning canvas bag. "I go now," he added a bit viciously.

"You put that bag away," Jack rasped. "You stay on the job, Wong."

"Me go now," reiterated the old Chinese sullenly.

"Wong," Jack spoke quietly, "old Mark wouldn't like you and me to lie down on the job. He was our friend, Wong."

"You allee same damn fool," grunted the Chinaman. A grim smile creased his brown wrinkled face. "Wong allee same damn fool too. Wong no go." He upended the partially-stowed bag and shook out its contents. "You allee same bet your life me no lay down on job."

"Have a smoke, Wong." The warm smile on Jack's tanned face said more than words as he handed tobacco and papers to Wong's claw-like hand.

As the two sat there in the big kitchen smoking their cigarettes in troubled silence, Belle Gerben was remonstrating sulkily with Mel Destrin.

"What's the big idea, tellin' Jack Fielding I'd go live in that Kelly dump? I wanna stay at the Palace and have some fun. I seen that Kelly place when we drove past this mornin'. Looks like a nice home for old ladies if you ask me."

The lawyer flicked his whip at a dusty flank. "I've my reasons," he told her curtly.

"Why?" The blonde girl gave him a cross look. "I've just been askin' you."

"You can keep your ears open, and your eyes," the lawyer said with a sly grin. "It's like this, Belle, Ma Kelly is a nosy old devil we want to throw out on her ear. It fits in fine for Jack to want you to go and stay with her. She'll take you to her bosom and if you're smart, you can pick up a lot of tips we can use."

"I get you," the girl spoke sullenly. "Gosh, Mel Destrin, wonder what scheme you'll think of next." She repressed a shiver, and leaned her trim supple self away from him. "You give me the creeps." Belle's laugh had a shrill note. "Wouldn't put it past you to get to schemin' things about *me*."

The ugly glint in the lawyer's eyes as he glanced at her, made Belle wish she had held her tongue.

CHAPTER TEN

Don Vicente Torres rode up the wide floor of the Chuckwalla Wash on his proud-stepping Palomino stallion. At his back, slouching in their huge saddles with the easy grace of their kind, followed the faithful Diego and Estevan, eyes wary under the shadowing brims of their high steeple hats. Don Vicente was apt to rely on their ceaseless vigilance for his safety the while he composed sonnets to the eyes of his latest inamorata. The two hard-visaged vaqueros adored their gay and always-too-reckless young master. Since the days of the Conquistadores there had always been a Torres lording it over the vast rancho granted by a king of old Spain to Don Vicente's valiant ancestor, and always had there been a Diego and an Estevan serving a Torres.

"He rides like a man who is in a dream," grumbled the fierce-eyed Diego to his companion and half brother, for they both boasted the same Yaqui chief for their father. "It is good we are with him when he suffers these moods."

"We are his eyes," muttered Estevan, his gaze roving the waste of sand and boulders. "Our master would have died long before this, but for our eyes, our ears and these." He patted the rifle across the saddle bow.

"He is always this way when his mind is on a pretty one." Diego's tone was gruffly affectionate, tolerant. "A true Torres, our young master, easily beguiled by a woman's eyes and her smile."

"Cease your chatter! He would speak with us." Estevan sank in huge spurs. Diego followed more slowly, wary gaze raking across the wash.

Don Vicente looked at them with dancing eyes when the two pulled rein in front of him as he wheeled his horse.

"Listen, hombres, at last the lines come. You shall be the judges.

Eyes that make the night bright day,
    Ah, lovely One!
Your eyes are stars to lure my heart
    And draw me ever to your . . ."

A sharp exclamation interrupted the poet and the next instant smoke was pouring from Diego's long rifle and his voice was lost in the staccato crash of hastily-flung shots.

" '. . . and draw me ever to your side,' " finished Don Vicente in an annoyed voice as he reached for his holstered gun.

"The last line does not sound quite right," Diego said, lowering his rifle and staring at a patch of willows.

"It is so, Señor Vicente," agreed Estevan politely, also watching off at the willows, "the line does not have the true measure, as Diego says."

"Let it pass." Don Vicente waved his hand carelessly. And like the others he stared with unconcealed interest at the fringe of willows. "You shot well, Diego," he added, "and with a quickness that saved my life." He slipped off the silver-braided chin strap and took off his flat-brimmed hat. The two vaqueros stared gloomily at the bullet-mark that nicked the silver-encrusted band.

"Not quickly enough," grumbled Diego, his face paling. He spurred away in the direction of the willow thicket.

132

Don Vicente and Estevan galloped after him and found him bending over the limp body of a man sprawled face down behind a boulder half-concealed by the green growth.

"The gringo," Diego growled, looking up at them.

"Ah!" Don Vicente glowered down at the dead man, "the Señor Fargo Laben. He will not make a second escape from you, Diego." He smiled his satisfaction.

"At least we know he will not carry tales back to his master. It might have been unfortunate for my good friend Juan."

Diego swung up to his saddle and the trio rode on their way up the twisting course of the great wash. The affair had quite driven poetic thoughts from Don Vicente. There was a frown on his brow, and the dreamy look was gone from his dark eyes.

It was unfortunate that the gringo Laben had managed to escape from Diego the night before. True, the man was now very dead, but it was also true he could no longer prove the source of information Jack Fielding had hoped he would.

A thought smoothed the frown from the don's face. Carlos Montalvo had hinted there might be word of vast importance in the affairs of Jack Fielding. A smile played over Don Vicente's haughty face. Little did his friend Juan dream of the secret eyes watching in his behalf. Juan had no idea of the sources from which Don Vicente obtained the information that sent the Hawk winging over the range to strike so swiftly and terribly at his enemies.

Presently they heard the roar of the cascades, where the Chuckwalla River made its plunge down from the great gorge of the San Jacinto. Once the river bed had been the big wash up which Don Vicente and his two companions had ridden, but great cloudbursts had gouged out a new channel and the river now flowed across the wide valley that was the range of the Bar 7.

Don Vicente's hand lifted in a signal. The three horsemen drew rein behind a great clump of smoke tree bushes, and at a nod from his young chief, Estevan climbed from his saddle and went on noiseless feet up the twisting floor of Dry Creek.

In the time that it took for his companions to smoke tiny cigarettes, the vaquero was back. His expression was reassuring.

"All is well," he told them, "the vaqueros are working cattle in Tule Flats. Carlos waits for us at the camp. Our uncle is with him," he added, grinning at his brother.

"I will keep watch from the butte," Diego said. He swung his horse up the slope while Don Vicente and Estevan pushed into the twisting ascent of Dry Creek.

The Chuckwalla Crossing Camp consisted of a

rude hut, roofed with tules, a tepee tent occupied by the cattle boss and a pole corral for the *remuda*. A fat Mexican cook was bending over his pots at the fire, stirring something that sent out appetizing smells and at the sounds made by the approaching riders he straightened up, head craning round for a look at the newcomers.

"*Buenas dias*," he grunted, recognition in his eyes. His voice lifted. "It is the Señor who comes."

A man suddenly appeared from the tent, his gaze fastened on the two horsemen coming up the slope from the deep gorge of the creek. He was a lean, rather small man with a high-boned dark face and deep-set watchful eyes. His hand lifted in a gesture of recognition as he moved leisurely toward the pole corral to meet his visitors. He walked lightly, with the lithe ease of a great cat, and indeed there was something pantherish in his noiseless approach and watchful eyes.

"*Buenas dias*, Señor," he spoke softly, his teeth showing white in a brief smile that included Estevan.

"*Buenas dias*, Carlos," returned the don graciously. His glance flickered at the blaze-faced sorrel horse in the corral. "Where is Pedro?"

For answer, the cattle boss clapped his hands smartly and from the tent emerged the paunchy, elderly Mexican who was his uncle and the uncle of Estevan and Diego.

Don Vicente dismounted from the Palomino and went leisurely to a cottonwood tree. "We will rest in the shade while we talk," he said, beckoning for Carlos and Pedro to join him. Estevan remained in his saddle, his eyes roving alertly.

Don Vicente sat on his heels and proceeded to make a cigarette while his eyes questioned the cattle boss. The latter nodded and gestured at the elderly Pedro.

"He brings news, but not enough—not what you must know, before the time comes to strike a last blow for the young Señor who now rides the saddle of the Señor Severn."

"I listen." Don Vicente's gaze commanded the old Mexican to speak.

"Two nights ago it was planned to slay the Señor Fielding," began Pedro. "The plot failed . . ."

"I know of this plot," smiled the don. "It failed because I was there with your nephews."

"The men concerned were much troubled because the one sent to slay the young Señor did not return."

"The man is now very dead," said Don Vicente, his voice a satisfied purr. "Already the buzzards gather in the wash of the Chuckwalla."

"*Bueno*," muttered the old Mexican. His sunken eyes gleamed. "The mystery of his disappearance has brought fear to the hearts of these others whose names you know. Also, they are like wild men about the affair of the Cole raid and the killing in Topaz Basin. Fear lives with them since that night."

The three men exchanged grim smiles, and Carlos said softly, "I know only what my uncle tells me, my Señor."

"One man alone lived to carry the tale," Don Vicente said with a careless gesture. He suddenly frowned. "One other man was given his life, by the foolish kindness of our friend Juan. I think though, he is by now very far from this part of the country."

"His name, Señor, this one who was given his life?" Carlos Montalvo's tone was harsh.

"Starke Quintal, a young brother of the man you hate, is the man who escaped our guns."

"I will remember the name," the cattle boss nodded. "Perhaps some day I will kill him, as I surely will kill the other Quintal."

"Go on with your tale, Pedro," commanded Don Vicente. "Have you yet uncovered the trail to the one whose orders are obeyed by these men we know by name?"

The Mexican shook his head gloomily. "His trail is well covered," he answered. "His name is never spoken. I know only that he is called the Big Boss." An amused smile creased his face. "Yesterday the Señor Curt Quintal came with his vaqueros to my place on the mesa and I was ordered to make a visit to the Bar 7 on pretense of seeing my nephew, Carlos, but really to learn if the Señor Fielding had returned to the ranch, and if possible, solve the mystery of Fargo Laben's disappearance."

The other two laughed softly as if in enjoyment of a good joke.

"These men do not yet suspect you," gloated Don Vicente. "You have been very clever to keep them fooled."

"I would not be here if they suspected me," said the old Mexican simply. He drew a long knife and pointed it significantly at his brown throat.

"You are brave," declared Don Vicente, and Carlos Montalvo nodded, a gleam of admiration in his eyes as he looked at his rather unprepossessing uncle.

"I spoke to the young Señor Fielding," went on Pedro. "He is a good man, worthy of the old señor's trust."

Don Vicente drew himself up proudly. "He is my friend," he said. "He commands your loyalty, the same loyalty you give to me."

"My life's blood will empty from my body before I betray him," vowed the Mexican solemnly. "He carries on for the old señor who was good to me. I serve him as I served the old señor, as I serve you."

Don Vicente's smile was approving, and after a brief silence, he said thoughtfully, "You must carry some news back to these dogs who think you are their spy. Else they will begin to lose confidence in you."

"It is a good idea," agreed Pedro.

"You can tell Curt Quintal that while riding the trail to the camp to see your nephew, you met the man, Fargo Laben, whom you recognized by the scar on his cheek."

"Quintal spoke of such a scar," Pedro said.

"You can tell Quintal that the man stopped you and asked about waterholes in the badlands. The story will lead them to think Laben lost his nerve and fled rather than face them."

"It will be a good story," agreed Pedro.

"*Bueno!*" Don Vicente pinched out his cigarette and stood up. "On your way back to your mesa, hombre." His face darkened. "I would you had brought us the name of the one who schemes so evilly against my friend Juan."

"He is a cunning devil," muttered the old man, "but some day he will leave the mark of his cloven foot on the trail and then you shall have his name, my Señor."

The shrill scream of a hawk drifted down from the high butte above the gorge of Dry Canyon.

"Diego signals us!" exclaimed Don Vicente, glancing towards the top of the cliff.

"The vaqueros," reassured the cattle boss. "They return for the midday meal." He glanced at the simmering pots.

"It is well we are not seen here," Don Vicente

said quickly. "There may be a spy among your gringo riders." He went hastily to his horse and swung into the saddle with lithe grace. "*Adios,*" he called back softly, and was gone into the depths of the gorge, Estevan following at the Palomino's heels.

CHAPTER ELEVEN

Jack was talking to Pop Shane in the latter's tiny office, rich with the pleasant smells of leather and sweet hay.

"I see the reward for the Hawk is up another thousand," he observed.

The liveryman chewed gently on his cud of tobacco. "Sheriff Slade is some peeved," he spoke cautiously. "Seems awful upset about somethin'."

Jack grinned. "I suppose you've been hearing talk about the Topaz Basin affair," he said.

"Topaz Basin?" Pop hesitated, gave him a sly look, and after a moment he rose from his chair and pushed the street door shut. "Mebbe I've been hearin' things," he went on, resuming his seat, "and mebbe I ain't."

"You mean Quintal and the gang are keeping mum about what happened in the Basin?"

"Why, son? What just *did* happen in the Basin?" Pop's tone was bland. "How come you know

140

what Quintal and Bert Cross and Ace Coran ain't shoutin' out loud to the public?"

"Things get around," grinned the young man. "You know plenty, Pop."

"Well," admitted the liveryman. "Monte Boone was hintin' at some sort o' play pulled off in the Basin." He gave Jack a searching look. "From what Monte let slip I'm guessin' that what happened is somethin' Bert Cross and his friends ain't carin' to talk about." His tone was dry, touched with sly humor.

"They can't talk about it without admitting they were stealing Bill Cole's cows," chuckled Jack.

"You know all about what took place, huh?" Again the dry humor in the liveryman's voice.

"Well," Jack shrugged his shoulders, "I'll tell you this much, Pop. I ran into Bill Cole and he gave me a yarn about a raid on his place and then finding his cows right back on the home range the very next morning."

"Jibes with the story Monte says Bill gave him when he was in town last night," Pop commented. "Monte said Bill was tellin' him about a lot of dead hombres layin' in the Basin. He recognized two or three Arrow men among 'em, Bill told Monte."

"Which is why certain gentlemen in this town are sure keeping their mouths shut," pointed out Jack.

Pop Shane stared at him with narrowed eyes.

"Them fellers ain't keepin' their mouths shut to Slade," he mused. "The reward for the Hawk is up a thousand dollars, which proves Slade knows all about it." Pop wagged his gray head. "Son, I'm greatly fearin' that our noble sheriff is hand-in-glove with that damn bunch o' crooks."

"I wouldn't bet against your guess, Pop," murmured the young cowman. His face darkened. "What's your idea about the Jake Kurtz killing?"

"Same as yore's," drawled Shane.

"They wanted him eliminated," muttered Jack. His tone was worried. "Pop, I'm in a stew about Ma Kelly. She's not safe a minute in this town."

The old man gave him a shrewd look. "Was wonderin' some about them two young gun-slingers boarding their broncs with me." He chuckled. "Told me the Bar 7 would foot their bills while they was restin' theirselves up at Ma Kelly's."

"I sent 'em," admitted Jack tersely.

"Figgered it was on the widder's account," Pop said. He straightened up in his chair, a curious look in his eyes. "I'm forgettin' about the girl, the one Mel Destrin is tellin' round is Mark's granddaughter."

"Have you seen her, Pop?" Jack's tone was non-committal.

"Right smart-lookin'," Pop answered cautiously. "I reckon you're mighty pleased, son."

Jack was silent, his moody gaze fixed on a

spider that was sliding down its gossamer thread. Pop Shane stirred uneasily, watching him under sleepy-lidded eyes.

"Wasn't exactly what I was lookin' for in old Mark's granddaughter," he said finally.

Jack's eyes lifted and met the old man's gaze a bit defiantly. "She's Mark's granddaughter, Pop." He spoke harshly. "Don't you forget it!"

Pop Shane snorted. "Awful touchy about her, seems to me." He sent a dark brown stream with destructive accuracy at the dangling spider. "I ain't likin' the girl," he declared frankly, "an' you ain't foolin' me none, young feller. You ain't likin' her yore ownself."

"Damn you, Pop!"

"Damnin' me won't make you like the gal, nor me like her." The liveryman spoke grimly. "I'm sayin' that she looks awful phony to me, son, phony as hell."

"Wong doesn't like her, either," muttered Jack miserably. His voice hardened. "Just the same she *is* Mark's granddaughter, Pop. She's got the letter he wrote to her mother when she sent him the picture. No use trying to make me believe she's phony."

Shane sighed, shook his head sorrowfully. "Well, all I've got to say is I'm kind of glad old Mark ain't here to see his grandchild. He'd say the breed had fallen off awful bad."

Jack uncoiled his length from the rawhide-bottomed chair. "So long, old-timer. Got a date with Mel Destrin at his office, then I'm heading for Ma Kelly's."

"So long, son," grunted the old man a bit sourly. The talk had put him in a bad humor, and for long minutes he sat there, gazing through the open door with angry, bitter eyes.

"Mebbe she ain't phony," he reflected gloomily. "Mebbe she *is* Mary Severn's daughter, but she's a bad filly just the same, else she wouldn't be so thick with Bert Cross an' Ace Coran, and her in town, less than a week."

Grumbling to himself, the old liveryman lifted his wiry frame from his chair and sauntered out to his favorite seat under the shady cottonwood tree, where he could see what went on in the street. What instantly drew his gaze was a group of men in front of the sheriff's office. Pop jerked out of the rawhide rocker and went pounding up the boardwalk.

Sheriff Slade's voice was loud and angry. "You mind yore own business, Jack Fielding! I'm arrestin' this young feller for good reasons!" He glared at Johnny Archer, who stood backed against the wall, hands lifted above head. "I'm puttin' him behind the bars, also that other young hellion he pals with."

Jack shook his head. "Johnny and Smoky work for the Bar 7, Slade." He spoke quietly. "You're not arresting them."

"I'm warnin' you, Jack, don't you go interferin' with the law."

"Take your gun off him," Jack said, his soft tone in sharp contrast to the sheriff's loud, bumptious voice.

The burly, red-faced officer looked at him, his bravado melting under the hard steel of the younger man's eyes. His gun lowered.

"I've a mind to throw you in jail with 'em," he blustered. His gaze went uncertainly to Bert Cross, watching from the hotel porch. A slight young girl in summery blue stood by the tall Arrow man's side, a little blue parasol swinging in one hand.

"What's the charge against the boys?" Jack's curt question brought the sheriff's wavering attention back to the matter.

"There ain't no charge," blurted Johnny Archer contemptuously. "He's fixin' to frame us because that Quintal coyote egged him on."

Pop Shane shouldered through the group of bystanders. "What's the trouble?" His usually mild drawl was ominously thin and he gave the sheriff a hard look. "I know this young feller, Slade. He ain't no crook."

"How come he an' his friend are loafin' round in Coldwater?" demanded the sheriff in his loud blustering voice. "Been too much cow stealin' goin' on an' I aim to ask 'em where they get the money they're spendin' so free."

"I told you they're working for the Bar 7," reminded Jack. "You're crazy with the heat, Slade."

"Why ain't they out on the ranch 'stead of loafin' here in town?"

Jack ignored the question. He was looking at Johnny, whose hands now hovered lightly over his gun butts. "What's he mean by this money he claims you and Smoky are spending so free?" he asked.

Johnny reddened. "I sat in on a game over at Coran's the other night," he confessed. "Smoky wasn't feelin' so good . . . figgered he'd take it easy at Ma's." Johnny grinned significantly at his boss. "Reckon you savvy how it is with Smoky." Reassured by Jack's scarcely perceptible nod, Johnny's grin widened. "Sure was lucky at Coran's that night . . . cleaned up more'n a hundred bucks."

Pop Shane chuckled. "Reckon that settles about the money the boys is spendin' so free," he said to the sheriff. His drawl took on the ominous thin edge again. "Also, an' I'm repeatin' it loud, Slade, Johnny an' Smoky are friends o' mine."

Sheriff Slade reluctantly holstered his gun. "I ain't finished with this business yet," he said in an ugly voice looking at Jack. "I'm thinkin' Curt Quintal ain't so wrong when he figgers the Hawk's got friends in this town." He stamped arrogantly into his office.

Pop Shane followed Jack and Johnny to Mel Destrin's office door. The liveryman's expression was worried.

"There's more than meets the eye," he muttered. "Slade knows well enough the boys are workin' for you, Jack."

"The man who gives Slade his orders doesn't want them at Ma Kelly's," Jack told him. "He suspects why I'm keeping them at the 'Dobe House." He was looking across the street, at the trim young girl in laughing conversation with Bert Cross. The sight of Mark Severn's granddaughter obviously on friendly terms with the Arrow superintendent depressed him. Pop Shane saw the look, read his thoughts.

"There's more important things to worry about," he said significantly. "Slade's pass at you about the Hawk, for instance." He glanced at Johnny Archer. The latter was staring intently up the street at a far-distant trailing haze of dust.

"I'm telling the boys," Jack spoke softly. "They'll have to know."

"You can trust 'em," muttered Shane. "Wish you'd keep 'em close to you, Jack."

"I can look out for myself," Jack assured him. "Ma Kelly can't."

"That reward is gettin' too big," worried Shane. "I ain't quite trustin' some of these hombres the Hawk's been helpin'."

"You're crazy!" Jack spoke impatiently.

"Bill Cole, for instance," pursued the old liveryman. "Never thought much of that feller. He's got a yeller streak in him."

Johnny Archer's voice drew their attention. "Looks like the Arrow bunch ridin' in," he muttered, gaze on the lifting dust. "Quintal will be with 'em." His tone was hopeful.

Jack gave him a hard look. "Listen, Johnny, you go back to the 'Dobe House and stick there close."

"I sure crave to lock horns with that Quintal skunk," grumbled the young puncher.

"First time I'm hearin' a skunk has horns," chuckled Pop Shane.

"The horns I mean make plenty smoke," grinned Johnny, unabashed.

Jack scowled at him. "You get back to Ma Kelly's. Quintal can wait."

"I'm on my way, boss." Johnny went clattering up the sidewalk. Jack gave the liveryman a brief nod and turned toward the lawyer's office door. Mary Severn was climbing with a flutter of summery frock into Bert Cross's red-wheeled buggy, he noted.

Mel Destrin was watching the performance from his window and Jack shrewdly guessed the lawyer was not over-pleased. After all, the girl was the owner of the Bar 7 ranch, and a decided catch. Destrin was a bachelor and might easily be jealous of the Arrow man's attentions.

The lawyer plumped himself angrily into his

chair and stared at his caller. There was something snake-like about his hunched-forward head, his glittering black eyes.

"I'm glad you dropped in, Jack."

"I got your message, that's why I'm here."

Destrin tapped some documents spread out on his desk.

"You may not know it, but I've a claim against the Bar 7," he said abruptly.

"No, I don't know!" Jack looked at him with some surprise. "What kind of claim?"

"I loaned Mark Severn ten thousand dollars last fall and the note is months past due."

Jack stared at him in silence. Mark Severn was not one to borrow, and yet it was possible.

"What was the security?" he finally asked.

"Mortgage, real estate, the cattle . . ." Destrin smiled. "Really a personal transaction between friends. For Mark's sake, I didn't put the papers on public record. Knew Mark was good for the loan." The lawyer shrugged his black-garbed shoulders in a poor imitation of sympathy. "Trouble now is Mark's dead."

"The ranch is worth many times ten thousand dollars," pointed out Jack.

"I'm needing my money." The lawyer's tone was sour. "There is no money. Your cattle shipment won't more than take care of running expenses."

"Won't even do that," murmured the young

149

man. "I was planning to borrow from the bank at San Carlos."

"You can't," declared Destrin. "I'm holding a blanket mortgage. You'd have to pay me off first."

"I can't pay you off, not now."

"I'd hate to do it, Jack." Destrin's tone was regretful. "It means I must foreclose."

Jack looked at him with doubt and growing suspicion in his eyes. "You mean the Arrow would buy in the Bar 7 for a song, huh, Destrin?"

The lawyer gestured. "How do I know who'd be the highest bidder?"

"Do you know who really owns the Arrow, Destrin?"

"Why don't you ask Bert Cross?" retorted the lawyer.

"Some day I'll be asking him a question he won't like," Jack said grimly. He pondered for a moment, perplexity deepening in his eyes. "Seems a bit rough on the Severn girl, taking her ranch after all the trouble you've had in finding her. This foreclosure talk of yours doesn't make sense, Destrin."

"I don't want to foreclose," declared the lawyer. "It'll be up to you, Jack."

"No savvy."

"You step down from the saddle and make way for my own man to run the ranch. You agree to that and I'll nurse things along until Mary Severn is out of debt and sitting pretty."

"Who's the man you have in mind for my job?" With an effort Jack curbed his growing rage and spoke quietly.

"Bert Cross is the best cowman in the country." The lawyer was watching him intently. "His work with the Arrow proves he knows his business."

"So that's the play," muttered Jack, half to himself. More loudly he said, "Let's have a look at this mortgage of yours, Destrin?"

The lawyer pushed the paper across the desk. "It's legal enough," he sneered. "You heard my terms. It's up to you whether or not I foreclose on the Bar 7."

Jack was scrutinizing the heavy-handed signature, undoubtedly Mark Severn's handwriting, and yet there was something there, or not there, that brought a puzzled frown to his brow. Suddenly memory came to his aid. His gaze lifted in a long searching look at the lawyer, then with an angry gesture, he pushed the papers away.

"Destrin," he spoke softly, "you're a crook, and I'm telling you to your face that you won't get away with this play." He stalked from the office.

Mel Destrin's gaze followed him, then slowly went to the papers on the desk. He picked them up, studied the signature intently. Presently he stuffed the papers into a drawer and leaned back in his chair, a baffled look in his eyes, a growing fear. Nothing wrong with the signature. Mark Severn himself would have hesitated to deny it, and yet something about it had aroused Jack Fielding's suspicions.

The baffled lawyer huddled deeper into his chair, his eyes foul pools of evil as he pondered.

Jack found old Pop Shane lounging near the door. The old man met his enquiring look with a sheepish grin.

"Somethin' I figgered I'd best say to you," Pop explained. "It's like this, Jack, why don't you call for a showdown right now and get Bill Cole to swear it was Arrow men that rustled him? Bill saw enough of 'em layin' there in the Basin."

"Slade would say Bill was crazy," demurred the young cowman. He shook his head. "The time's not ripe for a showdown, Pop. I want the man who's backing these men. When I know who he is, I'll know who's responsible for the murder of my father and Mark Severn." Jack paused, his thoughts going back to the lone rider he had glimpsed vanishing into the upper Topaz. "Has the old Indian turned up yet?" he asked. "Tomi?"

"Ain't seen him round yet," returned Pop. "No tellin' when that Injun will show up."

"I'd give a lot to have a talk with him," muttered the young man. He was staring fixedly at something up the street, a red-wheeled buggy in front of Ma Kelly's 'Dobe House. "So long, Pop," he added hurriedly, and started away, then changed his direction toward the saloon across the street. Monte Boone had furtively beckoned him, craggy face peering between the swing doors.

The cool barroom was deserted this midafternoon, but not for long, if Johnny Archer had rightly guessed the meaning of those approaching banners of dust.

Monte slapped a bottle down in front of him. "Jest for looks," he muttered. "Know you ain't a drinkin' man." He filled a glass. "We didn't connect that evenin' we was talkin'," he went on in a husky whisper.

"You wanted to tell me something," Jack said. "Was it about Jake Kurtz, Monte?"

The barman shook his head and glanced off nervously as a shadow darkened the swing doors. "Don't you go thinkin' I knew about *that*. I'd have tipped off Jake my own self." He paused, then reassured as the man outside moved away, he leaned closer over the bar. "Was overhearin' Curt Quintal, the same day, talkin' as how him an' a bunch of fellers was to meet over on Bill Cole's range."

"I get you." Jack's eyes narrowed in a searching look at the face opposite him. He was wondering how far he could trust the likable old rascal.

Monte seemed to sense his doubts. "I knowed yore pa afore you was born," he said a bit reproachfully.

"I'm listening," Jack said patiently. "I'm not admitting I know what you're talking about."

Monte gave him a sly look from red-rimmed

eyes. "I ain't wantin' you to admit nothin'." He spoke earnestly. "I was wantin' to tip you off that night when I seen you about this here talk o' Quintal's." His voice lowered. "Heard Quintal say somethin' about the Hawk was to be charged up with a lot more killin's and sow stealin'. I figgered you'd want to know what was up."

"Seems like the Hawk got wise and spoiled Quintal's play," Jack said in a noncommittal tone. "I reckon the Hawk is obliged to you just the same, Monte."

"Don't you go to thinkin' I got any idees about that bird," muttered the barman. An oddly defiant look crept into his eyes. "Wouldn't tell on him if I *did* know."

"*Adios*, old-timer." Jack gave him a cheerful smile and pushed through the swing doors. Monte Boone's glance tentatively regarded the untouched glass, then with a grin, he picked it up.

"Here's to you, young feller." The silence in the long barroom was broken by a gurgling sound as the whiskey vanished down Monte's throat.

CHAPTER TWELVE

A man standing in the doorway of the General Merchandise Emporium hailed Jack as the latter crossed the street from the saloon.

"Can I have a word with you, Mr. Fielding?"

Jack followed him into the pleasant coolness of the big store.

"What's on your mind, Carson?" He looked at Jake's assistant curiously. He knew little about Will Carson. Jake Kurtz had picked him up in San Carlos.

The young man licked dry lips nervously. He was sandy-haired, and his thin, snub-nosed face was covered with large freckles.

"I'm wishin' I could quit this job," Carson said. Fright stared from his pale blue eyes. "I'd like to quit," he repeated.

"Why don't you?"

"Well, I kind of hate to go back on Jake. He was awful good to me. He took me in when I was broke and starvin'. He give me a good job and his trust."

Jack looked at him with growing interest. He was in a hurry, but something held him. "What's getting you scared, Carson?" His voice was sympathetic.

"It's the way folks look at me," muttered Carson. "I get to feeling they think I, I killed Jake for his money." He paled under the freckles. "Folks don't know much about me and if I was to quit now, I'd maybe have the sheriff after me."

"I wouldn't worry too much about it," advised Jack quietly.

"I'd quit at that, if it wasn't for somethin' else that keeps me," Carson told him a bit wildly. "You see, Mr. Fielding, it's the talk that Jake left no will and that the county people will have to sort of wind up things for him. The sheriff said I was to stay on the job and keep the store runnin' until the Administrator come."

"Somebody's got to keep the store open," Jack said. "Only store in Coldwater."

"Sure!" Carson nodded. "Can't let the store close, but it ain't true about there being no will." He glanced around nervously. "You see, I know there was a will, 'cause I was a witness."

"You're sure, Carson?"

"There was more than money took from the safe. Jake's will was taken along with the money." Carson lowered his voice. "That will would have made Mrs. Kelly owner of Jake's store, owner of all he had."

Jack pondered for a moment, his face hard. "I'm glad you told me, Carson," he said finally.

"I kind of thought I could trust you," muttered the freckle-faced young man. "Something about you, Mr. Fielding, and Jake Kurtz thought an awful lot of you."

Jack said thoughtfully, "Keep your mouth shut about this will, Carson. Might be bad for your health if you let on you know there's a will."

The young man gave him a panicky look. "You, you bet I'll keep my mouth shut! Gosh, Mr. Fielding, the feller that knifed Jake might be layin' for me if he thought I was wise about that will!"

"That's why I'm advising you to keep quiet about it. Don't even tell Ma Kelly. You leave it to me, Carson, and in the meantime carry on with the store like the sheriff tells you."

Carson nodded, "Thanks." His tone was grateful. "Gosh, it's done me good to tell you."

A rancher came in for a set of harness he had ordered, and as Jack went out to the glaring sunlight he saw that the fright had left young Carson's eyes. His manner was alert, almost cheerful.

"Acts like he's shed a wagon-load of worry," Jack reflected as he continued his interrupted journey to the 'Dobe House.

The red-wheeled buggy was still in front of the gate, and as Jack turned in, he met Bert Cross sauntering down the path. He also glimpsed a flutter of blue skirt disappearing through the door. Jack guessed that the Severn girl and Cross had been enjoying the bench under the shady chinaberry tree. The tall Arrow man gave him a bland smile.

Jack answered with a curt nod and would have passed, but the other man barred his way.

"Don't hold it against Slade—the play he pulled off awhile back." Bert Cross stroked his trim black mustache. "Slade's awful jumpy these days. He thinks every stranger comes to town is spying for the Hawk."

"Johnny Archer's no stranger," retorted Jack.

"He was pretty flush with his money," pointed out the Arrow man. "Can't blame Slade for wanting to question him."

"Slade's *your* sheriff." Jack's tone was thin. "You maybe know what he's up to, Cross, and from what Johnny said, it was Quintal who sicked him on the kid." His pause was significant. "Quintal takes his orders from you," he added.

Cross reddened angrily. "Some day there'll be a showdown between you and me." His tone was vicious.

"Can't come too soon," Jack countered. "When that day comes, there'll be an explosion that will blow you and your friends to hell."

He pushed past the other man, and when he glanced over his shoulder, the latter was climbing into his buggy, momentarily obscured by dust that trailed in the wake of some half score riders loping up the street. Jack paused for another look. One of the horsemen was Curt Quintal. Johnny

Archer's guess had been correct. The Arrow outfit had come to town.

Jack went thoughtfully round the rambling adobe house to the kitchen door.

Mrs. Kelly and Maria, the cook, were expertly regarding a big roast in the oven and at Jack's step, the widow swung around with a low exclamation.

"The start you give me, lad!"

Jack looked at her shrewdly. The flush on the comely widow's cheeks was not entirely from the heat of the stove, and the undoubted pleasure of his sudden appearance had not quite banished the angry sparkle in her handsome eyes.

"I'm that glad to see you, Jack Fielding!"

"I hope so, Ma." He smiled teasingly. "Wasn't so sure from the look of you."

The color deepened in Mrs. Kelly's cheeks. The long fork in her hand swished viciously. "I'm that angry, Jack! The impudence of the man, darin' to foul me own doorstep with his dirty feet."

"Meaning the Señor Cross?"

"The very same!" Mrs. Kelly sniffed. "For two pins I'd order that Severn girl out of me house, bringin' the likes of Bert Cross home with her."

"You can't do that, Ma." Jack shook his head disapprovingly. "She's Mark's granddaughter. We've got to look out for her."

Mrs. Kelly gave him a searching look. "What do you think of the girl, Jack?" There was a curious note in her voice, and after a quick glance at the cook, she pushed him through the door into her little office. "I'm askin' what you think of this Severn girl now that you've found her." Mrs. Kelly sank into her chair, her smile tinged with sarcasm.

He frowned at her. First old Wong, then Pop Shane, and now Ma Kelly.

"Why, Ma," his tone was cautious. "I've only seen her once—the day Destrin brought her out to the ranch."

Mrs. Kelly sniffed scornfully. "Tell the truth an' shame the devil," she said acidly. "You don't like the girl any more than I like the hussy, for that's what she is, just a painted hussy."

"I've been talking to young Carson," Jack said, abruptly changing the subject.

"A worried young man he is," declared the widow. "He was wantin' to quit the job but Sheriff Slade told him to stay in town or he'd be thrown into the jail." Mrs. Kelly reddened angrily. "Slade sort of hinted folks might get to thinkin' the lad was the one who killed poor Jake if he got up an' left Coldwater too sudden."

"Lives with you, doesn't he, Ma?"

Mrs. Kelly nodded. "Jake liked the lad an' asked me to take him in."

"Any idea what will become of the General Merchandise Emporium?" asked Jack.

Mrs. Kelly shook her head. She had no notion

save it would be in the hands of the Public Administrator. "I'll tell you somethin', Jack," she went on, "when the time comes, it's in me mind to make a bid for the business. There's good money in the store," she mused, "an' I'd put young Will Carson in charge and make him me partner. He's shrewd and has a good way with the customers."

"Not a bad idea," assented Jack. He was silent for a long moment, and then said, "You've seen Mark Severn's signature, haven't you, Ma? His business signature, I mean."

"Many the time," answered the widow. She looked at him sharply. "Why, Jack?"

"How would Mark write his name to something important—his checks or a legal paper?"

"Why," Mrs. Kelly's smooth brow wrinkled as she pondered, "why, Jack, he'd a way of workin' in his Bar 7 brand, a tiny little iron he'd had made for the purpose. Mark would stamp the brand on first and write his name over it."

"He was proud of his Bar 7 brand," Jack said. "He always signed important papers that way." His tone was hard. "I'm thinking somebody slipped badly, Ma, slipped so badly that maybe he'll feel a rope slipping tight around his neck."

"Land sakes!" Mrs. Kelly gave him a wide-eyed look. "What have you stumbled on, lad?"

He told her briefly about the mortgage Mel Destrin held on the Bar 7. Mrs. Kelly was frankly skeptical.

"It's a queer business," she declared. "I'll not be believin' Mark would slap a mortgage on the ranch for a measly ten thousand dollars. He could have gone to a dozen places and got the money on his word." Mrs. Kelly nodded vigorously. "It's the truth. Mark could have gone to old Jim Cary for any cash he was needin'. They was that close friends."

Jack nodded. He knew of Jim Cary of the big Smoke Tree outfit. Jim Cary was now governor of the state and he was Mark's executor.

"I've a notion to write Jim about this mortgage Mel Destrin claims Mark give him," Mrs. Kelly fumed. She sighed a bit. "I can't help but wish that son of his was back from Europe. Lee would be a mighty good one to get advice from. You wouldn't be rememberin' much about the way he wiped out El Capitan's gang some years back. You was away at school then."

"I've heard about that fight," smiled Jack. "I reckon we need a few like Lee Cary in Coldwater these days."

"A cool one he was," recalled the widow, "an' sure I'll never forget how he saved Nan Page from them murderin' scoundrels." She chuckled. "Fell in love with the girl an' married her, an' now it's off in Europe the two of 'em are, and Lee studyin' all about irrigation schemes, him plannin' to make the desert bloom, so he says." Mrs. Kelly paused, looked soberly at Jack. "You're a lot like

162

him," she declared. "You've the same look about you, cool an' steel-like." She nodded. "You'll not be needin' him to help you clean out this gang that's got the Chuckwalla by the throat. I'm bankin' on you, Jack Fielding."

"*Gracias*." Jack's smile was a trifle dubious.

"You'll be stayin' for supper?" Mrs. Kelly's tone was hopeful.

"Wasn't planning to stay. Got to get back to the ranch."

"You can take them two boys back with you," tartly said Mrs. Kelly. "I won't have 'em loafin' here at the 'Dobe, wastin' Bar 7 money on my account."

"I'd feel easier in my mind if you weren't here, Ma." Jack's tone was grave. "I wish you'd come out to the JF and bring Maisie with you and stay until, well, until things clear up."

Mrs. Kelly stared at him. "*Me,* go out to your JF and take Maisie! Of all the cracked notions!"

"You're not safe in Coldwater."

Mrs. Kelly looked at him, more impressed than she cared to admit.

"At that, Maisie an' me could put in some good licks puttin' things in order at the old house," she mused. "I'll bet that Mexican woman you've got don't hurt herself none keepin' things clean."

"Haven't been over to the JF since I took hold of the Bar 7," Jack confessed. Noting the light in the widow's eyes, he cunningly added, "Juana isn't much on housekeeping, Ma, and it would be a favor if you'd stay there for a few days and boss Juana a bit and put the old house in decent shape."

"I'll run out there tomorrow," decided Mrs. Kelly briskly. "Maria and Jose can hold things down here at the 'Dobe while I'm gone." She read the question in his eyes. "Yes, I'll be takin' Maisie along," she chuckled.

"I'll tell Smoky and Johnny," gratefully said the young man.

Mrs. Kelly started to protest. Jack grinned. "No use, Ma. Those boys stick with you."

Again the frank worry in his eyes, an anxiety that his smile failed to cloak, caused the widow to yield.

"I declare, you'll have me tremblin' at the sight of me own shadow," she said with an uneasy laugh at his disappearing back.

Jack went upstairs and found his two protégés good-naturedly wrangling over a game of cards.

"This feller's too lucky," complained Johnny Archer. "Good thing you showed up, boss. I sure ain't holdin' the aces today."

"You owe me four bits," reminded Smoky Tucker, "an' also it's yore turn to let me do the talkin' to Maisie when we eat dinner tonight. You sure lost plenty." His tone was triumphant.

"Lost plenty is right," groaned the blond-haired cowboy. He grinned sheepishly at Jack who was looking at them rather soberly. "You see, boss, we kind of make side bets an' the loser has to keep his mouth shut an' let the other man do the talkin' to Maisie when we eat."

"I see." Jack's smile was a trifle bleak. Smoky and Johnny exchanged glances and the latter said in a curious voice, "Don't matter which of us does the talkin', boss, when it comes to what we talk about." He chuckled. "You see, Maisie just won't talk about anythin' but you. All the time askin' questions about you."

"That's right," chimed in Smoky a bit dolefully. "Maisie sure likes to talk about you."

For some reason Jack reddened and was acutely aware of a sly exchange of amused grins. His tone unnaturally curt, he told them of Ma Kelly's proposed visit to the JF ranch.

"That's sure good news!" exulted Johnny Archer. "I'm fed up plenty with this town o' Coldwater an' its mangy coyote of a sheriff."

"Me too," muttered Smoky, his eyes suddenly pin points of fire at the reference to Sheriff Slade. He had heard Johnny's account of the attempted arrest.

"I'm putting you on the JF pay roll," Jack told them. "If things go right, boys, the JF will be a real ranch again. And I can't keep you out there and have you draw Bar 7 money," he added with a grin.

"Suits us," chorused the pair joyously.

Jack looked at them steadily. "You've heard of the Range Hawk?"

"Havin' lived here all our lives, we done heard of that bird plenty," commented Smoky, surprise in his voice.

"I'd sure like to meet up with the Hawk," declared Johnny. "I'd be ridin' with him, if I knowed him."

"You're looking at the Hawk now," Jack said quietly.

They stared at him, amazement growing in their eyes as the meaning of his words struck home. Smoky Tucker's eyes narrowed to cold glittering slits.

"Should have figgered you was the Hawk," he muttered. "The Hawk would be yore sort o' man."

Johnny Archer came to with an excited grunt. "You've said it, feller! Me an' you was always sayin' the Hawk would be a man fellers like us could tie to."

"You still want to work for me?" Jack gave them his slow smile. "Slade accuses the Hawk of a lot of killings and offers big money to the man who'll nab the Hawk."

"Knowin' *you're* the Hawk is plenty for us," declared Johnny. He glanced at Smoky.

"Slade's a lousy liar," grunted the latter.

"I'm trusting you a lot," Jack told them.

"You can trust us all the way to hell an' back," assured Johnny vehemently.

"Ma Kelly knows, and Pop Shane," Jack informed them. "You can trust Pop Shane, boys. Call on him in a pinch."

"Hope there ain't too many others knowin'," muttered Smoky, thinking of the reward posters.

"They're all my friends," Jack reassured him. He broke off, turned a startled face to the window. Mrs. Kelly's voice, shrill and terrified came from somewhere in the garden below.

"She's yellin' for the doc!" ejaculated Smoky Tucker, reaching frantically for his gun belt. Jack was already leaping into the hall. The two cowboys pounded at his heels, their pale faces betraying the ghastly fear that rode them—fear that death had reached for the woman Jack had told them to protect.

A door flew open in front of them and Doc Manners sprinted for the stairs, a bag in his hand. Jack's longer, faster stride carried him by the anxious-faced doctor.

"Somebody's been shot!" gasped the latter, as Smoky and Johnny pushed past with wild clattering leaps. The doctor's feet faltered and glancing back, Jack saw him halt midway on the stairs, his face contorted with pain.

"One of you boys help him down," he commanded sharply. Johnny turned reluctantly to obey and Jack hurried into the garden. He was vaguely wondering at the doctor's presence in Mrs. Kelly's house.

Smoky caught up with him, the waning sun glinting on the barrel of his drawn gun, and drawing cold fire from the gun-metal of his narrowed eyes.

Mrs. Kelly was talking excitedly to young Jose. The Mexican was in a state of panic, almost unintelligible, as he answered the widow's frantic questions.

The sight of her drew a relieved exclamation from the young cowboy racing at Jack's side, but the latter's face went the paler.

Ma Kelly's first words made him almost dizzy with relief. Not Maisie, not Maisie! Ma was talking about young Carson.

"Jose found Will layin' on the floor," cried the widow tearfully. "The poor lad's been killed, Jack!"

"*Si!*" The Mexican youth nodded. He'd gone to store for some things Maria needed and found young Carson lying like one dead.

"There was much blood," Jose finished with a shudder.

Doc Manners came up, leaning on Johnny's arm. Mrs. Kelly gave him a distracted look.

"I'm all right," grunted the doctor. He opened his bag and swallowed a small white pill he took from a bottle. "My heart," he explained with a wry smile, "acts up sometimes when I get too excited."

"Can you make it to the store, Doctor? 'Tis poor Will Carson needin' you. He's been shot."

"I'm all right," repeated Doc Manners. "Come

on." He turned toward the gate, and Jack sensed that the spasm of pain in his eyes was not caused entirely by a tricky heart. Doc Manners' conscience was hurting him.

A man drove up in a buckboard as they reached the gate. Mrs. Kelly gave a little squeal.

"It's Tim Hook!" She seized the doctor's arm. "In with you, Doc. Tim'll drive you to the store."

The big Diamond D man did not pause for questions. His reaching hand dragged the doctor into the seat and in a moment the buckboard was rocking up the street in a cloud of dust, with Johnny and Smoky hanging on behind.

As Jack ran up the street, he was suddenly aware of light feet keeping pace with him. Maisie was running by his side.

She met his astonished, sideways glance with a cool little smile.

"I've had a year's training in a hospital," he heard her say. "I can help the doctor, if it's not too late."

She ran with lithe ease. She was amazingly strong, Jack saw with some surprise. She was as strong as good steel, for all her slim delicacy.

Doc Manners was bending over the limp form lying on the floor when they reached the store. Big Tim Hook watched with the calmness of a man accustomed to such scenes. Gun wounds were no novelty to the Diamond D man.

"He'll be all right when you stop the bleedin',

Doc," he declared in his hearty booming tones. "The feller that shot him was in too big a hurry. He bungled his job."

Doc Manners got to his feet and looked at Ma Kelly as the widow pushed her way through the growing crowd of bystanders. "We'll take him to your place," he said curtly.

"Of course," assented Mrs. Kelly. She gave the unconscious Carson a horrified look. "The lad's not dead, you're meanin'?"

Maisie took the older woman's arm. "No," she said quietly. "He's not dead, Ma."

At a gesture from Jack, the two cowboys carried the hurt man to Tim's buckboard. Maisie climbed in by Tim's side. "I know how to hold him," she said quietly. Tim turned the team and they drove slowly up the street. Mrs. Kelly paused a moment on the sidewalk.

"I won't be goin' to the JF tomorrow," she said in a low voice. "Not with poor Will Carson so bad hurt and maybe dyin'."

He nodded gloomy assent. "No chance, Ma," he agreed, and added, "I'll be staying with you tonight."

"It'll be a comfort to have you in the house," Mrs. Kelly told him with a catch in her voice. She hurried on her way back to the 'Dobe House, and obeying Jack's look, Smoky and Johnny went clattering behind her, faces hard, eyes wary.

Jack turned back to the store. His face had a

drawn look. He was upbraiding himself for the attempt on Will Carson's life. He should have remembered that Carson had witnessed the slain Jake's will, that Carson's name was on the will. It was inevitable that the man who had stolen the will would plan to speedily remove the one person who knew of its existence.

Gloomily he pushed through the crowd into the long store and came face to face with Sheriff Slade. The latter's face was red with anger.

"You've got a nerve, rushin' young Carson off to Ma Kelly's."

"Tell it to Doc Manners," rasped the young cowman.

The sheriff's gaze roved around at the circle of faces fastened on Mel Destrin, as the latter appeared in the doorway.

"Ain't it so, Mel?" the officer's voice rose to a shout. "Ain't it my dooty to keep an eye on Carson? He'll maybe talk and tell me the name of the hombre who shot him."

"It's your right, Sheriff," agreed the lawyer smoothly. "In the interest of justice, the law demands that you have the man where you can question him when he is able to talk." Destrin shouldered his way to Slade's side and looked indignantly at Jack. "Carson must be turned over to the sheriff," he declared. "His story must not be tampered with by persons who may have good reason to influence him."

The sheriff glared triumphantly at the young cowman. "You heard the law on it, Fielding. It's my dooty to take charge of Carson an' you ain't got a word to say."

"Just what do you mean, Destrin?" Jack stared with chill eyes at the lawyer. "Who do you suspect wants to tamper with young Carson?"

Destrin's glassy eyes glinted viciously under their snaky hoods and with a fox-like grimace he looked at a man who had slouched in at his heels. "You tell 'em what you saw, Redden."

Redden's bloodshot eyes roved around at the tense faces. He was a scrawny hard-faced man and wore a red calfskin vest and dusty brush-scarred leather chaps. Jack looked at him with a puzzled frown. There was something vaguely familiar in the tilt of that battered sombrero, under which hung a dank black fore-lock.

"Tell 'em about that man you saw leaving the store awhile back," prompted the lawyer.

"Was comin' out of Coran's place acrost the street when I seen a feller make a quick sneak into the alley back of the store," Redden said in a high nasal drawl.

"What made you look at the man when he ran through the alley?" again prompted Destrin.

"I'd jest heerd a shot. It sounded like it come from inside the store," explained the man. "Stopped dead in front of the alley, wonderin' what the play was, an' then I seen the feller hightailin' away from there."

Sheriff Slade's blustering voice broke in excitedly. "You seen the feller, Redden? You'd know him ag'in?"

"He was a Mex," Redden answered with a sly glance at Jack. "He sure was on the run."

"Huh!" grunted the sheriff, "a Mex hombre, you say. Ever seen this Mex hombre before, Redden?"

The man rolled his sly bloodshot eyes in a vindictive glance at Jack's stern face. "Sure I seen him before," he returned. "Works for the Kelly woman down at the 'Dobe."

There was a silence, and then Jack said quietly, "Jose came to the store on an errand and found Carson lying unconscious on the floor. Naturally he was frightened and ran. I was at the 'Dobe House when he came with the news." Jack's tone hardened. "You're a liar, Redden, if you claim you heard that shot just before you saw Jose run down the alley."

"I'm believin' Redden's say-so," broke in the sheriff harshly. His hand went to the gun in his belt. "I'm thinkin' the 'Dobe House ain't a good place for Carson to be took. I'm takin' him away from there, Fielding, an' I'm throwin' that Jose hombre into jail."

"You're crazy," retorted Jack.

"Sheriff Slade is within his rights," declared

Mel Destrin with malicious satisfaction in his voice. "You can't buck the law, Fielding."

Jack appealed to the crowd. "You people know Ma Kelly . . ."

"She's mixed up in this business," interrupted Slade blusteringly. "I've a mind to throw her in jail too." He looked at Destrin for support. The latter nodded.

"Might be a good idea, Sheriff," he said with a malignant grin. "It's quite possible that Mrs. Kelly knows more about the mysterious killing of poor Jake Kurtz than we suspect or *have* suspected," he added significantly.

"You're crazy," repeated Jack. He was studying the crowd for friendly faces. With one or two exceptions, only hostile eyes met his look. These men were the border scum that had gradually filtered into and fouled the life of once-decent Coldwater—renegades, all of them, with a sprinkling of hard-faced Arrow riders. He spoke again, coolly fighting for time, fighting for a break. This sheriff too, was a renegade, his brutal purpose plain to read. Slade's intent was to ruthlessly destroy one more who stood in the path of the schemer he served.

For a moment Jack saw red. Once Ma Kelly was in jail there would be no saving her from the sinister web of conspiracy that sought her life. She would die in that jail and into the records would be written the story of a suicide. The archvillain behind the curtain was indeed using a cunning and deadly hand.

Jack thought despairingly of gay, reckless Vicente Torres. Desperately he wished for him and his fighting brood.

CHAPTER THIRTEEN

Even as Jack heard his own voice shearing like cold steel through that grim silence, he was amazed to glimpse the tall, swaggering form of Don Vicente suddenly framed in the doorway, and peering over the Mexican's shoulder, a pair of blazing blue eyes that could belong only to old Pop Shane.

"You're not taking Jose or anybody else from the 'Dobe House." Jack's look was stabbing at Mel Destrin. "Put the sheriff right about it, Destrin, or you're dying where you stand." Jack's gun was suddenly in his hand. "Talk fast, man!" he urged in that same low stiletto voice. "Tell Slade he's wrong, awfully wrong."

Again the ominous hush, broken by Don Vicente's soft laugh, his voice.

"*Si*, obey quickly, it ees the comman' of my frien', Señor Fielding."

"You bet, Destrin," said Pop Shane, his voice thin-edged with rage, "call off yore sheriff damn *pronto.* My trigger finger is sure twitching bad."

The lawyer stood like a man turned to stone, save for the flicker of his restless eyes at the gun in Jack's hand.

Horsemen suddenly filled the street in front of the store—swarthy, fierce-eyed men, with sunlight drawing flashes from their gun barrels. Destrin's quick, furtive look took them in.

"You heard me," warned Jack, "there'll be men killed, Destrin, and you will go first." A quick glance told him that Pop Shane's huge Sharps was leveled at the dumfounded sheriff. The lawman's face was pale, as under the menace of Pop's ancient rifle, he slowly lifted his hands above his head.

"You're committin' a crime, Shane," he mumbled, and rolled his eyes at the grim-faced liveryman.

"No crime to hold a gun on yore kind," Pop rebutted scornfully. "You never was elected sheriff proper an' 'cordin' to law, Slade, I'm proclaimin' loud that you're nothin' but a hired gunman, the Arrow's hired gunman."

There was the sound of hurried, booted feet in the back of the store. The door flew open with a crash, revealing big Tim Hook with a gun in each hand. The bearded rancher was breathing hard.

"What sort of hell's going on here?" His voice was a low rumble of fury. His gaze fastened on

176

Jack. "Figgered they'd gang up on you, huh, the mangy cowards!"

Jack grinned, but it was Destrin's voice who answered the enraged cattleman.

"Been a little mistake, Mr. Hook." The lawyer's tone was precise; he might have been arguing a case in court. "Sheriff Slade was only attempting to do his duty as he saw it. Naturally he resented what appeared to be an attempt to smuggle Carson away right under his nose."

Jack scarcely heard him, he was staring incredulously at the slight figure hovering behind Tim Hook. Maisie, a gun in her hand, stood with cool, watchful eyes! She met his astonished look with a faint, composed smile.

The sight of her standing there directly in the line of fire, if one of the glowering renegades attempted a shot at Hook, sent a chill through the young JF man. His voice lifted tense and deadly and cut the lawyer short. "Reach for the sky, all of you. Slade, Destrin, you're dead men if one of you go for your gun."

Reluctantly there was a display of hands above heads. Again Jack spoke, "All right, Pop, take their guns."

The liveryman nodded. "Line up ag'in' the wall," he ordered, stepping into the room. "Belly up close as the blood-suckin' ticks you be."

"Make it fast," warned Jack's chill voice. His gun menaced Destrin. The latter, his face a sickly

177

gray, turned to the wall. Slade ranged alongside, his frightened eyes signaling frantically at the sullen-faced men grouped inside the door. There was the scrape of booted feet on the heavy planked floor, the press of bodies against the adobe wall. Pop Shane passed down the line of backs, deftly plucked guns from holsters and tossed the weapons through the open window into the alley.

"Reckon their teeth is drawed proper," he announced grimly, as he disarmed the last man in the row. The liveryman's voice took on a startled note as he added, "I'll be dingdonged if it ain't Scorpy Redden lined up with this bunch o' p'ison snakes!" He pulled the last disarmed man around from the wall. "See you still fancy them red calfskin vests, huh, Scorpy?"

The renegade's eyes glinted venomously and darted a nervous glance at Jack, who was staring at him with suddenly aroused attention.

"Thought you was in the pen, where Mark Severn sent you for brand-blottin'," went on Pop Shane. "Looks like you broke jail." Pop's voice broke off in a startled gasp as Redden's hand made a lightning reach for the gun in the old liveryman's holster. In another lightning move the gun was menacing the girl who had edged closer to Tim Hook.

"I'm killin' her if yuh start shooting," warned the desperado in a husky whisper. His eyes bored at the big Diamond D rancher who stood like one petrified, his own weapons covering the line-up of men facing the wall. "Drop yore smoke-pots," Redden said in that same snake-like hiss. "Move away from that door, mister."

Tim Hook obeyed, his face gray with fear for the girl at his side. The guns fell with a clatter to the floor, and slowly he edged away from the door. The others watched, helpless to resist, helpless because of the instant death that would reach for the young girl. But for her the crash of guns would have shattered that stillness.

Even though the balance of power had swung so suddenly in their favor, the men facing the wall seemed reluctant to break the line-up. They were unarmed, their weapons in the alley, and it was plain they distrusted Redden's ability to save them from the blasting fire of the guns in the hands of Jack and the Mexicans. They chose to remain sullenly inactive.

Redden never even glanced at them. Slowly he moved toward Maisie and suddenly snatched the gun from her lowered hand. Obeying his fierce gesture, the girl turned and preceded him into the deeper gloom of the storeroom piled high with boxes of miscellaneous goods. The desperado's husky voice came back to the others.

"Keep as yuh are," he warned. "I'm killin' the gal if I hear a move from yuh."

Tim Hook began to mutter low, bitter oaths, his gaze helplessly on Jack. The latter's face was like gray granite. Seeing the agony in his eyes, Don Vicente, still standing just inside the doorway, lifted his hand in a warning gesture to the riders in the street.

"Do not so much as jingle a spur," he told them in Spanish. "Have a care or the señorita dies."

Scorpy Redden was hurrying the girl into the alley. His breath came hot on her neck. "Mind what I tell yuh and keep movin'. Head for them broncs yonder."

Maisie obeyed and walked swiftly with the press of his gun hard in her back turning her flesh cold. One mistake and she knew that gun would blast the silence in the street. But she would not even hear that death-dealing roar. She would be lying very still in the dust of that alley.

In another minute they had crossed the street about a block down from the store, and using one hand, Redden loosened the tie rope of a rangy-looking pinto horse. He swung into the saddle and motioned for the girl to mount the bay animal alongside the pinto.

"Push on," he muttered. "I'm ridin' on yore tail." His gun barrel whacked the bay's rump and the horse broke into a gallop. Maisie heard the man's voice close behind her. "Head for that barranca and keep yore bronc movin'."

They tore into the wide gulch and soon were

following a trail that twisted into the maze of bleak desert hills south of the town.

Presently they were riding up the floor of a deep gorge. The pinto forged alongside the bay and Maisie felt Redden's cold eyes studying her. She turned her face and looked at him with chin up.

"Why take me any further?" she spoke coolly. "You can ride faster without me."

The desperado's grin was admiring. "You don't scare easy," he said.

"Would you *really* have shot me?"

"Sure I would." His tone was matter-of-fact. "Mebbe I'll be leavin' you lay round for the buzzards yet."

"You, you wouldn't . . . ." Maisie's voice was unsteady. "You, you wouldn't kill me now."

"I aim to git clean away," declared Redden frankly. "I'm not takin' chances on yuh tellin' which way I rode."

The girl's thoughts raced desperately. She knew that somewhere not far away those barren hills spread over the Mexican border. Redden would not halt until he was safely in the vast reaches below the line. She looked at him nervously.

"What are you going to do with me?"

He gave her a mirthless grin. "I'm keepin' yuh"— the girl's heart sank—"till we git to the border, and then I'm turnin' yuh loose."

Maisie drew a quick breath. He was not taking her over the border. He was turning her loose.

181

"I'm kind of likin' yore pluck," Redden said. "Would have been a lot of killin' if yuh hadn't acted sensible back there in the store." His cold eyes were appraising her slim grace. "Was figgerin' some of takin' yuh to the hogan down in Mexico, but yuh're kind of skinny. I ain't carin' for skinny gals," he added frankly.

"Oh, of course!" Maisie couldn't keep from smiling, despite the horror of her situation. She was vastly relieved to know that Redden found her not to his liking.

They rode on in silence and the girl saw that the desperado was alertly listening for sounds of pursuit. Of course they would be promptly followed, she reflected. The thought made her apprehensive. It was best now for Redden to reach the border before her friends could overtake them. He had promised to turn her loose at the border. To be overtaken now would mean a fight, perhaps dead men. Redden would fight to the death. He would promptly shoot her down the moment his pursuers showed themselves.

From far behind came the sound of hammering hoofs. Even Maisie recognized that unmistakable, if scarcely heard, drumming noise. She darted a frightened look at her sinister companion. He was scowling.

"Comin' like bats out o' hell," he muttered. His reaching hand grasped her bridle rein and swung her horse into a growth of bristling giant cactus.

"Climb down," he told the girl curtly.

Maisie slid from the saddle, wondering wildly if the man was going to kill her. She faced him, her knees horribly wobbly, and seeing the panic in her white face, Redden shook his head.

"I'm tyin' yuh up," he said briefly. "Don't yuh git scared, gal."

In a minute she was lying on the hard gravelly ground, bound hand and foot with Redden's bandana securely drawn tight over her mouth.

"They'll be findin' yuh," he muttered, as if to reassure her. Again his mirthless grin. "*Adios*, kid, thanks for the hand yuh give me." He sprang into his saddle and with something of a shock, the helpless girl saw the gun leap from his holster and the next instant the bay horse sank on buckling legs and toppled over, inert and lifeless.

Maisie could have screamed in horror at the cold-blooded killing. She could only watch with shocked eyes, as the killer spurred from the scene.

For long moments she listened tensely, until at last the hammering of the pinto's hoofs faded.

She began to work on the rawhide ropes that bound her. Redden had made the knots too secure, but finally she managed to get a piece of the bandana between her teeth. She chewed furiously at the fabric, working the tip of her tongue against the shreds until finally her strained jaw ripped out an opening. She drew a long breath and filled her lungs with the fresh air. At least she could scream now, when those distant horsemen poured up the trail.

Maisie listened tensely. The hammering hoof-beats were drawing nearer. With an effort she twisted around, so she could face the trail below the steep slope. Something stirred in the brush. A sound that brought a startled gasp to her lips made her heart jump madly.

Slowly she turned her face and stared at the big rattlesnake coiled against the roots of a shading greasewood.

Maisie held her breath, but even in that dreadful moment she found herself thinking of the deadly eyes she had glimpsed in Mel Destrin's face when the lawyer faced the wall under the threat of Jack Fielding's gun.

The rattlesnake's flat head lifted. Maisie shuddered and recoiled from the evil menace in those obsidian eyes.

CHAPTER FOURTEEN

The rataplan of galloping hoofs, as Scorpy Redden fled up the street with his captive, released Jack from his frozen crouch. A leap carried him to the door in time to glimpse the outlaw and the girl disappearing in a cloud of dust. Even in that desperate moment his mind automatically registered that the horse under Redden was a rangy red and white pinto, the same pinto he had glimpsed disappearing into the upper reaches of the Topaz. He knew now why Redden had seemed vaguely familiar. The man was the murderer of Mark Severn.

Don Vicente was climbing hurriedly into his saddle, his voice rasping commands to his riders. Jack interrupted him harshly.

"No! Redden will kill her! Stop your men, Vicente!"

The Mexicans reined their horses and Jack's gaze went a bit wildly to Tim Hook and Pop Shane as they hurriedly emerged from the store. The latter nodded agreement.

"Redden's a killer," he said, "a damn killin' scorpion! The gal's a goner, if we foller him too close."

"We got to figger some play fast," muttered Tim Hook. He glared at Pop Shane. "You was clumsy, Pop, lettin' him grab yore gun."

Jack's irate glance silenced him, and Don Vicente said thoughtfully, "He will make for the border." His look went to the restless-eyed Diego. "You ride for Paso del Lobo, Diego," he commanded in Spanish. "All of you, and ride like the wind. It is possible you will come upon the man face to face and take him by surprise." He looked at Jack for approval.

"A good idea," agreed the latter, and obeying

his gesture, the Mexicans spurred up the street. Don Vicente alone held his horse back, his gaze on Jack. "I ride with you, my friend," he said quietly. "Do not despair. We will save the young señorita from harm."

Mel Destrin emerged somewhat hesitantly from the store, the sheriff at his heels, and behind them crowded their followers. Destrin spoke, his voice oddly subdued, apologetic.

"My God, Fielding, the fellow had me fooled. Never dreamed he was Scorpy Redden, that outlaw killer. Slade says the same."

The sheriff nodded. The bluster had gone out of him. "Sure am sorry for this business, Jack," he spoke humbly. "Like Mel says, I was fooled by his talk . . . gettin' me to think Jose had shot young Carson."

Jack looked at them dubiously. He was finding it hard to believe them, but there was no time for argument or recriminations. His gaze shifted down the street. Smoky and Johnny coming on the run. He waved them on to the livery barn.

"Get your horses!" he shouted. "Throw my saddle on Red!"

"I'm riding with you," exclaimed Tim Hook.

"No!" Jack's tone brought the big rancher to a standstill. "You stay with Ma Kelly, Tim."

Something in his tone made Tim blink. Then with a startled grunt he started on the run toward the 'Dobe House. Mel Destrin, after an oblique glance at the hurrying rancher, turned to Slade.

"Get busy," he snapped. "It's up to you to nab that Redden man before he harms the girl."

"I'm ridin' now," grunted the sheriff. "Git yore broncs, fellers. I'm deputizing you." He went clumping across the street to the horses at the hitch rail in front of the saloon.

"You bet we'll git that skunk," muttered a hard-faced Arrow rider in an aside to Jack, who sensed the man was attempting to reassure him. "Don't hold to treatin' gals like *he* done." With a grim nod, the cowboy ran to overtake his fellows.

"Come on, Pop," Jack said curtly and turned toward the livery barn. Don Vicente swung his horse and followed, his eyes warily watching Slade and his men as they scrambled for their horses. Jack halted and looked over at the sheriff.

"Slade, you and your posse can head for where you please. Only you don't follow Redden's trail direct. I'm following *that* trail, savvy?"

"I'm headin' for Paso del Lobo, same as the other fellers," shouted the sheriff from his horse. "You can ride where you damn please." He spurred away, a half score of men lining out behind him.

Smoky and Johnny were tugging at their saddle cinches when the others ran into the long barn. A Mexican hostler was throwing Jack's saddle on the big red horse.

"I'm ridin' with you," announced Pop Shane, as he dived into a stall.

"You needn't, Pop!"

"You bet your life I am!" yelled the wiry old liveryman. "I got a slug o' lead for that Scorpy hombre's guts."

They tore up the street, five furious-eyed men. Bitter rage blazed in Johnny Archer's blue eyes as his blue roan spurted dust alongside Smoky Tucker's fast sorrel horse.

"Some feller run off with Maisie!" he yelled. "Boss says it's Maisie!" The young cowboy's voice choked to a mumble of curses for which he would be forgiven. Johnny was praying, but didn't know he was praying. Smoky Tucker was praying too, and his eyes were pin points of cold fire as he rode. He was praying that old Pop Shane would have no chance to empty his gun into the man who had carried Maisie away. Smoky had two guns and he wanted to empty both of them into the man whose trail they followed.

Don Vicente talked coolly to Jack as they raced through the chaparral, and the latter, only half listening, for he was alertly watching the trail for sign, began to understand the manner of his friend's opportune appearance in Coldwater.

"The news came to me of the man who killed the Señor Severn." Don Vicente leaped his sleek Palomino stallion over a boulder. "The man had boasted in a *cantina* that I know in Santa Ysabel.

We went to take him, found him gone, and so followed him to Coldwater."

"Redden!" Jack lifted his voice high above the clatter and scramble of flying hoofs. "I have already guessed the truth." He lifted the big red horse in a jump that carried him over a suddenly yawning chasm.

"*Si!*" yelled the young don as the Palomino rose to the jump. He talked on jerkily as the horses tore across a stretch of mesa. He had paused at the 'Dobe House and had found the young señorita talking to Tim Hook, pleading with the rancher to hasten to the store.

"They start running up the street," shouted Don Vicente, "so all of us ride fast, and there you have it, Juan *mio*. We come to you in what you say, the neek of time, no?"

"The price was too big," Jack was thinking miserably. "Maisie was too big a price for his life, for the lives of all of them."

A gunshot came faintly to their straining ears.

Jack flung the Mexican an agonized look and both put spurs to their near-winded horses. Something suspiciously like a curse came from Smoky Tucker on the sorrel horse close on their heels.

They breasted a steep slope and went thundering down the side of a gorge bristling with great cactus. Jack suddenly brought his panting horse to a standstill.

"A voice!" Don Vicente reined the foam-flecked Palomino. *"Por Dios!"*

Smoky and Johnny came to a plunging halt, but Jack was suddenly spurring furiously up the slope toward a clump of giant cactus.

The first thing that caught his raking glance was the dead bay horse, and then Maisie, lying still as death near a big greasewood. In that instant he also saw the cause of the horror that stared from her eyes. His gun went up, and with its staccato crash, the venomous flat head went hurtling from the thick sinuous coils of a rattlesnake less than three feet from the girl.

In a moment Jack was bending over her, lifting her into his arms. She read the horror in his eyes and gave him a faint smile of reassurance.

"No, I, I wasn't bitten, but *oh . . .*" She could say no more.

The others stared down at her from their horses, their faces as pale as they ever would be.

"Por Dios," muttered the young Mexican, "that was close."

"Some shootin'!" Smoky Tucker spoke softly, awe and admiration in his voice.

Pop Shane came up the slope, excitement making his eyes an arresting blue in the mahogany of his face. One look at the headless writhing coils told him the story. "The killin' varmint," he grumbled, "leavin' the gal layin' 'longside a damn rattler."

190

The rawhide knots came loose under Jack's tugging fingers. Maisie leaned against him, her faint smile playing round on the grim faces of her friends. "At least, he didn't, didn't harm me," she said quietly. Her look went shudderingly to the flat, venomous head. "I don't think he knew the snake was there. You see, Scorpy was in a hurry."

"I'm followin' him, followin' him to hell," announced Smoky Tucker.

"Me, too!" ejaculated Johnny Archer violently.

"He's making for the border," Maisie told them. "You won't catch him now." Then, a bit wildly she added, "Oh, let him go. He could have killed me, but he let me go."

Reaction was taking her, Jack saw. "Some other day," he said, looking at the other men, "we'll settle with Redden, but right now we're taking Maisie back to Ma Kelly." He chuckled a bit. "First thing we know Ma will be coming in hot chase if we don't get back and relieve her mind."

Smoky and Johnny exchanged disappointed looks, and the latter suddenly grinned. "Reckon that's right, boss. Ma'll sure be hightailin' this way *pronto* if we don't get Maisie home awful quick."

Pop Shane was eyeing the dead black horse. "Some Arrow feller's lost him a good bronc," he opined, "which kind o' indicates that one of us does some walkin', or else rides double."

"Maisie rides Red," Jack said quickly. "Red can

carry the two of us." He swung the girl up lightly and stepped into the saddle and felt the girl's arms go round his waist. It was not an unpleasant sensation, feeling the light press of her against him.

"Don't weigh more'n a basket o' roses," chuckled old Pop, and added gallantly, "an' a dang sight prettier."

Maisie's low laugh mingled with their chuckles. To be a little foolish was good after those tense, never-to-be-forgotten moments. Pop Shane was nice, she thought. All of them were nice, and fine, but none quite so nice and fine as the man in front of her. There was something reassuring in the feel of the hard shoulders against which she leaned.

They rode down the rocky slope, envy in the eyes of Johnny and Smoky as they trailed the procession, a good-natured envy, mixed with tolerant understanding. The two young cowboys shrewdly suspected the real reason for the starry look in the girl's eyes.

"That boss of ours is sure lucky," muttered Johnny to his companion. "My gosh, feller, I'd be feelin' like the king of this whole world if she was settin' my bronc, and *me* in the saddle."

"He don't know *how* lucky," rejoined Smoky Tucker a bit resentfully, "an' she feelin' the way she does about him."

Smoky was wrong, but then, how could he know the thoughts of the inscrutable-faced man on the tall red horse? Only the keener Don Vicente suspected that perhaps Jack's heart was beating a little faster, and that perhaps he was wishing he might ride through all the years with Maisie.

CHAPTER FIFTEEN

Belle Gerben stood at the wide bedroom window. There was an absorbed look in her hard brilliant eyes, a breathless parting of her full red lips. It was not the vast sweep of the Bullion Mountains that gave her that expression of eager interest, nor was it the more distant peak of San Jacinto lifting ermined crags to the blue desert sky. She was watching a tall figure in the horse corral beyond the trees. There was a lane through the green tamarisks, and it was like looking into a telescope, with Jack Fielding cleanly focused in the bright sunlight. It was not the first time Belle had watched Jack through that green leafy vista.

Elation darkened her eyes as she saw him slip the rope on the neck of his red horse. Her full lips tightened with resolution, and with an almost defiant gesture, she went quickly to her mirror and examined her reflection critically.

"Not so bad," she murmured. "You sure look swell in this outfit. That's what a figure like I got does for a gal—slim and straight as they come and all the curves in the right places. That's little Belle Gerben, or Miss Mary Cameron, beautiful young owner of the Bar 7 Ranch, or what have you." She made a wry grimace at the face in the mirror. "Damn Mel Destrin anyway!" With a final glance into the mirror and a shrug of her slim shoulders, she picked up a riding-crop and went quickly from the room, her shiny boots tapping smartly and her silver spurs tinkling as she ran down the stairs.

Old Wong was leisurely dusting a rack of guns in the hall. Belle halted and made a slow pirouette in front of him.

"How do you like them, Wong?"

The Chinese looked her over with inscrutable eyes. "No good," he said blandly, "allee same look like hell."

Belle flounced away indignantly. "Crazy old chink!" she muttered. "I'll tie a can to that slant-eyed pain in the neck or my name is, is Mary Cameron." Again the angry grimace spoiled the smoothness of her face.

Despite Wong's bluntly expressed criticism, Belle made an attractive figure as she sauntered through the big grove of trees. Her riding coat fitted her snugly and the jaunty black Stetson looked well on her short blonde curls. She walked slowly, her expression thoughtful.

"Been here a week," she reflected, "and that man still acts like I was something he didn't see."

Her small white teeth clicked. "He's goin' to learn I'm alive, learn I'm a woman, and kind of crazy about him. My Gawd, who does he think he is, acting so offish?" She halted and stared uncertainly through the trees at the man saddling the red horse. "He's different from the other fellers, different from that smart-aleck Bert Cross, not that I care a small red penny for the four-flusher." Belle's red lips puckered scornfully as she thought of Bert Cross. So he figured he could play around with her, and she knowing he was daffy about the doll-faced Maisie. Belle told herself she wouldn't be in *her* shoes, not with that slimy devil after her. The girl's face hardened. She would like to put one over on Bert Cross and that snaky Mel Destrin. She could do it too, if Jack Fielding would back her up and play the game with her to the finish. With a little gesture she went swinging from the covering trees across the yard toward the corrals.

"Hi there, mister man, going riding?" Her voice was shrilly gay.

Jack turned his head, his fingers busy with saddle leathers.

"It's a fair guess," he told her good-naturedly. His eyes widened a trifle as he looked at her.

"How do you like them, Jack?" The girl spoke with unaccustomed shyness and there was a hint of color in her smooth cheeks.

"Something new for this neck of the woods."

He picked his words cautiously. "Reckon they're all right, if you like 'em."

"It's what girls wear in the big towns," Belle told him a bit defiantly.

"The Chuckwalla is not exactly a city," laughed Jack. "You're in the Chuckwalla now, Miss Cameron."

She pouted. "Call me Mary, frozen man. That's what you are, a frozen man, cold as ice when I'm round."

"Sorry, Mary," he said, stroking Red's velvety nose. "Maybe I don't think about it much. Lot of grief on my mind these days."

"Look at me!" she commanded. "I'm worth lookin' at, mister frozen man!"

Jack obeyed, mingled amusement and annoyance in his smile.

"You're goin' to teach me all about this country," Belle said. "If you don't like my fancy ridin' clothes, I'll burn 'em." She laughed shrilly. "You give me a chance, Jack, and I'll be the darndest little sagebrush gal you ever saw—a true daughter of the rangeland."

His smile grew more friendly. "You'll learn," he said good-naturedly.

"I want to learn all about the ranch and the cattle." Belle's eyes sparkled with growing enthusiasm. "Jack, we can be awful good friends, you and me. We'll make the old Bar 7 hum like it never did."

Jack swung up to his saddle. "That's the sort of talk old Mark would like," he approved. "Well, so long, Mary, I've got to be on my way."

"I'm ridin' with you," announced the girl. "You always slip away from me, but this time you're not shakin' me."

He frowned and shook his head. "I'm riding over to my JF ranch."

"I'm going with you." Belle's tone was desperate. "Please, Jack, you won't have to wait. I've got my brown mare all saddled and ready to go." She dimpled. "I was watching to see if you was riding this morning."

"Mrs. Kelly will be there," he argued. "You said you didn't like her."

Belle's lips tightened stubbornly. She was well aware of Mrs. Kelly's presence at the JF ranch house. The Maisie person was there too. Jealousy flamed through her.

"I don't care if the devil is there, I'm riding with you." She fled back to the trees for her horse.

Jack hesitated, then with a muttered exclamation, he swung his horse into the avenue and rode on toward the gate. Old Buck Wells called to him from the adobe house. Jack veered toward him through the trees and Buck got out of his chair and stood leaning on his crutch.

"Carlos Montalvo sent word he was coming in from the Crossing Camp," he began.

"Won't be back till sundown," Jack said. He

scowled. He was having bad luck with Carlos Montalvo. Either old Pedro had failed to deliver his message, or else Carlos Montalvo was avoiding the ranch. Jack had ridden twice to the Chuckwalla Crossing Camp, only to find the man mysteriously absent. Carlos was hunting strays, the Mexican camp cook had told him rather vaguely on his first attempt, and the second trip elicited the information that Carlos had gone to Santa Ysabel below the border. The thought of Santa Ysabel pricked Jack's memory as he looked at Buck Wells, recalling to his mind something Don Vicente Torres had said about a certain *cantina* in Santa Ysabel. It was from there his Mexican friend had followed Scorpy Redden's trail to Coldwater.

"I'll tell Carlos to stick around till you get back," Buck Wells was saying. "Reckon he'd have been in some sooner, but he's got an awful lot of range to cover down his way, now that I sent the outfit over to the Wild Horse camp. Nobody with Carlos 'cept that o' Mex he keeps to cook for him."

"Buck!" the younger man's tone was worried, "do you think this Carlos Montalvo is all right? I mean, do you trust him?" He was thinking with growing uneasiness of the man's presence in Santa Ysabel at about the time Scorpy Redden was seen there.

"Trust him?" Buck's tone was startled. "Sure I

trust Carlos! He's the best hand with cows we have on the pay roll."

Jack changed the subject abruptly. He saw that Buck could tell him nothing. The old foreman had no suspicion that Carlos Montalvo might not be all that he seemed. Again he wondered if there could be a connection between the man and Don Vicente, or was Carlos Montalvo a cunning foe to be reckoned with, a dangerous spy from the enemy's camp.

"How are things at Wild Horse?" he queried.

"Not so good," gloomed Buck. "The cut ain't what it should be by half, Jack."

There was a curious expression in Jack's eyes as he looked at the foreman. "Don't you worry, Buck, maybe a lot of steers missing from the Wild Horse range will show up soon and come wandering back to where they belong." He thought grimly of a certain valley in the vast reaches of Rancho del Torres, where Don Vicente's swarthy riders kept a zealous watch on several thousand sleek white-faced cattle. The Range Hawk had not swooped in vain on the marauders of the Chuckwalla. Numerous brands marked the hides of those bald-faces, among them the Bar 7 and Jack's own JF.

Buck Wells was plainly puzzled. "Ain't understandin' you," he complained. "When a steer's been rustled, he don't come back, far as I know." He was staring curiously at Belle Gerben riding toward them from the big ranch house. "Looks like Mary aims to ride with you." His tone was dry. "Sure looks funny in that rig she's wearin'." Buck shook his head. "I'm tellin' you, Jack, me an' Jennie don't quite savvy that gal now we've seen more of her."

"She'll learn," muttered the young man.

" 'Tain't that she's awful green." Buck frowned and shook his head again. "It's just that she ain't what Jennie an' me figgered Mark's granddaughter would be." His tone hardened. "She just ain't a Severn," he finished.

There was no answer from Jack. With a curt nod, he wheeled his horse and joined the girl as she reined up in the avenue. Buck Wells watched them, his face doleful. His wife appeared in the doorway behind him. Buck turned his gaze on her.

"He's thinkin' like we does," he said.

"She's a sly one." Jennie Wells spoke tartly. "Good as told me to mind my own business," she added angrily. "Was only trying to tell her things about the party she's givin' to celebrate her comin' to the ranch. And the way she talks to Wong is somethin' awful. He'll be quittin' cold."

"Nope." Buck shook his head. "Wong won't quit, Jennie. He'll stick. He good as told me he wouldn't be stampeded."

"I don't like the hussy," declared Jennie Wells.

Buck gave his wife a troubled look. "Wong said somethin' awful queer last night." The foreman paused, "What do you think he said, Jennie?"

"What are you scared of?" His wife looked at him worriedly. "Why don't you tell me?"

"Wong said, *'she allee same damn cheat, she no good.'*"

"My gracious sakes alive!" breathed the woman. She stared at her husband with frightened eyes.

Belle Gerben watched contentedly while Jack swung from his saddle and opened the wide gate. "Here's where we first met," she reminded him with an arch smile. "Remember, Jack?"

She rode through and Jack closed the gate. "Remember, Jack?" she repeated as he swung back to his saddle. "You saved my life," she added softly. "You, you were wonderful, Jack."

He chose to ignore the subject and put the red horse to an easy lope. Belle made a grimace at his back and spurred to overtake him. "Tell me about things," she commanded. "What's that funny snaky brush with the red flowers?"

"An ocotillo," informed Jack. He pointed out other things as they rode across the desert, showing her the difference between a mesquite and a greasewood and warning her against too close a contact with the deadly cholla.

"Seems awful dreary," observed the girl. "The wild flowers are kind of sweet, but the rest of it gives me the creeps. It's so kind of fierce and hard." She shuddered.

"I like it," Jack said briefly.

Belle gave him a sideways glance. He was fierce and hard too, this unapproachable man, but she'd get him, even if he was full of prickly spines like the awful cactus things that covered the slopes.

The trail pitched into a narrow canyon, a stream rushing noisily down from the distant snows. Jack took the lead, warning her to let the brown mare make her own pace.

Belle's chatter ceased. It was a narrow trail, in some places nothing more than a ledge cut in the face of the cliff. She was petrified with terror and carefully let the reins hang loose. The brown mare seemed to know more about it than she did.

"I'm one scared gal!" she exclaimed, when the trail leveled out on the canyon floor. She pulled the mare to a standstill and scrambled from the saddle. "That rock looks a lot safer than a saddle." She went limp-kneed to the boulder by the stream's edge and sank down. "Next time I ride with you it'll be on shanks' pony," she giggled.

"You'll get used to the trails," reassured Jack. He lit a cigarette and smiled at her through the blue smoke.

"Any more of those fly-on-a-wall places?" Belle wanted to know. She shuddered. "Somethin' tells me I made a mistake."

"Trail's good from here to the ranch."

"I'm not going back the way we come," declared the girl. "Once is enough for me."

Jack told her there were other trails back to the Bar 7.

"This is a short cut," he said.

"Short cut to hell maybe!" Belle's tone was resentful. The man had wanted to make the trip short as possible and scare the life out of her in the bargain. Her anger welled, but with an effort she curbed her tongue and forced a gay smile. "Get off your horse and sit for a while," she said, as she patted the nearby boulder. "I want to talk to you, Jack."

"No time to sit here," demurred Jack.

"I'm feelin' awful weak, after that cliff," Belle pleaded.

Reluctantly he climbed from his saddle and took a seat on a boulder opposite her, at which she shrugged her shoulders a bit pettishly.

It was pleasantly cool in the deeps of the canyon away from the baking sunlight. The girl's gaze idled up the cliffs, towering almost sheer for over two thousand feet.

"What do you call this hole in the ground?" she asked.

"Topaz Canyon, the lower Topaz." Jack's face darkened and he gestured upstream. "Your grandfather was killed about five miles away from this spot, in Topaz Basin."

The girl paled a bit. "He was murdered, wasn't he, Jack?"

He nodded briefly.

"Mel Destrin didn't tell me much, only that he was shot." She shivered. "I've been thinkin' some about it, wonderin' if he was murdered."

"My father was murdered too," Jack said in a low voice. "That's some of the grief on my mind, Mary. I'm going to get the men who killed my father and killed Mark Severn."

She was silent, absorbed in her thoughts. Presently her face lifted in a troubled look at him.

"I saw that paper—the will," she said. "You'd be ownin' the Bar 7 if Mel hadn't found me, wouldn't you, Jack?"

"Why talk about it?" He spoke gruffly, impatiently.

"Just suppose I hadn't turned up?" she persisted. "Just suppose Mark Severn's granddaughter hadn't been found?"

"I'd still be looking for her," answered Jack dryly.

Belle studied him slyly, and suddenly she leaned toward him. "Jack, just suppose I'm *not* Mary Severn—that I'm a fake Mel Destrin planted on you."

He gave her a disturbed look. "Don't say crazy things."

She watched him carefully, wondering how far she dare go. It was plain he regarded her talk as sheer nonsense.

"Jack, if you owned the Bar 7, would you be nice to me—maybe like me a lot?" Her color mounted. "I, I'm sort of crazy about you, Jack," she finished with a rush.

He was startled for a moment. Then suddenly he was smiling, his brown eyes dancing with amusement. "You're a funny girl, Mary."

"Why shouldn't I be crazy about you?" Her head went up defiantly. "You saved my life, didn't you?"

"If you're done talking nonsense, we'll be on our way." Jack pinched out his cigarette. "Didn't know you were romantic, Mary."

"Wait," she spoke desperately as he got to his feet, "you'd be the boss of the Bar 7 . . ." She floundered a bit. "Mel Destrin couldn't stop me from making you the owner of the Bar 7 . . ."

"Destrin couldn't stop me from marrying you, if that is what you mean." Jack's tone was indulgent.

Belle regarded him doubtfully. It was not what she meant, exactly. She bit her lip vexedly. She could make this man the rightful heir to the Bar 7 ranch. She had only to tell him the truth, but she wanted her price for that truth. She wanted him. Something warned her to beat a cautious retreat.

"I mean, as my husband you'd be the boss of the ranch." Her laugh rose shrilly above the roar of the rushing stream. "I guess Mel Destrin wouldn't have a thing to say about it if we did get married some day." Again her laugh was shrill, as she rose from the boulder and smoothed her wind-blown curls under the jaunty Stetson. "It's only supposin', Jack. It's fun to be foolish with you and make you look all scared and embarrassed. You're so darn stiff. I've been tellin' myself I'd get a rise out of you somehow."

He chuckled good-naturedly. There was more to the girl than he had suspected, even if her sense of humor was rather startling.

"Give me a lift," commanded Belle, standing by the brown mare. As she went lightly into the saddle, her face turned in an oddly earnest look at him.

"You're all right, Jack Fielding." Her voice was low, almost breathless. "You're a *man!*"

CHAPTER SIXTEEN

Mrs. Kelly was frankly pleased with the changes accomplished at the JF ranch house.

"It's a wonder what soap and water and plenty of elbowgrease can do," she told Maisie. "You've been a grand help, and I'm thinking Jack Fielding will open his eyes when he sees what we've done to the place."

"I've loved helping," the girl said simply, the color rushing into her face.

Mrs. Kelly looked at her quizzically, but wisely made no comment. She was thinking that the finishing touch would be Maisie herself, installed as mistress of the rambling old house built by Jack's father for his Kentucky bride.

"Plenty left to do yet," she observed, critically studying the smoke-blackened walls. "It's lucky that stone and adobe don't burn or there'd have been nothing but an ash heap of the old house, same as the barns and the rest of the buildings."

Maisie shook her bright head sorrowfully. "How can men be so wicked!"

"Shot old John Fielding down in this very same patio," Mrs. Kelly told her. "But the house he built still stands, and he's left a son that's a man, if there ever was one." Mrs. Kelly nodded and added softly, "I'm thinkin' there'll be happy times in this old garden again—in the happy voices of little youngsters playin'."

Maisie was silent, but there was a touch of color in her cheeks. Mrs. Kelly hid a smile. "The outside looks kind of dingy after the fire, but a bit of work will fix things good as ever and the vines will soon cover the walls again."

"I think I hear horses in the yard," Maisie interrupted. She listened, an eager, expectant look in her eyes.

"Jack Fielding!" exclaimed Mrs. Kelly, and then, as a girl's high laugh came to them, she frowned. "An' that Cameron girl with him!" She hurried to the patio gate. Maisie followed her, eyes widening a bit at the sight of the smartly-attired blonde girl on the sleek brown mare.

"Did you ever see such fancy togs?" marveled Mrs. Kelly. "You'd think she was a queen on parade."

"Hello, Ma!" Jack swung from his saddle.

"Glad to see you, lad." The blonde girl's voice interrupted Mrs. Kelly.

"Jack, give me a hand down, please." Belle's voice had an intimate, endearing tone that made Mrs. Kelly look at her sharply.

"Tryin' to show off and make us think he's at her beck an' call," inwardly fumed the widow. She darted a glance at Maisie. The latter's face was expressionless.

Belle visibly winced as she walked toward the gate. The new boots were beginning to hurt and the unaccustomed saddle had chafed her. Nevertheless, she managed a bright smile and waved gaily.

"Hello, there, folks! Guess you're surprised to see me, but then Jack fairly made me come, darn him." She winced again, pausing to rub a sore muscle. "Some ride for a gal who ain't done much ridin'," she added ruefully.

Jack reddened, annoyed at the inference that he had invited her to companion him. But the twinkle in Mrs. Kelly's eyes reassured him. Belle's remark had not fooled the widow.

"You poor dear!" Mrs. Kelly's tone was commiserating. "Them boots are pinchin' your feet somethin' terrible from the way you walk. You come right into the house an' Juana will get some hot water for you." Mrs. Kelly was enjoying herself hugely. "You can sit an' give your poor feet a good soakin' while Jack talks over the business he's come about."

"Thank you, but my feet are quite all right." Belle gave her an angry look and smiled condescendingly at Maisie. "Hello, there, kind of nice not to be waitin' on table, I'll bet."

Maisie's cool little smile masked her thoughts. She was miserably conscious of her own much-washed and faded blue jeans and her ragged flannel shirt—the articles of clothing Mrs. Kelly had commandeered from Juana's young son. They were scrupulously clean and she had enjoyed the comfort of them, but she was longing desperately to be in a dress. She felt like a boy in the presence of the elegant Miss Cameron.

Maisie would have been thrilled could she have guessed that Jack was secretly admiring the slim grace of her, revealed by Tony's old clothes; but Belle, sensing his thoughts, frankly pouted.

"Looks like the real thing in cowgirls, eh, Jack?" She giggled, staring at Maisie a bit enviously. "I'll have to dig up a pair of old pants and a ragged shirt and a pair of scratched-up boots."

"It'll be a long day before you'll ever look like Maisie," said Mrs. Kelly tartly. "Not that I'm meanin' you don't look real smart in your fine ridin' things," she added sweetly, too sweetly. The angry sparkle in Belle's eyes delighted her.

The latter's riding-crop beat a tattoo on her dusty boot. "I'm thirsty," she declared.

"Come along with me, darlin'." Mrs. Kelly's hand was on the girl's arm, urging her through the gate.

Belle went rather reluctantly, not willing to leave Jack alone with the cool-eyed girl who looked so attractive in her boyish clothes.

"You come, too," she said, smiling back at Jack.

He nodded, but instead of following, he turned to Maisie, leaning against the gate post, and met her faintly challenging smile with a long look.

She stirred uneasily and suddenly averted her eyes. "You, you seem disturbed . . ."

"It's seeing you here . . ." Jack spoke in a low voice that held a bewildered note.

"You knew I was here with Ma Kelly."

He nodded, his dark eyes intent on her. "Of course, but it's something else that startled me when I saw you coming from the patio. I felt that I'd seen you before . . ."

"Waiting table in the 'Dobe House," interrupted the girl, darting him a sideways glance.

"I don't mean *that*," Jack frowned. "The feeling that came was, was that you reminded me of some one familiar . . ."

She looked at him strangely for a moment.

"Perhaps you have seen somebody who may have looked like me." Her voice was almost a whisper. "Perhaps there *is* a reason why I remind you of somebody you have known."

"It isn't the first time," muttered Jack. "Keeps coming to me that you remind me of somebody."

"Did she wear cowboy clothes like these?" Maisie dimpled a bit and looked down at herself. "They're Tony's," she informed him. "Smoky's been teaching me to ride, and Ma said it couldn't be done in skirts."

"I like it." He looked at her approvingly. "You seem so natural, as if you have always lived here or belonged here."

She flushed a bit, then suddenly her eyes danced. "You are forgetting Miss Cameron, and after fairly forcing her to come!"

Jack grinned. "She didn't like the Topaz," he confided.

"I've never been in the Topaz," Maisie said, feeling a bit jealous. "I'll ask Smoky to take me."

"Smoky won't," Jack told her with a frown. "I'm leaving orders for him to keep you away from that canyon." He began to worry about her rides with Smoky.

"We don't go far," Maisie reassured him. She gave him a slow, demure smile. "Smoky is quite crazy about me and I think he'd take me over to the Topaz, if I asked him, even if you told him not to take me there."

"He'll be hunting a new job." Jack's tone was grim. "I'm serious about this, Maisie."

"Why is it more dangerous for me than for Miss Cameron?" Maisie asked in a cool little voice.

Jack pondered. It hadn't occurred to him to worry much about Mary Cameron's safety. Perhaps it was because of Mel Destrin. He was her friend and for some queer reason, Destrin's friends were safe from the dangers that threatened Ma Kelly and himself. Maisie was watching him intently.

"What do you really think of her?" she went on, not waiting for an answer to her first question.

He looked at her blankly, and Maisie said in a curious tone, "Ma Kelly has been telling me about her."

"You didn't know?" Jack looked at her in surprise.

"Not until a day or two ago," Maisie informed him. "Of course I knew she was Mark Severn's granddaughter, but I didn't know she'd been lost since baby days, that old Mark Severn had never seen her, and that you had never seen her until she turned up in Coldwater about the time I did."

"It was Mark Severn's dying wish that I find her," Jack said. "You see, years ago his daughter ran away and got married. All Mark knew was that she was dead and that there was a baby girl." Jack paused, his expression gloomy. "Mel Destrin found her through an advertisement.

That's all I know, Maisie." His tone grew bitter. "I'll admit I've been kind of glad, at times, that Mark isn't here to see his granddaughter."

"I, I think I understand," Maisie spoke compassionately, then in a harder tone, "I wonder if you have ever thought she might *not* be Mark Severn's granddaughter."

"But she is!" Jack's voice was resentful, more than surprised. He was growing impatient of these ever-recurring doubts raised against Mary Cameron. "She has the proof. Mel Destrin says any court would accept the letter Mark wrote to her mother as ample proof." He glowered a bit. "What makes you ask such a question?"

"Oh," she faltered, then lifting candid eyes to his, "perhaps it's because I don't like her much, and because of the way Ma Kelly talks about Mark Severn, how fine he was, and, and . . ."

"Yes, go on," Jack spoke curtly.

"Well, Ma Kelly thinks Mark Severn would be awfully upset if he could know the sort of person his granddaughter *is*."

"I see." Jack's face was hard and after a moment he said quietly, "We must give Mary Cameron a chance. We don't know the sort of life she's lived or the hard knocks she's taken. It is not her fault she was left alone and helpless, to the care of strangers. She'll be all right. She's a Severn and that means she's got the right stuff in her."

Maisie was silent, her eyes downcast, her small

brown fingers plucking nervously at the empty pistol holster hanging from the belt about her trim waist.

"I'll get you a gun for that holster," Jack said, suddenly smiling at her.

"Smoky Tucker is fixing one for me," she murmured absently. "Something was wrong with the trigger and he wanted to fix it." Her gaze lifted. "You're thinking it's mean and small of me to say things about Mary Cameron."

His smile grew and brought a warm light to his dark eyes. "You'd be surprised if you knew what I'm thinking?"

Color waved into her cheeks and suddenly Jack reached out to take her hand in his. "I'm thinking I'd give a lot if only *you* were Mary Cameron, and that's the truth, Maisie."

"Would you be glad, Jack?" She was suddenly pale and again she gave him that strange look. "Would I make a good Mary Cameron, the sort of granddaughter Mark Severn would have loved?"

He was very still, but she felt an almost imperceptible tightening of the strong brown fingers over hers. She leaned back against the gate, breath quickening, lifting the swell of her firm young bosom. She was aware in that lengthening silence of a strange quality in his continued careful attention. It was as if he were endeavoring to see behind the veil of the mystery which surrounded her. Her head went back a bit, caught brightness from the hot sun, and color suddenly waved into her cheeks. Her lips parted in a faint smile.

"Isn't such talk silly?"

He shook his head, still regarding her with that same odd intensity.

"I was thinking how truly you do seem to belong here." He spoke musingly, almost regretfully. "Yes, old Mark Severn would have, have loved you, Maisie . . ." He broke off, an oddly startled look in his eyes. "Maisie," he repeated, "do you know, it seems absurd, but that's all I do know of your name, Maisie." His smile came, whimsical, amused. "Never heard Ma Kelly call you anything else, but I suppose there's more to your name than just Maisie."

The girl laughed softly and withdrew her hand. "You've never asked me, before." She looked quickly at the house. "Ma is calling us. She's made lemonade."

Jack hesitated and shook his head. "I'll be in later," he said. "There are some things I want to do first."

Maisie gave him a bright smile and went swiftly towards the house. Jack watched her for a moment. There was something strong and vital about her for all her slim and delicate body, a hardiness that fitted naturally into the harsh frame of the desert landscape. He went thoughtfully across the yard to the corrals and found Johnny and Smoky squatting on their heels in the shade of the new barn. The latter was sandpapering the trigger of a .32 Colt.

"Reckon she'll pull easy, now," he greeted, as Jack paused. He clicked the trigger rapidly.

"Fixin' it for Maisie," informed Johnny Archer, critically examining the skin of a rattlesnake which hung across his knees. "Make a sure fine band for her hat, huh, boss?"

Jack grinned. "Looks like Maisie's keeping you both busy," he commented dryly.

"She's a peach!" declared Johnny enthusiastically. "Boss, she takes to a bronc like she was born in a saddle."

"Can shoot the eyes out of a fly," chimed in Smoky, rubbing the little gun with his shirtsleeve. "I've got her so she can handle a smoke-pot like she was an old-timer."

"What do you know?" Jack's tone was suddenly grave. "Anything new?"

The two cowboys exchanged looks, and Johnny said slowly, "There's things been happenin', but Smoky an' me stick around close, like you told us. Nights when Smoky's snoring his head off, I'm keepin' my eyes plenty open." He grinned at his glowering friend. "Ain't been any trouble round here," he went on, "but maybe you'll learn more if you mosey up the Honda Wash." His tone was significant.

Jack nodded and turned to his horse. "Ma's making lemonade," he told them over his shoulder.

"I'm samplin' that lemonade!" Johnny was on his feet in an instant. "Come on feller! Mebbe if you mind yore manners, Maisie'll fill a glass for you." Expectant grins on their faces, the pair clattered off to the house.

CHAPTER SEVENTEEN

Jack rode past the corrals. His expression was grave. Johnny Archer had hinted he would learn things in the Honda Wash.

The trail worked up a long slope through tangles of greasewood. The red horse moved briskly, his shod hoofs crunching on flinty rock.

He topped the rise and drew rein for a brief survey. In front of him the land stretched away to dark ridges of hills and barren slopes of strewn slab rocks, laced with sprawling clumps of catclaw and dotted here and there with the cylinder shapes of barrel cactus.

He pushed on through a big grove of paloverde that was brightening with tiny yellow blossoms and dropped down to the wide boulder-strewn floor of Honda Wash.

For some fifteen minutes he followed the

wash up its northerly course, working the horse through clumps of smoke tree bushes, and finally swung up the opposite bank and drew rein in the shade of a tumbled mass of boulders.

For the space of half a cigarette, his eyes roved alertly. Satisfied, he topped the ridge. Again the desert rolled away in great heaves of cactus-covered hummocks reaching into the horizon to saw-toothed peaks darkly cut under the sun's steely glare.

For some ten minutes he rode up a shallow ravine, choked with dense thickets and ribbed in places with the soft, luring green of treacherous catclaw. A gully came twisting sharply down from a steep rise of barren hills on his left. Jack reined his horse. He sat relaxed, but his eyes were wary and alert. The red horse blew softly and drooped his head, tail switching at a big fly darting savagely at his flanks.

The heat closed in, and a stillness, above which rose the occasional buzz of the darting fly. From far away a coyote's howl made a thin, high note.

Jack's gaze was intent on a high black butte, pinnacled with spearing upthrusts of rock from which spurted faint puffs of smoke. His gaze roved quickly from peak to peak of the encircling low hills. From three points, other puffs of smoke lifted, hung for a moment in the air, and as suddenly faded.

Jack relaxed again in the saddle, his gaze now

steadily fixed on the mouth of the gully some hundred yards below him. Suddenly in its dark opening appeared a faint moving shape. Jack's hand lifted, he kept it high for a moment above his head. As he did so, the indistinct shape took on the form of a man. The hand of the latter went up, and drew down sharply in an answering gesture. In a moment, Jack was riding down the slope.

The man drew back into the deeper shadows of the gully. He was heavily armed, two guns in his holsters and a rifle in his hand. A brief smile lit his dark face as Jack reined up.

"*Buenas dias*, Señor."

Jack returned the greeting, smiling warmly. "You keep good watch, Diego," he said in Spanish. "I was reading your smoke talk just now."

"*Si*, Señor, the Hawk has many and sharp eyes." The Mexican grinned. "We have known ever since you left the corrals, Señor, and have been waiting for you."

Jack nodded contentedly. "It is certain no enemy can approach the ranch house unseen by my friends," he said.

"Estevan and his men watch from the hills across the river, and Pepe Moreno and those with him wait like hawks along the slopes of the Chuckwalla." Diego's tone was grim. "Death awaits any man who dares come near the *casa*." His glance went significantly to a great tumble of slab rocks that overlooked the heaving floor of the desert. Jack had to look twice before he made out the crouching form of a man in the shadows of the massed boulders.

"One of us," Diego murmured softly. "Forty others make the big circle, Señor," he gestured. "No one shall harm the señora or the señorita while the eyes of the Hawk keep watch."

"Don Vicente does well," muttered Jack. "I'll not forget the goodness of the men of the Rancho del Torres."

"We are your friends," answered the man simply. "You saved the life of our master, and more than his life. We of Mexico do not forget a debt, Señor." He gestured, "Come with me, Señor. I have a man you may wish to question."

Jack followed him for some hundred yards up the gully, and suddenly a sharp bend disclosed a wide sandy clearing dominated by a lone venerable cottonwood tree. Horses browsed the sparse, short grass and some half score swarthy-faced men lounged under the brush roof of a *ramada*. A freshly-killed yearling hung from a limb of the cottonwood. Jack guessed that the meat simmering in the pot on the fire of grease-wood roots was from the same animal. His gaze went to the lone figure sitting with his back to the big tree. The man's legs were tied, he noted, but his hands were free and he was smoking a cigarette. Surprise widened Jack's eyes as he stared at the prisoner. Diego looked at him grimly.

"I see you remember him, Señor."

Jack's own face wore a bleak expression. "Where did you nab him?"

"Word of him came from Estevan," the Mexican said. "We picked up his trail which led to the corrals. It was there we found him, skulking, apparently spying for his masters." Diego shrugged skeptically. "He swears he meant no harm, that he wanted to see you about an important matter."

"Any other prowlers?" asked Jack.

Diego lifted two fingers. "They will be seen no more in Coldwater." His tone was grim. "We wasted no time with them, for they were known to us. Their purpose was plain, so we made them into food for the buzzards, the coyotes." The Mexican's look went to the prisoner. "The man yonder would have shared their fate had I not remembered his face and recalled your words that night in Topaz Basin."

Jack nodded. "I'll have a talk with him," he said, moving toward the tree. Two of the men lounging in the shade of the *ramada* left their companions and rode down the gully. Jack guessed they were on their way to relieve fellow lookouts. The *ramada* was a hastily-erected affair, he noted, roofed with tules and palm branches the vaqueros must have dragged up from the creek bottom. Strips of rawhide bound the brush roof to the slender poles strung like rafters from

221

corner posts of alder and sycamore. The result made a comfortable protection from the sizzling glare of the sun.

He came to a standstill, his bleak gaze on the man humped against the big cottonwood.

"Thought I told you to clear out of this part of the country," he said harshly. "I told you to keep traveling and never show your face here again."

Starke Quintal looked up at him sullenly, cigarette smoke curling from his nostrils, and after a moment he spat the twist of brown paper from lips that tightened to a thin bloodless line. Jack studied him curiously.

"You're in a tough spot, Quintal."

"Not much use of me talkin'," muttered the youth. His eyes had a hopeless look. "Might as well get through with it."

"Do you know what they call this place—this tree you're under?" Jack's tone was significant.

Starke Quintal shook his head. "Reckon any tree will do . . ."

"You're in Arroyo los Coyotes," Jack told him softly, "and this is Slade's Tree, young fellow."

"Ain't forgettin' what you said about Slade's Tree," muttered the young outlaw. "Yore dad dangled the sheriff's brother to this old cotton-wood I'm hearin'." His chin went up defiantly. "I ain't the skunk you're thinking. I was born decent and had a decent dad, like you had—cattleman down on the Pecos." He paused and gave his listener a troubled look. "Reckon Curt's ridin' the hoot-owl trail sure enough, but I wasn't knowin' his play when he sent for me to join up with him at the Arrow. It's the truth, Fielding. He give me a song an' dance about the Range Hawk hombre rustlin' the range an' I figgered I was ridin' on the law's side."

"What are you doing down here in the arroyo?" queried Jack harshly.

"You won't believe me, but I was wanting to see you . . . tell you something you'd like to know." Starke Quintal shrugged. "I let those Mex fellers grab me on purpose."

Jack looked dubious. "How about the Cole raid?"

"Curt told me it was a private deal he'd made with Bill Cole, that Cole was scared out by the Hawk and was quittin' the country for keeps." Starke Quintal's mirthless smile came again. "Been doin' some thinkin' 'bout the Range Hawk . . ."

"Yes?" Jack's tone was mild. "What kind of thinking?"

"You're him," Starke Quintal's eyes narrowed in a long searching stare, "an' you're no damn killin' rustler. That's what Curt an' his Arrow gang are—killin' rustlers." His voice hardened. "You're the Hawk, but you're ridin' with the law, kind of . . ."

"You know Curt is not dead?"

Young Quintal nodded. "That's why I'm here.

Curt sent me here to lay for you and kill you. Only I planned to fool him, double cross him if you like . . ." The youth's half smile was something terrible to see. "Sure, it's the double cross an' mebbe I'm lower'n a snake, but I can tell you all the things you want to know—things that'll help you clean up this range and fill a lot of trees with fellers dancin' on air."

Jack suddenly swung from his horse, and stooping over, he jerked the rawhide ropes from Quintal's legs. The latter drew a deep breath and got unsteadily to his feet.

"You're believin' me? You're not swingin' me?"

"I'm believing you," Jack said quietly. A glance over his shoulder told him that Diego was watching them with disapproving, scowling eyes. Jack gestured to him.

"Have your cook fix some food for this man," he called.

"*Si*, as you wish, Señor." His expression indicating grave doubts, the Mexican went back to the *ramada*.

"You're sure one white man," muttered young Starke Quintal. The sullenness was gone from his eyes and his hard young face took on a boyish look. "Them Mex hombres would have killed me, if you hadn't showed up."

He followed Jack to the shady side of a mass of boulders and gratefully rolled a cigarette from the packet of papers Jack offered him.

"What's this information?" asked the latter abruptly, as Starke put a match to his cigarette. "How much do you know?"

"Enough to hang Curt an' a dozen more," returned the boy. He broke off with a queer little choke, spun on his heels, and as he slid limp and lifeless down the side of the boulder against which he was leaning, Jack's startled ears caught the crack of a rifle. Even as he sprang for the shelter of the boulder, a second bullet spat viciously against the rock. He flung himself full length behind the boulder and heard the crash of rifle fire as the lounging vaqueros jumped into action.

"Señor!" Fright was shrill in Diego's voice as he raced up. "*Por Dios*! You are shot!"

Jack's face came round to him and reassured him. Diego halted, staring at the limp form of Starke Quintal. "*Por Dios*!" he exclaimed again, "the gringo, he is dead!"

A faint yell floated down from the cliffs beyond the creek, and the staccato drumming of six-guns, and again silence. Diego muttered something in Spanish and after a glance at the prostrate Starke Quintal, Jack went to his horse and pulled his binoculars from their case.

"You look, Diego . . ." He handed the glasses to the Mexican and went sorrowfully to the dead youth. There was nothing he could do, save turn the lifeless body over, and close the staring eyes.

Starke Quintal would never speak again, never tell him the things he wanted so desperately to know. Death had sealed the boy's lips.

Cold rage grew in Jack's eyes as he stared down at the dead youth. He well knew the reason for that bullet. Starke Quintal had been followed, and the man watching from the cliffs had grown suspicious and decided to close young Quintal's mouth forever. As from afar, Jack heard Diego's voice.

"I see Pepe Moreno on the ledge. He bends over something lying there. *Si*, a dead man . . ." Diego lowered the binoculars and rapped out a command to one of the vaqueros. The latter fired his gun twice, and from the cliffs came an answering double report. "Pepe will be with us soon," Diego muttered. He glanced at Starke Quintal, then looked shamefacedly at Jack. "It was close, Señor! Don Vicente will not like it that I allowed you to be followed, and your life attempted while in our midst."

"It was Quintal they wanted," Jack told him gloomily. "Starke Quintal was going to tell me things, Diego, but they've closed his mouth for keeps."

"*Dios!*" muttered the Mexican, "the young gringo was not one of the dogs who seek to kill you, then?"

"He was a brave man!" Jack spoke sorrowfully. "I'm taking him back to the ranch, Diego. I'm not leaving him here for the coyotes. His father was a cattleman. His grave shall be in a cattleman's garden."

"*Si*," murmured the Mexican, looking with a new respect at the slain youth. "His own horse will carry him to the rancho, and Ramon will ride with you, Señor."

By the time the body was lashed to the saddle, a lean young Mexican made a soundless appearance at the *ramada*. Diego fired a curt question at him.

"*Si*, the man is very dead," Pepe Moreno told him with a shrug. He scowled. "Another with him made good his escape."

"Don Vicente will slice your ears," snarled Diego. "Careless fool, only a miracle saved Don Juan from death!"

"Do not blame Pepe," intervened Jack. "He did well and bravely. At least the murderer is dead."

Pepe Moreno's fierce eyes thanked him, and with a sudden laugh Diego waved him to the cooking pot. "Eat quickly and get back to your post. But remember, no more must you fail to hear even the scrape of a snake's belly."

In a few minutes Jack was pushing his horse out of the darkening gorge. Ramon followed, leading Starke Quintal's horse with the slain youth roped to the saddle.

Already the shadows were creeping up the slopes. Jack kept the red horse moving briskly. Mary Cameron was waiting for him to take her back to the Bar 7. She'd likely be furious, fearful of the long ride in the darkness. Serve her right for forcing her company on him. He'd half a mind to take her home by way of the Topaz and scare the wits out of her. With a grimace, he dropped Mary Cameron from his thoughts, reflecting with grim amusement on what Mrs. Kelly would say if she knew of the ring of guns he had placed around the JF ranch house. Ma had rebelled indignantly at his insistence that she and Maisie leave the 'Dobe House. There was no sense to it, Ma Kelly had maintained. She didn't see how they could be any safer at the ranch than in Coldwater. Smoky and Johnny would be helpless if the place was again raided. It was only old Tim Hook's added pleas that won Ma over to the plan. Jack had privately informed the Diamond D man of his purpose to encircle the ranch house with Don Vicente's hard-fighting vaqueros, and Tim and his men had agreed to keep watch from their side of the Honda.

It was a sound plan—the only thing to do that would insure the safety of Mrs. Kelly. Such an armed guard in Coldwater would have been impossible. Jack was satisfied that Ma Kelly was safe as long as she stayed close to the house. He'd speak to Smoky and Johnny about riding Maisie too far. He chilled a bit at the thought of what could happen to Maisie if her young protectors relaxed their vigilance and let the girl have her way with them. Smoky and Johnny would die smoking their guns for her, but their dying wouldn't do Maisie any good if she were snatched from the security of the ranch house.

Clouds were gathering about the lowering sun as the red horse climbed out of the Honda Wash. A dark night ahead, perhaps a gale and driving rain, by the looks of the sky.

Jack frowned. No sense returning to the Bar 7. No telling what might happen, and with Mary Cameron on his hands he'd be in a tight spot if he ran into trouble. He'd stay the night, and then, there was Starke Quintal to care for—a grave to prepare for the slain brother of Curt Quintal. Young Starke had paid his debt, or tried to, in the best way he could.

His decision to stay the night rather warmed Jack. He would have a chance to see more of Maisie. His moments with her had always been too brief. He mentally counted the times he had seen her—only four times, but things had a way of developing amazingly fast these past few weeks. He could still feel her arms clinging to him, feel the quick beat of her heart as he held her close that moment in the chaparral when he found her bound and helpless. Jack repressed a shiver. A prayer had gone with that bullet he'd sent at that swaying flat head so close to the girl's terrified face. It was the quickest and best shot he had ever made—that shot that had torn the rattler's head from those writhing coils. Without knowing it,

Jack's hand went down to the gun in his holster, his strong brown fingers tensed over the walnut butt.

Wind began to whip through the bristle of cacti and the clouds curled in long red streamers over the mountains. Jack was not caring now. He would stay the night and talk to Maisie, and perhaps again glimpse that fleeting look in her eyes. He had felt oddly shy talking to her at the patio gate; shy and vaguely perplexed by her likeness to somebody he had known, or seen before. She had looked at him so strangely when he spoke of Mary Cameron.

The thought of Mary Cameron returned the frown to his brow. Mary Cameron would be there, too, and there would be small chance to talk to Maisie with Mary Cameron on the scene.

He wondered grimly if the blonde girl would ask Ma Kelly and Maisie to the big barbecue she was giving to celebrate her homecoming to the Bar 7. He hoped Mrs. Kelly would not refuse. He wanted Maisie to come to the party. It would be a nicer party if Maisie could be there.

For some reason, Jack found himself suddenly smiling as he rode into the reddening sunset toward the old ranch house showing through the trees.

CHAPTER EIGHTEEN

Mrs. Kelly leaned over the patio gate, with something like disapproval in her handsome eyes.

"I'll not have you riskin' the girl's neck on that colt!" she called. "Where's your brains this mornin', Johnny Archer, puttin' Maisie on that piece o' Satan? You know better than that!"

"Why, Ma, this here mare's gentled fine. Rides like a rockin' chair." The red-headed cowboy's tone was nettled. "I wouldn't let Maisie ride her if she was outlaw."

Maisie smiled confidently from her saddle, a hand patting the arching neck of the red, bay mare under her. "Rosita is as gentle as a kitten, Ma, and I don't mind if she does buck a little."

"Sure," grinned Johnny, "you can just about ride anythin' with hair on. Never saw a female take to the saddle like you, Maisie."

"The beast's got a mean eye," grumbled Mrs. Kelly, "but don't you be ridin' too far from the house," she warned. "I heard Jack tellin' you to be careful, Johnny."

"Only to the arroyo," promised the girl. She laughed teasingly and jerked her gun from her holster. "I'm not afraid of trouble now Smoky has taught me how to shoot." She sent the red mare into a dead run down the long yard with her gun blazing. A coffee can perched on a fence post went spinning into the air.

Mrs. Kelly watched nervously, but admiringly. No doubt but what the girl was born to it. She rode with the easy sureness of any cowboy. Mrs. Kelly stifled a shriek. Rosita, not yet broke to gunfire from her back, went suddenly into a wild orgy of bucking. A startled yip came from Johnny Archer. High-heeled boots spurted dust as he ran. The girl's voice, shrill and fierce, rose above the hammering of plunging hoofs.

"Don't you touch her, I'll ride her . . ." Maisie's voice ended in a breathless gasp as the red mare went into another frenzy of bucking.

Johnny's expert eyes saw the girl was weathering the storm. He slid to a halt, and suddenly the mare was running smoothly around the big yard, her brief rebellion over. Maisie pulled her to a standstill by the patio gate.

"You frightened the wits out of me," wailed Mrs. Kelly.

"She's bucked all the bad out of her system." Maisie laughed, shaking back bright wind-blown curls. "I'm glad it happened. I'll never be afraid of a horse *now.*"

"You're born to the saddle," declared Mrs. Kelly. "It's in your blood, lass."

Johnny Archer hurried up through drifting dust, followed by Smoky Tucker, the latter carrying the girl's fallen gun. Their tanned faces were pale. Maisie looked at them composedly.

"Scared the wits out of you, didn't I?" she jeered.

"I ain't bein' scared no more!" Johnny's tone was deeply admiring.

"Me neither," chuckled Smoky. He handed up the gun. "Wouldn't want you pullin' trigger on me, the way you sent that can spinnin'."

"She's born to it," repeated Mrs. Kelly. She broke off, her eyes widening at an approaching cloud of dust. "Doc Manners is comin', and I declare if it ain't that smart-aleck Mel Destrin with him."

The buckboard whirled into the yard. Doc Manners climbed out and reached for his bag.

"Good morning to you, Mrs. Kelly." The gray-faced doctor's greeting was formally polite as always. "Mr. Destrin insisted that he companion me when he learned I was coming for a look at our patient." His glance went to the patio garden where Will Carson sat in a home-made willow chair. "How is the young man?"

"Will's doin' just fine," reported Mrs. Kelly. She gave Destrin a frigid nod. "Is it some business with the lad that brings you out to the JF, Mel?"

Mel Destrin gave her his fox-like smile, glancing curiously at the flush-faced girl on the red mare. "If Carson is strong enough, I'd like to talk with him about certain matters concerning the store," he answered.

"I'm leavin' it to Doc Manners to say," Mrs. Kelly said, staring at the lawyer suspiciously. She opened the gate. "You go right in, Doctor. I'll be with you in a jiffy."

"Thank you, Mrs. Kelly." Doc Manners bowed and went on down the flagged walk. His face had a worn, drawn look, the widow noticed. Mel Destrin started to follow. Mrs. Kelly swung the gate in his face. "Just what is it you want of the lad?" she asked sharply.

The lawyer hesitated. "I fear you are not pleased to see me, Mrs. Kelly." His tone was mildly resentful.

"I'll not say that's a lie," retorted the widow. She opened the gate. "We'll sit here on the bench in the shade whilst Doc Manners takes a look at Will," she added reluctantly.

Destrin followed her to the rustic seat, an unpleasant look in his eyes. Johnny muttered something to Smoky, who nodded. Maisie spoke a bit impatiently from her saddle.

"Well, let's ride."

Johnny shook his head and moved close to her side. "Won't be ridin' this mornin'," he told her in a low voice. "The boss said for Smoky an' me to stick round close if, if that feller showed up here."

"That's right, Maisie." Smoky's tone was grim.

The girl looked at them for a moment, then with a brief nod, she swung the mare toward the barn. "I'll unsaddle, you needn't come," she called softly over her shoulder.

Her two admirers exchanged pleased looks. "Sure is smart," murmured Johnny. "Got plenty of savvy, that girl."

"What the boss says goes with her any time." Smoky's grin was rueful. "She wasn't stoppin' to argue when you told her it was the boss's orders." His gaze went in a hard look at Mel Destrin on the bench under the chinaberry tree, and after a moment, he sauntered over to the fence and leaned up against a post. Johnny knew his friend would stay there until the buckboard had carried the lawyer away. His own eyes frosty pin points, the red-headed cowboy pushed through the gate and sauntered to the wide porch steps. Jack Fielding's heart would have warmed to see the careful attention his two protégés were giving Ma Kelly's unwelcome visitor.

The widow was frankly admitting her uncordial thoughts. "You've never been welcome at the 'Dobe House, an' you're not welcome here, Mel Destrin," she told the lawyer. "I'm not trustin' what you want with young Will Carson."

"He's sent in a bid for the General Merchandise Emporium," the lawyer said, unperturbed by her plain talk. "His bid was accompanied by a thousand dollars in gold, Mrs. Kelly." Destrin's tone was silky. "Sheriff Slade is wondering just how young Carson happens to possess so much money."

235

"Sure now an' Slade might do better 'tendin' to his sheriff business," retorted Mrs. Kelly. "Why don't he catch some of these murderers runnin' loose round here 'stead of pokin' his red nose into decent folks' affairs?" She sniffed scornfully. "Not a thing has he done about that Scorpy Redden man."

"Redden got clean away across the border," remonstrated the lawyer. "Slade can't follow the man into Mexico."

"I'll bet Redden's in Coldwater this very minute," declared Mrs. Kelly. "I'll bet Slade knows just where that killer hangs out, but he won't touch him. Slade an' Scorpy Redden take their pay from the same man."

"You've a dangerous tongue," murmured the lawyer, staring at her with sudden interest. "Might get you into trouble, Mrs. Kelly." He returned to the matter of Carson's bid for the late Jake Kurtz's store. "It is not unnatural for the sheriff to wonder about this one thousand dollars in gold which young Carson sent in."

"Yes?" Mrs. Kelly's tone was acid. "Meanin' just what, Mr. Mel Destrin?"

"The safe was robbed the night Jake was killed," reminded the lawyer softly.

"Meanin' that young Carson killed Jake?"

Mel Destrin regarded her intently. "I'm not accusing him of killing Jake, but he could have robbed the safe after the murder was done."

"You're plain daft," derided the widow.

"The chance was handmade for him," insisted Destrin, "with Jake lying there, dead and all that money in the safe his for the taking." The lawyer gestured skeptically. "After all, this Carson is a stranger in Coldwater. We know nothing about the man."

"So were you a stranger, couple of years or so ago," reminded Mrs. Kelly tartly.

"He'll have to explain that money," persisted Destrin. "Slade sent me to question him."

"The money is easy explained." Mrs. Kelly's eyes twinkled triumphantly. " 'Twas me own money Will Carson sent in with his bid. I'm buyin' the General Merchandise Emporium if I can get it, an' Will Carson is me partner in the deal."

Destrin looked a bit crestfallen. "I'll tell Slade," he finally muttered. He laughed unpleasantly. "And now Slade will be wondering where you dug up all that gold coin."

Mrs. Kelly's eyes flashed indignantly. "Slade knows I've got more money than he ever saw," she flared. "Just let him *dare* to make talk again that I had poor Jake murdered! Why I could have bought Jake up a score o' times, an' Ace Coran, an' you too, Mel Destrin, for how *you* make any money in Coldwater unless it's by cheatin' at cards, I'm not knowin'."

"You must be rich," murmured Destrin softly.

"I'm not poor," declared the widow complacently. "I've plenty to buy the store if my bid is accepted."

"Ace Coran is sending in a bid," commented the lawyer. "He wants the store, he told me."

Mrs. Kelly was frankly worried. "I'm sorry to hear it." She shook her head. "There'll be crooked work I'm thinkin'."

Destrin said nothing; he was watching Maisie sauntering through the gate. "She's the good-looker Bert Cross is raving about," he smiled.

"He'll do his ravin' at a distance," Ma Kelly said curtly.

"Bit of a mystery, isn't she?" The lawyer's tone was thoughtful.

"Her business is her own," Mrs. Kelly told him crossly.

"Never told you what brings her to this country, has she?" queried Destrin, ignoring the reproof in the widow's voice.

"If she did, I wouldn't tell *you*." She looked round at Doc Manners, as the latter slowly approached. "Well, how's the lad, Doctor?"

Doc Manners halted and stood staring at her. His face was ashen and there was a wild, stricken look in his eyes. Mrs. Kelly gazed up at him curiously, uneasily, struck with his ghastly appearance. The man was ill, terribly ill. He forced a faint smile.

"Carson's doing well," he said with an effort. "A

little feverish. I, I've given him some medicine."
The doctor staggered slightly and caught hold of
Destrin's arm, as the latter sprang to his feet.
"Feel, feel faint," he muttered, "my, my heart . . ."
His voice faded to a whisper and suddenly, giving
Destrin a dreadful look, he jerked from the
lawyer's grasp and went lurching unsteadily back
to Carson.

Mrs. Kelly was on her feet now, and watching
distractedly. Doc Manners was drunk again, no,
not drunk—just very ill, like a man out of his
mind. He was fairly running, with hands reaching
wildly toward Carson. "No, no!" he shrieked the
words incoherently as he ran, "don't, don't drink
it!" He dashed the glass from the bewildered
Carson's hand, and stood on wavering legs, with
mingled pain and relief in his contorted face.
Maisie, looking back from the porch steps, uttered
a little cry and ran to him, followed by Smoky
Tucker. They were all running toward him now,
all save Mel Destrin who stood watching coolly.
Doc Manners slowly turned his face and looked
at him, then with a queer little sigh, he crumpled
to the flagged walk. They stared at him with
shocked eyes.

"Good Lord!" Mrs. Kelly spoke in a horrified
whisper. "The man's dead—his poor heart!" Her
gaze went to Will Carson's white face, then to the
broken glass on the walk. A tiny pink pool had
formed on one of the flags. "He was callin' you

not to drink it," she said worriedly. "Did you drink any of it, Will?"

He shook his head, and suddenly there was a startled cry from Maisie.

A gray cat was writhing in agony by the side of the little pink pool and in an instant had stiffened in death.

"It, it drank some of that stuff," Maisie told the others in a shocked voice. "It, it was *poison* in that glass!" Her horrified gaze went to the dead man sprawled across the walk. "He, he knew it was poison . . ."

There was a stunned silence, broken by Mel Destrin's voice. He came up quietly and stood looking down at Doc Manners sorrowfully.

"The doc was absent-minded," he said slowly. "Gave young Carson poison by mistake. It came to him what he'd done and the shock killed him —weak heart you know." Destrin's gaze went to Carson. "Lucky for you he knocked that glass from your hand, young man. You'd be as dead as that cat."

"Poor man!" Mrs. Kelly sighed. "He's been tryin' so hard, keepin' away from the whiskey. A good man. I'm sorry for him." She wiped a tear from her eyes.

Mel Destrin's eyes gleamed queerly. "Absent-minded," he repeated. "That's why he came to Coldwater. He killed a patient once because he was absent-minded."

"You'll have somebody send for him, Mel?" asked Mrs. Kelly in a troubled voice. "I'm so upset I can't think straight," she added.

"I'll tell Slade," assented the lawyer. His lips twisted in a sardonic smile. "Doc Manners was coroner, but this time he won't be taking charge of the remains."

"You're a cold-blooded wretch, Mel Destrin," snapped the widow. "Get off with you, and send somebody in a hurry. Smoky," she added, "you help Johnny carry the poor creature into the house. We'll not leave him lyin' here on the cold stones."

The two cowboys exchanged looks, and Johnny said, "Tony can help me with the doc, Ma." He beckoned the young Mexican and bent over the dead man. Tony ran up, his eyes rolling with fright, and took hold of the doctor's legs. Smoky looked at Mel Destrin and gestured toward the gate.

Something in the dark-browed puncher's chill eyes seemed strangely to affect the lawyer. He turned a sickly green and throwing Carson a furtive glance, he went with quick jerky steps down the flagged walk. Smoky followed close on his heels.

Mrs. Kelly's troubled gaze followed the lawyer. She was recalling the curious look of fear in Doc Manners' eyes as he had joined them, the dread-ful grimace he had given Destrin. Her

241

blood ran cold. Doc Manners had known poison was in the medicine he had given young Will Carson—he had known, *and it was not another absent-minded mistake.* Carson would have died, with nobody the wiser. Doc Manners was the coroner—nobody would have known the truth.

Maisie put an arm around her. "You're trembling."

Mrs. Kelly leaned on her, her face white, and horror in the look she gave the body Johnny and Tony were carrying into the house. "I'm feelin' awful queer," she said with a shudder. To herself she was saying, "He was goin' to murder Will Carson—was goin' to murder him, and then he got sorry, *sorry . . .*"

Mel Destrin climbed into the buckboard and gathered the lines in shaky hands. He saw that Smoky was moving on toward a chinaberry tree under which stood a saddled horse. Fright grew in the lawyer's eyes. He felt stealthily for the gun in the shoulder holster under his coat.

Smoky swung into his saddle and rode up to the buckboard. "I'm ridin' far as the canyon grade with you," he said.

"I know the road," demurred Destrin with an uneasy laugh. "Thanks just the same, young man."

Smoky's answering smile was mirthless. "You got here safe 'cause you was with Doc Manners, but you won't be ridin' back to Coldwater with the doc this time."

"What are you trying to tell me?" The lawyer's smile was a wolfish snarl.

"You won't get back to Coldwater if I don't ride far as the canyon road with you—not that I give a damn if you get a dose o' lead poisoning." Smoky's tone was indifferent. "Ain't tellin' you more, mister."

For answer, Destrin's whip cut viciously at the team. With wheels grinding spurts of dust, the buckboard whirled out of the yard. Smoky put spurs to his horse. His expression was bleak as he followed through the lifting yellow haze.

CHAPTER NINETEEN

The strip of mesa where Pedro ran his sheep followed the north rim of the Chuckwalla River for several miles. Jack recognized the place as Bear Flats. Bears were plentiful in the rugged, back country.

He reined his horse in the shade of a manzanita bush and reached for his binoculars. From what Buck Wells had told him the tiny hut showing vaguely against a dark blur of trees would be Pedro's sheep camp.

There were questions Jack wanted to ask the uncle of Carlos Montalvo. The latter had mysteriously disappeared.

The cattle boss had not kept his promise to meet Jack at the ranch, and Buck Wells was frankly worried. It was not like Carlos to break his word. The foreman feared the worst. He was annoyed by Jack's growing skepticism regarding the Mexican. He was sure of Carlos Montalvo's loyalty.

Jack was unable to share Buck's faith. He wished he had asked Don Vicente about the man. If Carlos was unknown to Vicente the chances were he might be a dangerous spy. In the meantime had come the decision to learn what he could from old Pedro.

The brush-roofed hut was plainly visible through the powerful glasses. The door, made of cowhide, stretched over a light pole frame, hung open, and a faint curl of smoke indicated that Pedro was at home. A dog was dozing in front of the door.

Jack turned the glasses on the horse, somnolent in the shade of a cottonwood tree in the pole corral. It was a gray, with black mane and tail, the same one the Mexican had ridden the day Jack had seen him at the ranch. A flop-eared burro and a ram with great curling horns were drinking at the little stream flowing from the spring Buck had mentioned.

A slide of rock had dammed the tiny creek near the mesa's edge, forming a marshy pool. There were clumps of tules and willows, and perhaps a score of cottonwood trees. Sheep browsed in the chaparral beyond.

As Jack studied the scene, the dog suddenly sprang up, and as its bark came faintly sharp through the thin air, Jack saw a horseman emerge from a gully that broke down from the hills on the left.

Pedro appeared in the doorway and stood watching the approaching rider. The latter rode up close to the old Mexican. Jack caught a movement of his hand, an upflung gesture that flowered in a burst of smoke. Pedro staggered and was suddenly a crumpled heap in front of his door.

The two gunshots seemingly came to Jack's ears minutes after he had seen the smoke, but even as he heard them, he was leaping for his horse. He had just witnessed a cold-blooded murder and he was raging to come to grips with the cowardly killer.

He put the buckskin horse to a dead run. He was not riding Red. The big horse had earned a few days' rest, but the buckskin was fast and sure-footed.

The killer was riding slowly back toward the gully. Something about him, the way he slouched in his saddle, brought a startled grunt from Jack. The man was not riding the red-and-white pinto, and the distance was too great for a clear view of his face, but he did not need the glasses to prove the identity of the murderer.

The hammering of the buckskin's hoofs on the flinty ground must have reached Scorpy Redden's keen ears. He looked around, jerked his horse to a halt, and snatched his rifle from his saddle-boot.

Jack swerved his horse toward a thick growth of sumac. Scorpy was taking deliberate aim. The rifle's report sounded like the sharp crack of a whip. The buckskin shuddered and was down. Jack flung himself clear of the dying horse. Again the rifle cracked, but the bushes now effectually screened him from the deadly marksman.

With a longing look at his rifle pinned in the saddle-boot under the dead horse, Jack pushed on cautiously through the brush. An attempt to recover the rifle would be certain to draw Scorpy's fire. The man could shoot. Jack was thankful it was not faithful old Red that had taken the killer's bullet.

The dog's furious barking now turned to a mournful howl. Scorpy was not lingering to meet the rider of the slain horse. Jack broke into a run. There was a chance that old Pedro was still alive.

The dog at first challenged him savagely but sensing a friend, drew aside, whimpering when Jack bent over the limp form sprawled in front of the door.

There was a flicker of life in the Mexican, but Jack saw at once that there was nothing he could do. Pedro was dying.

Jack straightened up, sorrow and regret in his eyes. No chance now for Pedro to tell what he knew. One sure fact loomed large. Scorpy had been sent to close the mouth of the old Mexican in the one way the gang knew best. Jack shrewdly guessed that it was Scorpy Redden who had escaped from Pepe Moreno when his fellow gunman had slain young Starke Quintal in the arroyo.

He went into the hut and rummaged for a stimulant, whiskey, or tequila, or something that might give Pedro sufficient strength for a few precious, enlightening moments. The Mexican's creature comforts were meager—a worn Indian robe spread over a bed of tules and dried leaves on the mud floor, a string of chili peppers strung from a rafter, and some odds and ends of clothing—but no whiskey.

Jack turned back to the door, pausing to glance at the pot of beans simmering on the fire. Pedro would not enjoy that appetizing stew now. Leaning near the door was a rifle. A belt, holstering an ancient six-gun, lay on the floor, under the Winchester. Pedro had not been expecting his murderous visitor.

A stealthy footstep outside sent a warning tingle through the young cowman. He whirled, hand reaching for his own gun. A voice, low and sibilant, held him in a frozen crouch.

"No! Lift your hands quickly, or I'll shoot." The

unseen man beyond the door spoke in Spanish. "Face the wall, keep your hands up."

Jack obeyed. The threat in that low, fiercely-flung command was unmistakable. He was at the speaker's mercy. He pressed against the mud wall. Whoever he might be the man was known to the dog. The dog had given no warning of his approach, indicating he was a friend. His only chance was to obey.

A shape darkened the doorway, shadowed the wall, and a hand deftly slipped Jack's undrawn gun from its holster.

"You can turn," muttered the voice.

Jack swung around and saw a swarthy face.

"Soon I will kill you, but first I would know why you have slain my uncle."

Jack started, eyes widened in a startled look. "Carlos Montalvo!" he exclaimed.

"Answer me!" snarled the Mexican.

"I've been looking for you, Carlos Montalvo."

"*Por Dios*," the Mexican glowered, "who are you?" His gun lowered, and after a moment he said, "You are the Señor Fielding, *si*? I make the mistake, you did not kill my uncle."

"While we talk, Pedro dies," Jack said. "Quick, Carlos, Pedro may talk before he dies . . ."

"*Si!*" The Mexican turned swiftly and in a moment was bending over the unconscious man outside the door. Jack followed and stood watching. Carlos Montalvo's ready acceptance of him was convincing. His swift abandonment of hostilities proved the man's loyalty.

Carlos straightened up and Jack saw from his expression that Pedro was dead.

"What happened, Señor?" He spoke wearily, like a man discouraged. Jack guessed that he was tired to the point of exhaustion. It was plain that Carlos Montalvo had been riding fast and far.

He briefly related what he knew of the killing, Scorpy Redden's attempt on his own life, and the man's escape into the dark gully.

Carlos nodded gloomily. Pedro had sent him word that he had learned the name of the man responsible for the death of Mark Severn. He explained it all unhappily.

"Alas, I come too late," he finished.

"Buck Wells was worried about you," Jack told him, studying him curiously. "You have been gone two days. You left no word."

"I went to Santa Ysabel," Carlos said. "I had no way of sending word to Buck, nor the time, for word had come that the Redden man had been seen again at the *cantina* of Luis Portola."

"Was it from Don Vicente Torres that you had this word about Redden?"

"*Si*, Señor." The cattle boss smiled faintly. "You are puzzled about me, Señor?"

"I'd like to know your connection with Vicente Torres," admitted Jack.

"I am his cousin."

"I thought you were a brother of Diego and Estevan."

"Diego and Estevan are my foster brothers." Carlos spoke reluctantly. "I am really a Torres, Señor, and perhaps some day, will take the name, as my cousin Vicente wishes."

Jack sensed a mild scandal in the family of the Torres and tactfully let the explanation stand. "Pedro is not really your uncle, then," he said, looking at the dead man.

"He is the uncle of my foster brothers." Carlos spoke sorrowfully. "I will yet kill this Redden hombre," he added with a fierce gesture.

"Tell me something, Carlos," Jack's tone was blunt, "was Pedro secretly spying on certain men you and I both suspect?"

"*Si*." The cattle boss gazed at the body of his foster uncle with grimly admiring eyes. "A brave man, Señor. His life was in hourly danger."

"They thought he was one of them and talked their secrets openly in front of him?" asked Jack.

"He brought their talk to me and to Vicente," admitted Carlos. Again he smiled faintly. "The Hawk found such bits of news helpful, Señor."

"You know about me, Carlos?"

"*Si*, Señor I have long known that the Señor Fielding was the man we call the Hawk."

"The Hawk doesn't know all his good friends," Jack said softly. He looked at the Mexican intently. "Vicente has never spoken of you," he

250

added. "I only knew of you from Buck's talk and that you were a friend of Mark Severn."

"It was the Señor Severn's wish for me to work in secret," explained Carlos, with a faint shrug of his dusty shoulder. "It was I who first told him certain things about Curt Quintal and made the old señor wish to learn more."

"He knew I was the Hawk," murmured Jack.

"*Si.*" Carlos nodded. "We thought it best if you knew nothing of Pedro and myself. Our enemies are cunning and would have been suspicious had they seen us together."

"You, too, were secretly spying on them?" Jack asked.

"I have been trying for months to learn the name of the man whose orders Curt Quintal obeys."

"Bert Cross?" Jack spoke the name softly. "Is *he* the man you suspect, Carlos?"

The Mexican shook his head and stared at the slain Pedro grimly. "I would have known his name but for this thing that has happened. Alas, I came too late."

"Pedro can never tell us now," muttered Jack. His face hardened. "Carlos, we've got to find out the man's name before it's too late. One by one he's picking us off." He gave the attentive Mexican a brief account of the killing of young Starke Quintal.

"The man is a devil," grumbled Carlos.

"It's a tough problem," mused Jack. "You see,

Carlos, it's useless to appeal to the law. We have no law, while Slade is sheriff."

"He is one of them," muttered the Mexican. He scowled. "Slade could tell us the man's name, Señor."

"Bert Cross," again suggested Jack.

"Cross is one of them, but not the head." Carlos gestured hopelessly. "You are the Hawk, with a price on your head! You cannot go to this crooked sheriff and tell him what you suspect. He already suspects you are the Hawk. In fact, he may even now know the truth about you."

"What do you mean, Carlos?" Jack looked at him sharply.

The Mexican hesitated. "Gold sometimes makes weak men traitors," he said slowly. "I have not told you all, Señor, about this absence of mine that troubled the good Buck Wells." Carlos smiled faintly. "A man you helped was greedy for the gold offered for the Hawk's capture."

"Cole, Bill Cole?" exclaimed Jack, frowning at him.

"The same," nodded Carlos. "We learned he was to meet a certain man in the *cantina* of Luis Portola in Santa Ysabel." The Mexican paused, gesturing significantly. "I do not know if the man got back to Coldwater with the information. I left him to the care of Vicente while I followed hot on the trail of the Redden man, suspecting his purpose here." Carlos shook his head sadly. "It was at the *cantina* that I found the message from Pedro, bidding me to come at once for the name of the man we seek."

"And Bill Cole?" Jack asked the question softly.

"He will not return from Santa Ysabel," Carlos answered with a cold smile.

"He is dead?"

"*Si*, but I did not kill him." Carlos spoke with some regret. "It would have pleased me to slice his throat, but the man sent from Coldwater to hear his story, killed him, Señor. No doubt he thought to keep the sheriff's gold for himself, or else it was the sheriff's own plan to have Cole murdered."

"I think you've hit it, Carlos," commented Jack. "Slade never intended paying all that reward money to Bill Cole. It was cheaper to have him murdered." He brooded for a long moment, and then said, "You think the other man got back to Coldwater, Carlos?"

The Mexican was dubious. He only knew that Don Vicente had picked up the man's trail and would follow him to Coldwater if necessary. There was a chance that Slade might be away when the man returned, if he did manage to get there before Don Vicente overtook him.

"There is one in Coldwater who would die for you," Carlos went on. "You would be surprised, Señor, if you knew his name, but he is secretly one of us, and will help Vicente."

"Monte Boone," hazarded Jack after a moment's reflection.

"It was he who sent us the word about Cole," admitted the Mexican with his cold smile.

Relief waved over Jack. It was his guess that Slade's messenger would make the saloon his first port of call upon reaching Coldwater, if luck was against Don Vicente. Monte Boone would be apt to size up the situation and act accordingly. The courier would never reach the sheriff, if Monte saw him first. Carlos Montalvo was speaking again, his voice despondent.

"Perhaps we must make force the law, Señor, gather all those we suspect, Bert Cross, all of them, and hang them without waiting for more proof."

Jack shook his head. "We want the wolf who leads the pack," he pointed out.

"He would be on the run, once we destroy his pack," argued Carlos.

"I want to hang him." Jack's tone was implacable. "The job's not done until we get this devil and stretch his neck."

"He hides behind a mask," muttered the Mexican, frankly pessimistic. "He has the cunning of a coyote."

Jack looked at him thoughtfully. "I've an idea, Carlos. It's been in my mind for some time and now I'm going to put it to work." He smiled grimly. "If this idea works, the law will be on our side."

Carlos turned toward the corral, his expression dubious. Jack suddenly remembered the dead buckskin.

"I want the gray horse," he called.

"I can use the burro," Carlos agreed. He got the animals from the corral and threw Pedro's saddle on the burro.

"I would not leave him here," Carlos muttered as they lashed the body of his foster uncle to the saddle. "He will lie with his people in the good earth of the Rancho del Torres." He swung up to his own horse.

Jack gripped the Mexican's hand. "*Adios, amigo.* I am glad to be the friend of another Torres."

"*Adios*, Señor. Vicente tells me you are the same as a brother. I am proud to be brother to the Hawk." He rode away, the burro trailing with its pathetic burden. The dog hesitated, whined, then at a word and a gesture from Carlos, the faithful creature headed in the direction of the little band of sheep. Jack knew the dog would remain on guard with the flock until help came.

He climbed on the gray horse and rode toward the slain buckskin to retrieve his saddle gear.

Jack urged Pedro's old pony into a stiff-legged run. Now that he had made his decision he was impatient to put his idea to the test. The time had come for a talk with Governor Jim Cary.

A buzzard winged heavily away as he

approached the dead horse. Jack was tempted to fling a shot at the carrion bird. But there would be other buzzards. He climbed down, made a hasty switch of saddle gear and in a few minutes was riding into the gorge that dropped down to the Chuckwalla. It was in his mind that he would need a better horse than Pedro's old nag for the long ride to the Smoke Tree. He would circle round to the JF and pick up a fresh horse. The thought brought a glow to him. He would have a few minutes with Maisie, also he wanted to tell Mrs. Kelly that nothing must induce her and Maisie to accept Mary Cameron's invitation to her celebration party at the Bar 7. He could not guarantee their safety beyond the vigilantly guarded con-fines of the JF ranch house. Mary Cameron would be in a temper about it and Ma Kelly, too, would probably scoff at his fears.

Jack's eyes narrowed thoughtfully. He'd give Smoky and Johnny an iron-clad order. No more riding for Maisie beyond the yard limits and no horses for Ma and Maisie if they tried to override his wishes about Mary Cameron's party.

Jack wrinkled his brows as he speculated about Mary Cameron. A queer girl, unstable and flighty. He did not understand her kind, and Buck's wife was hinting plainly that she and the old foreman would be seeking another home for their last years, had even suggested herself as housekeeper at the JF. Old Wong was managing to ignore the girl's jibing tongue, but for how long, Jack would not care to bet. He feared that some day soon Wong would be found missing from his kitchen. Jack scowled, as he recalled his ride back to the Bar 7 with Mary Cameron. She had acted very strangely. She was flirtatious and sulky in turns; at times oddly quiet, others, nervous, as though assailed by terrifying thoughts. Her behavior had puzzled and troubled him. When he asked if something had happened to upset her, she had flared up angrily and told him she wished she had never seen his horrid old house, adding, if he wanted the truth, she just couldn't stand that sly Maisie person.

A streamer of dust lifting from the road below him wrenched Jack from his somber thoughts. He halted his horse and listened intently, his expression a bit startled. Travelers seldom used the Bear Canyon road leading to the JF ranch out of Coldwater. Somebody was either heading for the ranch, or returning to town. Doc Manners, most likely. Don Vicente's riders had instructions to let the doctor pass unchallenged on his visits to Will Carson.

The rattle of buckboard wheels and the quick hammer of galloping hoofs drew nearer. Jack was suddenly concerned. Doc Manners was either in a mad rush to get somewhere or else his team was running away with him. Jack sank in spurs and sent the surprised gray racing down the trail. As he shot around the bend he glimpsed the buckboard whirling across the flats, dust trailing in a great dun plume. The driver was humped low in the seat, whip flailing at the horses. Jack let loose a startled yell and set out in furious chase. The man in the buckboard was Mel Destrin.

He drew alongside the swaying vehicle and after a quick sidelong glance in which lurked unmistakable terror, the lawyer pulled the team to a stand-still.

"What's your hurry, Mel?" Jack flicked a frowning glance at the blown mustangs. "Trying to kill your team?"

Destrin forced a sickly grin. His eyes had the hot gleam of molten lead which gave an insane look to his ghastly white face.

"Heard you up on the trail and thought you were after me." The words came in painful gasps. "Didn't know it was only you, Jack."

Jack's glance went to the horses again. Doc Manners' team. "Where's the doc?" Apprehension sharpened his voice. What sort of business had taken Mel Destrin to the JF, and what was he doing with Doc Manners' rig?

"The doc's dead." The lawyer was visibly struggling to regain his composure as he leaned forward to push the whip into the dashboard socket. "Keeled over dead while he was 'tending to young Carson."

Jack stared at him in shocked silence. Destrin

forced another grin. "Bad heart, you know, couldn't stand excitement."

"What got him excited?" Jack's tone was suspicious. He felt distrustful of Destrin. He was sure the man had lied when he spoke of an unseen horseman on the trail above him. Destrin could not possibly have heard Jack's horse above the uproar his own buckboard was making. Why had he lied?

"Plenty reason for him to get excited," the lawyer was saying. "Got his medicines mixed up and gave Carson a dose of poison by mistake." His tone grew sneering. "Not the first time the doc made a mistake."

"You mean Carson is dead, too?"

"No." Destrin shook his head. "Manners got to him just in time, knocked the glass from his hand, then dropped dead himself."

"What were *you* doing out at the ranch?" asked Jack curtly.

"Wanted to see Carson about the bid he sent in for Jake's store." The lawyer spoke sulkily. "If you're through asking me questions, I'll be on my way, Jack."

"Just a minute, Destrin." Jack was staring at him curiously. So Ma Kelly was sticking to her resolve to buy the General Merchandise Emporium, he thought. She had not mentioned it to him again, nor had he said anything about Carson's story of the missing will bequeathing her Jake Kurtz's estate. It was possible that Destrin had himself drawn the will for Jake. Something held him from questioning the lawyer, instead he said abruptly, "About that mortgage you claim Mark Severn gave you, Destrin. I've been doing some thinking about it."

The lawyer stiffened in his seat. "I'm collecting on that mortgage, and for all your thinking it's Mary Cameron's business, not yours."

"You're wrong, awfully wrong." Jack's face was a hard mask. "Mark Severn never signed that paper you've got."

"What do you mean?" Despite his show of indignation, fear was stark for a moment in the lawyer's slatey eyes. "Trying to make me out a crook?"

"I don't have to try," retorted Jack. "You *are* a crook, and I'm advising you to tear that paper up. It's not even a good forgery, Destrin, and you slipped badly when you tried it. Mark Severn never signed his name the way it appears on your fake mortgage."

For a moment the lawyer's eyes had the look of a striking rattlesnake. "I'll show you!" he shouted, almost screaming his defiance. "I'll show you, Fielding!" He snatched the whip from its socket.

"I'm not finished," Jack told him coolly. "I'm wanting to know how you got away from the ranch with the doc's buckboard."

"Drove it here!" snapped the lawyer. He quieted

down suddenly, stared malevolently at the young cowman. "One of your gunmen escorted me as far as the canyon road, said I wouldn't reach Coldwater alive if he didn't start me on my way."

"He wasn't wrong about it," Jack said with a bleak smile. "I'm telling you frankly, Destrin, no killer comes within a mile of Ma Kelly, after what happened in Coldwater."

"I'll tell the sheriff about it," retorted Destrin with his fox-like grimace. "He'll be wondering who your gunmen friends are. Maybe he'll be right in thinking you're the Hawk."

"I'll maybe have a talk with Slade myself right soon," Jack said softly. He gestured. "I'm not keeping you, Destrin, and you needn't run your horses to death. You're out of the woods—this time."

He waited until the buckboard dropped from view down the winding road, then swung the gray horse from the wheel-churned dust across the chaparral to a short-cut trail to the ranch. He was smiling grimly. Mel Destrin had been horribly afraid, which was why he had put his team to runaway speed. The man was a coward, as well as a crook. Jack's anger boiled as he thought of those livid welts marking the flanks of Doc Manners' horses.

A low voice hailed him from a butte overlooking the Honda Wash. Jack halted his horse and presently a Mexican emerged from the bushes.

"*Buenas dias*, Señor." Estevan's expression was a bit worried. "It is but a few minutes ago that Diego signalled he allowed a gringo to pass to the ranch house on the north road."

"Diego would not make a mistake," reassured Jack. "Did Diego say who the man was?"

"A tall old man who gave his name as Cary," Estevan told him. "He is a friend, Señor?"

Jack repressed an exultant whoop. "You bet he's a friend, Estevan!" He pushed on across the wide wash, all eagerness to reach the house. Jim Cary would be there, Governor Jim Cary, the man he wanted to see. No need now for the long ride to Smoke Tree Ranch.

CHAPTER TWENTY

Buck Wells brought the ranch buckboard to a standstill in front of the Coldwater Palace Hotel.

"You'll have to wait quite a spell," he said to the girl by his side. "The stage won't be in for a couple hours and Hardpan Jones most always eats supper before he heads back for San Carlos." He climbed out, reached for a small brown traveling bag. "You want for Jennie and me to wait and see you off, Mary?"

"I don't care what you do," Belle Gerben told him ungraciously. She sprang out and took the bag from his big-knuckled hand. "Sorry, Buck," she added with a brittle laugh. "Shouldn't talk to you like that."

"You're kind of jumpy." The old foreman's tone was troubled.

"Jumpy as a cat," agreed the girl with another shrill laugh.

"Be sure and let us know from El Paso when you're coming home," reminded Buck's wife from the back seat.

"You bet!" Belle spoke carelessly.

"We'll have the party when you get back," Jennie Wells said with a prim smile that just missed being genuine.

"You bet," repeated the girl. She was staring across the street at Mel Destrin's office. "Wait if you want to, folks." She nodded, forced a stiff-lipped smile and crossed to the opposite sidewalk. Mrs. Wells climbed down from her seat. "Might as well wait and see the girl off," she said to her husband. "I can do some shopping over at the store."

"I'll put the team up at Pop's barn for a feed," Buck agreed. He shook his head worriedly. "Mary sure acts awful queer, Jennie. Wish Jack Fielding was here so she could tell him what's devilin' her."

"She'll be tellin' Mel Destrin," commented Mrs. Wells. "He's her lawyer."

Buck went rattling up the street. Mel Destrin

263

was not in his office, he surmised. The girl was crossing back to the hotel, her expression petulant.

Belle took a chair on the shady hotel porch. She was wondering how she could endure the long wait for the sundown stage.

"My Gawd, what a town," she reflected bitterly. She made a face at Jennie Wells' plump figure which was just vanishing into the cool dimness of the store across the street. "You'll wait a long time for that letter telling I'm headed back to your ranch."

The drab street was stirring from its mid-afternoon drowse. A pair of dusty riders off-saddled in front of the saloon and pushed eagerly through the swing doors.

Belle watched them longingly. She could stand a glass of beer herself after the hot, dusty ride in from the ranch.

An old Indian rode up to the trough near the hotel and while the horse quenched its thirst he dismounted and slowly unfastened a bundle of hair ropes from his saddle. A voice hailed him.

"Hi, Tomi!" Old Pop Shane was sauntering up from his livery barn. "Seen yuh comin', Tomi."

The Indian's leathery face crackled in a smile of recognition.

"How!" he grunted. "Make um plenty rope. Me sellum rope now." He patted the coils on his arm.

"You come back to the barn with me, Tomi." Pop Shane paused to look curiously at the girl in the porch chair. "Howdy, Miss Cameron," his eyes flickered to the traveling bag, "looks like you was goin' places—"

Belle shrugged. "When that darn stage gets here."

"She'll be along," commented Pop. "Hardpan ain't one to keep his passengers waitin'." His attention went back to the Indian. "You come along with me, Tomi, maybe you can sell me a couple of them hair ropes." The liveryman grinned, added craftily, "You can give yore bronc a bellyful of free hay while we dicker."

"Me come," grunted the old Indian. He swung back to his saddle, followed Pop toward the livery barn.

The two cowboys emerged from the saloon, looking refreshed. Sheriff Slade appeared in the doorway of his office, watched sharply as the pair rode away. Ace Coran emerged from his saloon and crossed over to the sheriff. The latter's roving gaze fastened on the girl on the hotel porch. He stared intently for a moment, then spoke over his shoulder to somebody in the office. Bert Cross pushed out and leisurely strolled over to the hotel, giving the saloon man a brief nod as they passed in mid-street.

Belle watched suspiciously as the tall Arrow superintendent sauntered up. She tensed a bit in the chair and something like panic flicked across her face.

"Off on a trip, Miss Cameron?" The man looked pointedly at her bag.

"Who else wants to know?" Her tone was sullen, defiant. "My Gawd, can't a lady go some place without this town gettin' so nosy."

His smile was a thinly-veiled sneer. "Miss *Cameron* is an important lady in this town," he said softly. "Naturally her comings and goings interest us."

Mounting distrust was in the look she gave him, and unmistakable fear. He knows about me, she was thinking desperately. He's in with Mel Destrin in this dirty business. Aloud, she said, "I'll be seeing Mel before the stage leaves. He'll know about my little trip, Mr. Cross."

He stared at her doubtfully. "Kind of sudden, isn't it? What about your party?" He smiled. "I've been looking forward to your party."

Belle shrugged her shoulders indifferently, then sprang from her chair with a startled cry. A brief hush followed the two quickly-flung shots, followed by an uproar of excited voices. Cross started running down the sidewalk. Sheriff Slade burst from his office and ran across the street toward the saloon. Ace Coran went clumping at his heels. There was a slamming of swing doors as the men rushed into the saloon.

Belle was frightened, turned to run into the hotel lobby, and almost collided with the desk-clerk. He grinned reassuringly.

"Just some fellers smoking their guns at each other," he said. "Nothing to get scared about." He turned back to his desk.

Belle saw that the little groups in the street were already dispersing. She resumed her seat, then as quickly sprang to her feet again. A buckboard came rattling up the street. Dust lifting in its wake made a pale golden haze against the lowering sun. Mel Destrin climbed out and hurried into his office. The girl drew a quick breath and almost ran across the street.

The lawyer gave her a startled look as she hesitated in the doorway. His face was pale and drawn, his eyes dull leaden disks.

She stood for a moment, then drew the door shut behind her and sank into a chair. Destrin's look lowered to the bag in her hands. Belle's head lifted defiantly.

"I'm quitting," she said.

He was silent, removed his dusty coat and hat, hung them on a peg, then leisurely lowered his thin frame into the swivel desk-chair. Belle Gerben made a little choking sound as she leaned toward him.

"I said I was quitting."

Destrin stared at her over laced fingers, chin low, head thrust forward and his leaden eyes took on a glitter. "Not yet, Belle," he said, his head weaving slightly in a sideways motion, "you're not quitting until I say so."

"Don't wag your head like that at me," muttered the girl. "Makes me think of a snake." Her voice became louder. "You bet I'm quitting, leaving on the stage, making tracks away from this damn place."

"What's got into you?" grumbled the lawyer.

"I'm scared," said the girl frankly. "I'm finished with this business. Mel, I was a fool to listen to you and I won't go on with it."

He waited, eyes questioning her. Belle said abruptly, "Mark Severn's granddaughter has turned up right enough, but she ain't me. She's that Maisie person Ma Kelly's got with her."

The lawyer jerked upright from his slouch. The girl's lips twisted in a mirthless smile. "Gave you a start, didn't I? Well, it's true. Maisie is Mary Cameron."

Destrin swore under his breath. "What makes you think she's Mary Cameron?"

"I ain't thinking. I know she is." Belle told him in a flat tone. "I was over at Jack Fielding's ranch the other day. I stayed the night 'cause it got dark and kind of stormy. Jack said it wasn't safe for us to ride back to the Bar 7." She broke off, flushed under the lawyer's sneering look.

"You like him, don't you? You've kind of fallen for Jack Fielding."

"It's none of your damn business, and it's got nothing to do with what I'm telling you." Belle spoke with repressed fury. She went on more quietly. "They was short of beds, 'cause of the fire. I slept with Maisie. She had a picture on her dresser, and Mel, it's the same one you've got in your desk, showing the old man's daughter and the little baby."

Destrin's face went ghastly. "Go on," he muttered in a strangled voice, "what did she say about it?"

"Told me it was a picture of her mother and herself," Belle continued. "Seems that when her mother and father were killed in that train wreck some woman who was on the train took her and raised her. Maisie never knew the woman wasn't her own mother until one day when the woman was dyin', she told Maisie about taking her from the train wreck when she was a baby." Belle grimaced. "It's a damn queer story. All the woman knew was that Maisie's mother was on her way west to some cattle ranch in the Chuckwalla country. Maisie's mother was talking to this Kingman woman just before the accident. She didn't say her dad's name." Belle shuddered. "My Gawd, Mel, the woman was holding that picture in her hand, and the baby was in her lap, when the train crashed."

Destrin was frowning thoughtfully. "So the Kingman woman didn't know the mother's name?"

"The train caught fire and things was burned up," Belle said with another shudder. "All she saved was the baby and the picture," she gestured, "like the one in your desk."

"It's not in the desk," snapped Destrin savagely. "I gave it to Fielding last time he was in. He said he wanted to frame it for you, damn him." The lawyer clenched his fists. "Might have known he was up to something, thinking maybe you were phony." He broke off, stared at the blonde girl thoughtfully. "You're sure Maisie doesn't know her name's Cameron, or that her grandfather was Mark Severn?"

Belle shook her head. "Don't know a thing, only that her mother's dad had a cattle ranch some place out here."

"Why didn't you snitch that picture?" fumed the lawyer. "She can't prove a thing without that."

"I, I did think some of stealing it," confessed the girl. She reddened, then turned pale. "I, I just couldn't make myself do it," she confessed and in an almost inaudible voice she added, "She's in love with Jack, and he's kind of crazy about her, too."

"You fool!" snarled Destrin. "You're going back there and you're going to get that picture. We'll burn it."

"I won't!" Belle's tone was sullenly defiant. "I'm clearing out. Maybe I'm rotten, but I ain't mixing up any more in this dirty business. She's a nice kid and Jack Fielding's a swell feller. He ain't a smelly skunk like you."

He gave her a venomous look. "Is Fielding in

town with you? Does he know you're leaving, and why?"

She shook her head, dabbed at her eyes with a handkerchief. "He's out some place on the range, and, and anyway, I just couldn't face him to tell him I'm a low-down crook."

"Who brought you in?" Destrin was eyeing her slyly.

"Buck and his wife. They're round town some place, said they would see me off on the stage." She laughed shrilly. "I told 'em I was making a quick trip to El Paso and back, buying clothes for the party."

Destrin nodded. He seemed relieved. "Well, I can't stop you, if you want to skip out," he said with a shrug.

"You'll be damned sorry if you try," Belle said composedly. "I'll tell all I know, and that's enough to put *you* behind the bars."

His lip lifted in his fox's grin. "We'll have a drink on it," he said, pulling out a drawer.

The girl watched in silence while he carefully filled two glasses from a whiskey bottle. "Lock the door," he said suddenly, eyes intent on the brimming glasses. Belle rose to obey, turned her back to him. Destrin's hand made a lightning movement and when she faced round he was pushing the cork back into the bottle.

"Here's to a pleasant journey," he smiled, holding out one of the glasses.

"And no return," glibly responded the girl. She emptied the glass, shuddered, made a face, then suddenly gave him a startled look. "Tastes funny—" She broke off, swayed uncertainly and caught at the desk with her hand. "Funny," she repeated in a frightened whisper. Terror stared from her eyes.

Destrin rose from his chair, his expression malign. "No," he said softly, "you're not leaving on that stage, young woman."

Her knees were buckling. Destrin caught her as she collapsed. Belle was dimly aware of his face close to hers, felt the impact of his deadly eyes, heard his soft voice as from a great distance. "I'm keeping you, Belle, until I've finished with you, and then . . ." She heard no more, hung inert in his arms.

He carried her into the back room. The man was amazingly strong for all his slight frame. He put her down, none too gently, on a cot against the wall and swiftly tied her wrists and ankles. Somebody was knocking violently on the street door. It was Slade's voice, calling his name.

The lawyer glanced hastily at his senseless prisoner, nodded contentedly and left the room, closing the door as he went.

The sheriff pushed in excitedly as Destrin turned the key and pulled the door open. Bert Cross and Ace Coran crowded in, their faces grim and hard. The lawyer took one look at them, then quickly shut and locked the door.

"What's wrong?" He spoke coolly, his gaze raking his visitors with stiletto sharpness.

Slade said hoarsely, "Jack Fielding's the Hawk, he's the Hawk!" The sheriff was breathing hard, bloodshot eyes rolling triumphantly. "We've got him, we've got him in a box!"

CHAPTER TWENTY-ONE

A hush followed the sheriff's words, and then Destrin went to his chair and sat down. He moved with an odd deliberation, as if scarcely aware of what he was doing. The others, staring at him uneasily, sensed that he was in the grip of a dreadful fear. Slade broke the silence.

"Kind of took yore breath, huh, Mel?" His eyes gleamed wickedly. "Can yuh beat it? Young Fielding, the Hawk!" His laugh boomed and with an exultant oath he reached for the bottle of whiskey. "Here's to the rope, and a long, strong pull, huh, fellers?" He drank deep, proffered the bottle to Coran. The latter shook his head, but Cross seized the flask. His hand trembled perceptibly. Destrin spoke slowly, his voice husky.

"Fenton got back, then, from Santa Ysabel?" His head lifted in a hard look at the sheriff. "I told Fenton to come straight to me when he got back."

Ace Coran said, answering for the sheriff, "Fenton didn't say nothing 'bout you sending him off to Santa Ysabel, Mel. He come in an hour or two ago, but you wasn't around, and then . . ."

Sheriff Slade interrupted the saloon man. "Ike Fenton's dead," he said. "Monte Boone killed him." The sheriff shook his head. "Monte must have gone loco, pullin' his gun on Ike like he did."

Destrin regarded him thoughtfully. "Monte's an old-time JF man," he reminded, "used to work for Jack Fielding's dad." The lawyer swore softly. "I think that explains a few things. It explains how the Hawk's been kept informed of what goes on in this town. Monte's been double crossing us by tipping the Hawk off about our plans."

"Monte won't do no more double crossin'," muttered Slade. "Ike's bullet got him plumb center. Monte's done talkin'." He spat an oath. "Ike was dyin' when me an' Ace got there," he went on, "he says to us, 'I saw Cole. Tell the boss Jack Fielding is the Hawk.' " The sheriff gestured. "Them was Ike's last words, Mel."

"It's bad news," muttered the lawyer.

"Hell, it's good news!" exclaimed the sheriff. "I'll have Fielding swingin' from a tree damn quick."

"Fielding's clever." Destrin's lip lifted in a ghastly grin. "Don't forget, he's the Hawk." He broke off, listened intently. "Somebody coming in a hurry," he added nervously.

The drumming of horses' hoofs grew louder and drew into the street. Slade went to the door and looked out.

"It's Curt," he told the others over his shoulder. "Scorpy an' some of the boys with him."

There was a morose look on the burly Arrow foreman's hard face as he came in with Redden. He fixed blood-shot eyes on the lawyer.

"Starke's dead," he said in a strangled voice. "You shouldn't have sent the kid over to the Arroyo los Coyotes. Damn you, Destrin! I've a mind to fill yuh with lead!"

"You're crazy," grunted the lawyer. "It was your own idea to put the kid on Fielding's trail. You knew that every man we ever sent out to get Fielding never showed up again in Coldwater."

"Starke was supposed to keep tracks on him only when he come to town," grumbled Curt Quintal. He looked at Scorpy Redden. "Scorpy says you sent Starke with him and Solvang over to the Arroyo los Coyotes to watch that bunch o' Mexicans Fielding's throwed round his ranch."

Destrin shrugged his shoulders. "You tell Curt what happened," he said to Redden.

The gunman's unwinking gaze went slowly to the Arrow man. "The kid slipped away an' beat it down to the Mex camp," he said. "Solvang an' me figgered he'd turned yeller, planned to double cross us. We watched close and saw Fielding cut him loose, like he would if the kid had agreed to tell him what he knew. We wasn't takin' chances." Redden's smile was wicked. "Solvang got him first shot. I'd have got Fielding, but a fast-shootin' hombre jumped us and killed Solvang." The gunman was watching Quintal intently. "I beat it away from there. Too many rifles poppin' my way."

An oath frothed from Quintal and suddenly he was reaching for his gun. Redden coolly shot him neatly between the eyes.

Destrin's voice broke the stunned silence that followed the blast from Redden's gun. His tone was thin and charged with menace.

"Got anything to say, Bert?"

The tall Arrow superintendent's shocked gaze lifted from the shuddering heap on the floor. His face was a chalk white.

"Guess not, Mel—his own fault." Cross reached an unsteady hand for the whiskey bottle on the desk. "The boys won't like it."

"It's my pay roll they feed on," Destrin said in his deadly voice, "same as you, Bert, and you, Slade, and you, Ace." His gaze went to each of them, darting, stabbing looks that made them flinch. "We're all partners and friends together, and we must hang together or we'll hang separately, with Jack Fielding making a good job of it."

"Quin was a fool," grunted Slade. "You bet we stick together, Mel." He cocked his head, listened for a moment to the clamor in the street.

"You're the sheriff," said Destrin softly.

"You bet I'm the sheriff," growled Slade. He pulled the door open, glared at the gathering crowd.

"Curt Quintal got shot while resisting arrest," he told them blusteringly. "Figgered he'd buck the law, folks, an' got what was comin' to him."

An angry voice interrupted the sheriff. "Yore talk don't listen good, Slade! How come you wanted to arrest Quintal?"

The sheriff fastened a menacing gaze on the speaker, a lanky Arrow rider. "I'd plenty good reason to arrest him, feller," he lied smoothly, "Quin's been hand-in-glove with the Hawk." His voice lifted arrogantly. "Get yore broncs, fellers. We're goin' after the Hawk right now."

A hush followed the sheriff's announcement, broken by excited yells as certain of his listeners scattered in a rush for horses.

Slade's glance raked over the dispersing crowd. He knew most of the faces there, border renegades, hirelings of the man he himself served. Others were there in the milling crowd at whom the sheriff cast dubious glances. He saw Buck Wells of the Bar 7, old Pop Shane and one or two others who were known as friends of Jack Fielding.

Slade turned from the door, spoke hurriedly to Destrin. The latter nodded approvingly.

"Go to it," he said, "we'll take no chances of word reaching Fielding." Destrin paused, his smile sinister. "And Slade, don't try to arrest him *alive.*"

The sheriff grinned. "I savvy, the Hawk resists arrest, gets killed. The old Mex game of *ley fuego.*" He clattered out, drawn gun in hand.

Ace Coran chuckled. "Reckon I'll watch the play," he said. "Ought to be good, Pop Shane'll be some peeved." He hastened after the sheriff.

Two hard-faced men came in and dragged the dead Arrow foreman out, and obeying Destrin's gesture, Scorpy Redden closed and locked the door after a quick glance up the street. His dark saturnine face wore a grin as he looked round at the others.

"Slade's got old Shane, an' Buck Wells under his gun," he said with a chuckle, "he's marchin' 'em to the jail right now."

Mel Destrin nodded, a glitter of triumph in his eyes. "We'll see to it they never leave that jail alive," he murmured. His lip lifted in his cruel snarl. "Looks like fine weather ahead, boys." He broke off and stared questioningly at the gunman. "How about your little visit to Pedro?" he asked.

Redden's grin was significant. "Needn't worry about him no more," he said. "Pedro's done talkin'."

"Good work," grunted the lawyer. He scowled. "He had us fooled for a long time."

"Him an' Monte Boone," muttered Scorpy Redden. "Monte would pick up our talk in Coran's place an' pass it along to Pedro, an' Pedro passed it to the Hawk." The little gunman swore. "Reckon we was dumb, not gettin' wise quicker."

The twilight was fading. Destrin got out of his chair, lighted a lamp and drew the window curtain. Horses' hoofs went thudding past. The lawyer listened for a moment. Slade and his posse were headed for the Bar 7 ranch to nab the Hawk. Soon there would be no Hawk, no Jack Fielding to thwart his cunning schemes. Destrin went back to his desk, diabolic glee in his eyes. Soon the entire country of the vast Chuckwalla would be his own feudal barony. A few loose ends to catch up and tie, the Kelly woman, the Maisie person, this true granddaughter of old Mark Severn. But with Jack Fielding eliminated, these few loose ends offered no serious problem. Once the Hawk was dead his mysterious friends would scatter and give him no more trouble.

Wheels rattling up the street broke into the lawyer's reflections. It was the San Carlos stage. Bert Cross roused from his own thoughts was reminded of something by the arrival of Hardpan Jones.

"Saw Belle over at the hotel," he said. "She's skipping the country, Mel, leaving on the stage tonight."

Destrin smiled and shook his head. "Belle's

changed her mind." His glance went to the door of the back room. "Belle's taking a nap. She'll be going back to the ranch after we hear from Slade."

Bert Cross nodded. He had a shrewd idea of what had happened to Belle Gerben. The lawyer was speaking thoughtfully with gaze fastened on the Arrow superintendent.

"Kind of crazy about the Maisie girl, ain't you, Bert?"

Cross smirked, then scowled. "Never had a chance with her," he grumbled. "Might have had some luck with her if I could get her away from the Kelly woman."

"She's out at the Fielding ranch, you know that, don't you, Bert?"

The Arrow man nodded, looked suspiciously at the back-room door. "Sounds like something moved in there," he muttered.

"It's Belle waking up from her nap." Destrin spoke carelessly, and returned to the subject of Maisie. "The girl's yours if you get rid of Ma Kelly," he said. "How about it, Bert?"

"Suits me," laughed Cross. His eyes glinted as he rose from his chair. "I'll take her off your hands, Mel," he promised.

"I don't want Ma Kelly back in this town," Destrin said, "she's part of the bargain, Bert." His tone was significant.

"I'm no woman killer," grumbled his partner, scowling.

"You're going out to the JF tonight," coldly continued Destrin.

"The place is lousy with Fielding's Mex friends," demurred Cross sulkily.

"They'll be gone before morning," Destrin argued. "I'm not risking that Kelly woman getting away. She'd make trouble. She's a Tartar and she would never quit." The lawyer's tone lifted angrily. "You're going tonight. You'll get to 'em and I don't care what you do with the girl. Take her over to the Arrow and keep her there until you're tired of her." He grinned nastily. "She won't be staying round these parts when you've finished with her."

The Arrow man stared at him a bit contemptuously. "You're a devil, Mel," he drawled. "I'm no saint, but you turn my stomach."

"You don't fool me," sneered the lawyer. "I'll bet Maisie'd rather be dead than have you touch her. Don't be a hypocrite, Bert. You can scarcely wait to get your hands on her." Destrin looked at Scorpy Redden. "You go with him," he added. "I'm leaving Ma Kelly to you." His glance went significantly to the man's low-slung guns.

Redden nodded. "I get yuh, boss." His tone lacked enthusiasm and there was a curious look in his eyes as he unlocked the door and followed the tall Arrow man into the night.

Destrin went to the door and turned the key again, then stood for a moment, lighting a cigar

281

and staring thoughtfully at the back-room door. He suddenly stiffened. The footsteps were unmistakable. Belle Gerben had managed to free herself from the ropes. With a startled oath the lawyer ran to the door. It refused to open. She had turned the key on the inside. Destrin cursed himself for the oversight of leaving the key there.

In a moment he was back at the street door and frantically turning the key. He jerked the door open, then recoiled with a curious little animal cry, the agonized moan of a rabbit as it feels the crushing jaws of a hound. He backed from the door, hand lifting as if to fend away the tall shape filling the entrance.

Jack Fielding followed him in, gun menacing, and the ashen-faced lawyer read his doom in those implacable eyes. Jack had at last learned the truth. The latter spoke quietly.

"Mel Destrin, I arrest you for the murder of my father, John Fielding, for the murder of Mark Severn and for the murders of Jake Kurtz and old Pedro." Jack's voice hardened and sheared through the silence like cold steel. "The law will hang you, Mel Destrin—hang you by the neck until you are dead."

"You, you can't arrest me!" babbled the cowering lawyer. "You're not the sheriff."

Jack touched the star pinned to shirt pocket. "The governor's authority," he said grimly.

"But you're the Hawk, wanted by the law!" stuttered Destrin.

"The law rides with the Hawk, now," Jack told him tersely. "Hold out your hands, Destrin. I should kill you myself, but I'm leaving you to the law." A shot crashed out from across the street. Jack whirled, leaped to one side from the zone of lamplight in front of the open door. For a moment his gun was lowered. Destrin's hand darted under his coat, dropped again as the back door burst open, revealing Don Vicente framed there, gun leveled. Destrin gazed at him stupidly, saw Belle Gerben peering triumphantly over the Mexican's shoulder. In another moment Jack had the handcuffs on the lawyer's wrists.

The street was suddenly filling with the sound of trampling hoofs, the loud, excited voices of men. Another shot crashed out above the uproar, a second and a third. Belle Gerben suddenly pushed past Don Vicente.

"Jack, listen! Bert Cross and that Redden killer are riding to your ranch to get Maisie and kill Ma Kelly." The words poured from the girl frantically as she ran to him. "I heard them talking, Jack!"

Jack turned, wordless, went charging through the door, Belle at his heels. Don Vicente cat-footed toward the handcuffed lawyer, prodded him with his gun. Destrin tottered into the street, the Mexican's soft voice in his ears.

"He will himself kill you if harm comes to that girl, Señor Satan. *Si*, Juan will not leave you for the law to hang."

Horses and men were milling in the street. Destrin halted, gazed stupidly at a strange procession passing the office. Slade, handcuffed to Ace Coran, stumbling along, bewilderment, rage and fear, in their hard faces. A score of others trailed them, some wearing handcuffs, others strung together with rawhide ropes. Don Vicente looked at the lawyer mockingly. "Your sheriff wears his own handcuffs, Señor Satan." He rolled the name with obvious relish. "*Si*, we took your sheriff by surprise. The handcuffs he carried with him came in useful to *us*."

Jack's tall form emerged from the shifting crowd. Carlos Montalvo was with him, and Belle Gerben, the latter talking in a low agitated voice. Don Vicente gave them a questioning look. Jack seemed in no hurry to be on his way to save his friends at the ranch. He was smiling grimly, but there was relief in his smile.

"Redden killed Bert Cross in his hotel room," he told Don Vicente. "Don't know why Redden killed him, but that was the shot we heard. That is, it was the first shot. Then Carlos got Redden in the alley when he was trying to make for his horse."

"*Si*," Carlos spoke softly, contentedly. "*Si*, I have revenge the Señor Severn. I have kill the man who shot the old señor." The Mexican's eyes went suddenly hot as he looked at Mel Destrin and saw the handcuffs on him. "Not quite have I revenge the Señor," he muttered, "you are the dog who led the pack." Carlos was jerking at his gun. Don Vicente spoke sharply. "Not so, my brother. We leave Señor Satan to Juan's hangman. It is best."

"I will be there to see him strangle," muttered Carlos. He stalked away to a group of dark-faced grinning riders.

"Come on, Destrin." Jack's voice was harsh. "Jail's the best place for you." He prodded the lawyer into motion and drove him stumbling down the street.

Belle Gerben watched until their figures melted into the darkness. For the moment she was alone. Her glance went to the stage across the street. Hardpan Jones was coming out of the hotel lobby. With a gesture of decision the girl ran into the office, caught up her brown traveling bag and went flying out. Hardpan Jones was climbing up to his driver's seat when she ran up to the stage.

"I'm going with you."

Hardpan grinned affably. "You can set with me," he said, reaching down a helping hand. "Lucky you wasn't a minute later," he chuckled. "Won't be another stage out till mornin'." His voice lifted, the long whip cracked and the stage rocked away in a cloud of dust.

Belle Gerben drew a long breath. She was more

285

lucky than old Hardpan knew. She had been awfully close to missing his stage, and all the other stages. Too late she remembered with a qualm that she had not told Jack Fielding what she knew about Maisie, that she was the real Mary Cameron.

CHAPTER TWENTY-TWO

The sight of Mel Destrin and his hireling sheriff behind the bars considerably mollified old Pop Shane for his brief incarceration in Coldwater's jail.

"I reckon this here calaboose has got more fleas an' high stinks than any jail that ever was," he happily told the sullen and frightened deposed law officer. "You look awful natural, settin' there, Slade, you an' Ace Coran, an' Mel Destrin, an' all the rest of you dang sidewinders." Pop Shane chuckled grimly. "Only one other sight's agoin' to look more natural, an' that'll be when every last one of you is swingin' at the end of a rope."

There were those among the crowd milling around the adobe and stone jail who spoke loudly against any delay in making Pop Shane's picture a swift reality. Up and down the street sped the menacing growl of the mob. The reign of the mysterious despot was broken. Men no

286

longer would live in fear of the assassin's bullet.

"We want Destrin!" chanted hoarse voices. "We want Slade and Coran. Hang 'em, hang the bloody murderers!"

Jack was angry. "We can't stand for any lynching," he said to Tim Hook. "We've got the law in Coldwater now, and the law will hang these men, not a mob."

"Wouldn't mind pullin' on a rope myself," confessed the big Diamond D owner. He was burning with rage at the cold-blooded plot to destroy the Widow Kelly. "At that, hangin's too good for that skulkin' wolf."

"You'll be the next sheriff," Jack told him soberly. "You're starting this very minute to keep the law in Coldwater. I'm leaving it to you, Tim."

The big cattleman suddenly grinned. "I'm with you, Jack, you leave it to Sheriff Hook." His smile broadened. Ma Kelly wouldn't be saying no to the new sheriff, he was thinking. "I'll talk to these jaspers," he said bluffly, and he strode away, his big voice lifting above the roar of the mob. Suddenly there was a hush in the street, and the moon made pale light on a sea of faces turned toward the new sheriff as he addressed them curtly in the name of the law that at last had come to Coldwater.

Jack found Buck helping his rather limp wife into the ranch buckboard.

"I was never so scared in my life," wailed

Jennie Wells, "and never so mad, the way that awful Slade came pokin' his gun in Buck's back and takin' him off to jail."

"It's all done with, now," Jack comforted her. "Good times are coming now for the Chuckwalla."

"You're a wonder, Jack," beamed the woman. "Shouldn't be s'prised none if you was governor some day."

Jack winked at Buck. "You get her back to the ranch, Buck," he chuckled, "too much excitement in this town for Jennie."

The veteran foreman carefully eased into his seat. His leg still bothered him. "The gal lit out," he said tersely.

Jack nodded carelessly. He had glimpsed Belle Gerben as the stage rolled out of town. "She wasn't Mary Cameron," he told the pair in the buckboard. They gazed at him, too dumbstruck for words.

"It was a trick of Mel Destrin's," Jack said. "He knew the terms of Mark's will and saw a chance to get hold of the Bar 7."

"Reckon it's plain as day," muttered Buck Wells, finding his voice. "Destrin had Mark murdered, then rigged up a fake granddaughter."

"She told me the whole story," Jack said. "Destrin was to give her ten thousand dollars for the trick, and in a few months she would have deeded the Bar 7 over to him. Then she'd have cleared out of the country. Nobody would have ever known the truth." Jack shook his head. "Clever scheme, but it didn't work."

"The shameless hussy!" exclaimed Jennie Wells. "Old Wong was right. He saw through her from the very first." She spoke angrily. "You should have thrown her in jail."

"I'm glad she's gone," Jack's eyes softened. "She wasn't all bad, Jennie. She didn't know a thing about the killings, and anyway when she got to thinking she couldn't go through with it, she came in to tell Destrin she was going away, only he wouldn't let her."

"He would have killed her," shrewdly surmised Jennie Wells.

"Destrin's finished with his killings," Jack gestured. "All right, Buck, see you at the ranch."

The foreman looked at him curiously. "Looks like you're due to be boss of the Bar 7 for sure, Jack, now that there's no Mary Cameron to be Mark's granddaughter." He wagged his head. "Reckon there ain't no granddaughter, and that makes you old Mark's heir."

Jack gave him a worried look, and turned abruptly away. Jennie Wells frowned at her husband. "He didn't like you sayin' that to him," she scolded. "Let's get goin', Buck. I'm so tired an' nervous I could scream."

A voice hailed Jack as he rode past Shane's barn. Pop Shane beckoned him. "Just a moment, young feller." He hurried from the yawning doors. "Went clean out of my head, but I got that old Injun locked up in a grain bin—that Tomi feller you was askin' me to hold for you if he showed up."

"Won't be needing Tomi now," Jack pointed out.

"Sure, sure," agreed the liveryman. He grinned sheepishly as he scratched his thinning hair. "Tomi'll be some peeved at me for lockin' him up like I did," he worried.

Jack pulled a couple of gold coins from a pocket. "Buy all the ropes he's got with him, Pop," he said with an amused chuckle.

"Reckon that'll pacify the old Injun plenty," Pop Shane declared gratefully.

"Tell Tomi to come again next roundup," instructed Jack. "We'll take all the hair ropes he can make."

He rode on his way, and soon the town lights drew down to tiny winking points, then faded into the vast sweep of the night.

His thoughts were troubled, despite the swift succession of events that had unmasked Destrin and terminated the ruthless reign of horror that had terrorized the Chuckwalla.

Mark Severn's granddaughter apparently was as much a myth as ever. The problem of Mary Cameron stumped him. He would have to be careful of impostors. Mel Destrin's scheme had nearly worked. Destrin's cleverness had fooled all of them. It had been the attempt to poison Will Carson that had revealed the amazing truth about Destrin. From that moment, when he heard the story from Ma Kelly, he had been sure, and the presence of Governor Jim Cary at the JF ranch had armed him with the power to destroy the cunning and ruthless schemer.

The problem of Mary Cameron was still vexing Jack as he sat in the Bar 7 ranch office at old Mark Severn's desk. He unlocked a drawer and took out the enlarged photograph and studied it gloomily. It would be harder than finding a needle in a haystack. He could advertise, but advertising would bring a horde of impostors. How was he to know the real from the false?

He was suddenly listening tensely. The trample of hoofs in the yard was followed by the sound of voices, Ma Kelly's, Maisie's. Jack sprang from the chair.

Ma Kelly and Maisie were reining up their horses near the garden gate. Smoky and Johnny rode in attendance. Jack went with long hurried strides to the gate.

"Maisie was bound to come, lad," greeted Mrs. Kelly cheerily. "Oh, Jack, it's the grand news you sent us last night!"

"The war's over," Jack said. His eyes were all for the slim young girl scrambling from her saddle. She came up to him swiftly.

"I knew you'd win." She gave him a breathless

look of pride. "Oh, Jack, we had anxious moments until your man came with the news!"

"Only one thing wrong," complained Johnny Archer disgustedly, "me an' Smoky never had a chance to get in the scrap."

"Looks like all me an' Johnny is good for is to play nursemaids," grumbled Smoky as he helped Mrs. Kelly down from her horse. The widow's jeans were a tight fit. She calmly loosened the top button while roundly berating the malcontents.

"Don't you boys be talkin' nonsense," she scolded. "Maisie an' me might have been murdered a dozen times if you two hadn't been watchin' things so close."

A startled cry from Maisie interrupted Ma Kelly. The girl was staring wide-eyed at the photograph still in Jack's hand.

"Where did you get *that?*" Her voice was breathless.

"Why, it's, it's a picture of Mark Severn's daughter and her baby." Jack gave her a bewildered look.

"It's my mother—me!" exclaimed the girl. She began to tremble. "I, I have a picture just like that one."

Ma Kelly broke the sudden hush. *"Dear Mother of Jesus!"* Awe and repressed excitement shook her voice. "It's Mary Cameron you are, me darlin', Mary Cameron, the *real Mary Cameron.*"

Jack and the girl scarcely heard her. They were

looking at each other with eyes that hid nothing, but revealed all, and Jack knew that Mark Severn's granddaughter would always be only Maisie to him, his own Maisie.

About the Author

Although Arthur Henry Gooden was born in England, he was brought to the United States at the age of nine, where his family settled on a ranch in the San Joaquin Valley of California. He grew up there in the atmosphere and tradition of the Southwestern cattle country. From the beginning he helped out around the ranch and by the time he was sixteen or seventeen, he was a full-fledged cowboy. Not long after that, he was rated a top hand.

He was different from most ranch hands in that he had his nose buried in a book during his spare time and soon felt the writing urge. By the time he was twenty-one he was writing regularly for the magazines and soon after placed his first book, *Cross Knife Ranch.*

"However," he says, "in between times of book writing, I rode range and so the story of cattle became a real and thrilling thing to me. Years of later roaming in the Southwest has made me increasingly aware that it is a story that cannot be told too often. The source material is vast and unending. It is the heritage of all Americans, this early epic of the Westward Ho Trail. No fiction can be more adventurous, exciting and gallant than were the events that actually happened."

In addition to his books, Mr. Gooden spent sixteen years in Hollywood as a script writer during which time he wrote more than twenty serials in addition to feature pictures and shorts, including Westerns for some of the most famous of the old-time heroes.

Center Point Large Print
600 Brooks Road / PO Box 1
Thorndike ME 04986-0001 USA

(207) 568-3717

US & Canada:
1 800 929-9108
www.centerpointlargeprint.com